A Figure in a Black Commando Parachute Suit Appeared . . .

carrying a battered briefcase. "Buckaroo's getting in the Jet Car!"

"Crawling in" would be more like it. There was no door, only a window through which he slithered.

"Fire when ready, Buckaroo," came the voice of mission control, none other than Big Norse.

Buckaroo's hand moved to a final row of controls, the pulsating power of the jet behind him increasing with each successive throw of a switch until at last it seemed the car was a quivering caged beast. . . .

Eyes burning, Buckaroo Banzai pressed the final switch and threw the car into gear. In the swirl of flame and dust, to the observer it appeared that the hand of a giant had grabbed hold of the car and flung it as far as one could see in a single second, so fast did it dart toward the horizon.

Perfect Tommy, Rawhide, and I leaned forward, knuckles turning white, watching Buckaroo's progress on the monitor. Nearby, Professor Hikita furrowed his brow in resolute concentration. "Now it's in the lap of the gods," I heard him murmur.

BUCKAROO BANZAI

BY EARL MAC RAUCH

PUBLISHED BY POCKET BOOKS NEW YORK

Another *Original* publication of POCKET BOOKS

POCKET BOOKS, a division of Simon & Schuster, Inc.
1230 Avenue of the Americas, New York, N.Y. 10020

ISBN: 0-671-54058-0

First Pocket Books printing August, 1984

10 9 8 7 6 5 4 3 2 1

To Rawhide and the others
without whom . . .

To the Reader

IT WILL DOUBTLESS be charged by cynics that the compilation and publication of this volume have been done with an eye toward mass sales and nothing more; that the sensational elements of the case have been accentuated to serve the public clamor rather than the cause of accuracy. The truth is otherwise, however, as the most cursory examination of the facts will reveal. If anything, I have refrained from using much of the more lurid material on the grounds that it might invite panic among those unfamiliar with the story or in those of weak mental fiber. I do confess that in my zeal for getting an overview of the whole and a sense of perspective, I have found it necessary to recreate certain situations central to the drama where I could not have been a witness or where, indeed, no person now living (I use "person" in the sense of "intelligent being") could have been present. In all other instances, where possible, I have relied upon eyewitnesses, the corporate records of Yoyodyne Propulsion Systems, the kindly assistance of the Nova Police (the Planet 10 equivalent of Interpol), the documents of the Banzai Institute, and, of course, the Freedom of Information Act in obtaining U.S. government files. Throughout, I have endeavored to be as faithful as possible to the events as they actually occurred and would like to thank Mrs. E. Johnson, archivist of the Banzai Institute, for her valued help and her many hours of selfless labor on behalf of the project . . . and, of course, Buckaroo Banzai, M.D., Ph.D.

Reno

1

SITTING HERE SAFELY in the stained-glass enclosed study of the Banzai Institute for Biomedical Engineering and Strategic Information, I am at last able to look back on the events of the twelfth and thirteenth of June past with a certain remove and, I may say, a sense of profound relief that the worst did not occur when it seemed as though it might. For this, the world has to thank Buckaroo Banzai, that rare combination of cunning and civilized breeding, who was contacted by representatives of the Nova Police, whose very existence until that time was unknown to us; but perhaps I'm getting ahead of myself. A bit of history may be helpful here for our youthful readers.

One evening I made my way down from the bunkhouse, as the top floor of the Banzai Institute is called by those of us fortunate enough to be residents, and on passing the projection room looked in to see Buckaroo Banzai sitting alone while a faded eight millimeter home movie print flickered on the screen. It was a sight I had witnessed on more than one occasion, the man alone with his thoughts and whatever memories the images on screen rekindled, and I mention it here only because of the fortuitous timing. It was only days before the scheduled test run of the new Jet Car in Texas, and the events on the screen took on a special meaning, bearing as they did on the present.

On the screen, a Texas vista, made broader by the sweep of the camera, served as a backdrop for a 1950-model Ford automobile and an expedition of five individuals dressed in the style prevalent in that arid habitat, in boots and hats of the American Southwest. In my mind's eye now I see them smiling, waving at the camera. It looks more like an outing in the country than a scene of any scientific expedition. Certainly there is no presage of what is to come, not the faintest hint of danger. Comprising the group portrait are two Oriental men, two Caucasian men, and a single Caucasian woman. The sun is sweltering, thermal waves rising off the desert floor which is a dry lake basin. In one corner of the picture I recall surveying instruments, a theodolite. The operator of the camera shifts its focus repeatedly amongst the companions, his hand not the steadiest, and shooting from a lower angle relative to the subjects. He is in fact the young Buckaroo Banzai, a precocious boy of four years, and he now comes into view as one of the Orientals walks forward to take the camera.

Young Banzai is a boy like any other, racially mixed, wearing a red hat and a six-shooter, possessing what all children most require, a pair of loving parents. The Caucasian woman and the remaining Oriental embrace him warmly, and the film changes scenes.

Standing in the doorway of the projection room, I noticed Buckaroo stir. Something in him surged to his throat, and he exhaled audibly. More than thirty years later, the recollection of what was to follow on the screen still made it almost unbearable for him to watch. I must confess to feeling convulsed myself every time I have seen the footage.

Imagine a long torpedo with wheels and a cockpit cut into it so that it might accommodate a crew of two, and imagine yourself further to be the four-year-old Buckaroo watching from behind a sandbagged shelter as your father, at the wheel of the streamlined vehicle, presses the starter only to be engulfed in searing flames. Your mother screams, releases your frightened hand, and plunges herself into the fire in an effort to save your father. An explosion terrible to behold sucks the air out of your lungs, and only the body of your father's closest friend thrown recklessly across your own saves you from being pelted with bits and pieces of your parents.

For a long time after the film finished and slapped against the reel, Buckaroo did not move. Finally, because I suppose I could bear the pathetic sight no longer, I stepped forward, placed my hands on his shoulders.

"Buckaroo—?"

He looked up, trying to compose himself. "Hey, Reno—" he said, sitting up straighter. "I thought everybody was asleep."

"Just going downstairs for a beer. Can I get you one?"

"No, I'm all right. Think I'll go to bed. I was just trying to see if there was anything we could learn."

"Still think it was an incendiary device?" I asked, fully aware of the answer.

"It had to be."

I nodded. "Xan?"

"Who else? I can't prove it, though."

"What difference would it make if we could?" I said, knowing that getting Xan out of his stronghold in Sabah would be like extracting the incisors of a wildcat. No one knew this better than Buckaroo, who had actually been there and had seen the relic city of caves hacked out of mountainous jungle, teeming with brigands and assassins from every corner of the world, afforded by Xan a sanctuary from which they could come and go with impunity.*

Buckaroo stood up, resigned to going to bed. "Not a helluva lot," he said. "I can only kill him once. Good night, Reno."

"Good night," I said. "What time we leaving tomorrow?"

"Bus pulls out at ten-thirty."

"See you in the morning, Buckaroo."

He nodded. I took the film from the projector and went

---

* Note to the reader: In the adventure *Extradition from Hell*, B. Banzai went to Sabah under the protection of the beautiful zombie La Negrette, introduced to him by Seth. Seth told Buckaroo that his wife, poisoned by Xan, was not dead but alive in Sabah, having been injected with the nerve poison Talava which destroys mind and soul but actually improves one's health. B. Banzai failed to find any trace of her and barely escaped Xan's Nautiloids at sea.—Reno

down the hall to the archives to file it. As I suspected, Mrs. Johnson was still awake, listening to another batch of demo tapes submitted to the Hong Kong Cavaliers, the musical group of which Buckaroo and I were members. One of those persons who languishes by day and does not seem to come fully alive until the middle of the night, Mrs. Johnson, at nineteen the premature widow of Flyboy, was just gathering momentum. Over the indescribable din of a song called "Merry as a Monkey," she said hello and asked if Buckaroo had said anything about her going to the Jet Car test.

"To me?" I said. "Was he supposed to?"

"Well, it's been nearly six months."

By that I supposed she meant her apprenticeship which preceded internship, which in turn preceded residency. In the manner of a hospital, only interns and residents were allowed to go on actual operations, which I pointed out to her.

"But this isn't technically an operation," she said. "It's a tour."

True, we were presenting musical shows in three cities along the way, but that was mainly for gas money. Our clear mission was the Jet Car test, and beyond the Jet Car test there was the *real* Jet Car test of which only Buckaroo and the residents were apprised. And despite the perceived nature of the trip, *any* trip, there was always the lurking menace of Xan, capable of the basest atrocities. I said this to her.

"Anyway," I said. "The problem is that with the Seminole Kid, Pecos, and the Argentine with Cousteau on the *Calypso*, we're a little short around here."

"Go suck eggs," she said.

So much for my explanation. I smiled, remembering myself at her age when my quick temper had been legendary. Buckaroo in fact had more than once seen fit to needle me by reciting one of his Oriental maxims: "Young blood needs little flame to boil." I mentioned this to her, and she found it singularly amusing, as if I should have ever been her age.

"See you when we get back," I said on my way out the door.

"Good luck," she called after me.

2

THE MORNING OF the scheduled Jet Car test, I was awakened on the bus by the rude breath of Rawhide, who found it necessary to tell me that Buckaroo had been called away, and he, Rawhide, was going with him.

"Called away? What are you talking about?" I said, summoning the fortitude to look at my watch. It was barely four, and the test was to be in less than five hours, on top of which, there had been a concert in Amarillo the night before so that any foray at this hour of the morning seemed a particularly unappealing prospect.

"He has to go El Paso," Rawhide said in his typical humorless way. "He has to operate on an Eskimo."

I nodded, somehow knowing it was true. "What about me and Perfect Tommy?" I said.

"Buckaroo wants the two of you to go on out to the test site with Professor Hikita and stand by. We'll be there as soon as we can."

"Isn't the Secretary of Defense supposed to be there?" I asked, raising a small point.

"That's why we'll be back as soon as we can," Rawhide repeated and disappeared. "Try to keep him busy."

If I had dared to hope it was a nightmare, I was soon dissuaded by the anxious hands of Perfect Tommy shaking me awake for a second time.

"What is it, Tommy? Can't it wait?"

"Buckaroo's leaving."

He had heard the helicopter. I shouldn't have laughed, but no one ever told Tommy anything. He was the youngest of our number and the good-humored butt of our jokes. Again on this occasion he was the last to know.

"Well, what do we do now?" he said.

"Let's get some breakfast."

On our way back to the galley, we passed through that amazing section of the bus known as World Watch One, devoted to a constant monitoring of worldwide satellite and communications traffic. The intern on duty, a young Blue Blaze from Denmark who through no fault of her own had somehow gained the mismatched moniker Big Norse, immediately called to our attention a cryptic message just received from the Seminole Kid off the coast of Sabah, Malaya—a latitude-longitude fix and something about "death dwarves taken aboard."

I scratched my head, passed the wire to Perfect Tommy. "When did this come in?" I said.

"Just now," replied Big Norse.

Perfect Tommy proved as mystified as I. "Did you radio back?" he asked.

Big Norse nodded. "I didn't get an acknowledgement. There's a strange atmospheric disturbance going on, localized over this area of Texas. I don't know if they received."

"Well, try again," I said, at the risk of stating the obvious but not knowing what else to say.

"Death dwarves," muttered Perfect Tommy. "Some more of Xan's radio-controlled experiments?"

"Sounds like it," I said, as we were joined by Professor Hikita who insisted on knowing what the ruckus was about. "Xan up to his usual deviltry," was how I put it.

"Was there an SOS?" he asked.

Big Norse shook her head.

"Then perhaps we're getting worried for nothing," said the professor, wrinkling his brow, eyes twinkling. "Perhaps the message means they have taken death dwarves prisoner."

At that we all smiled, congratulating one another. "Of

course!" ejaculated Perfect Tommy. "That must be it! Otherwise—"

The professor cut him short. "Otherwise there is nothing we can do about it."

We knew the truth of that, all of us stonily grim. To mask his own fretfulness, the good professor forced a smile. "Anyway, we have problems of our own," he said. "I need some help with these Jet Car calculations, and we haven't much time."

3

BEFORE PROCEEDING, I must confess to being utterly lame of mind about the higher mathematics. Whatever explanation I can here contribute regarding that marvelous machine the Jet Car, keep in mind, reader, that it is the layman speaking, and the layman must inevitably rely upon poor metaphor, the turn of a phrase, to relate that which he fathoms only slightly. The result is to hold up one's hand and mark the spot, so to speak, mentioning almost merely in passing, "Here is where the great leap forward occurred. Now you know." All of this is by way of saying that it was Perfect Tommy, a whiz at figures in his own right, and not myself, who hovered near Hikita's shoulder in the desert blockhouse as the professor peered at the Jet Car through a viewfinder and read aloud a stream of computer data.

"T minus five hundred and counting," announced the professor. "Phaser positive. Latch compressor."

What thoughts went through his mind that morning I can only imagine, but no soul, not even the phlegmatic Japanese, could have been indifferent to the irony in the situation. Barely thirty years earlier on this same desert track, a vastly more primitive speed machine had poised for takeoff and disintegrated, taking three of its creators with it, among them Hikita's compatriot and mentor, Masado Banzai. It had been none other than Hikita who had thrown himself

16

across the young Buckaroo and just as selflessly from that day forward, reared the boy as his own blood.

"Power source output zero-zero-niner," he continued. "Multistage axial compressor latched."

I made a point at that time of jotting down an unusual personal observation in my notebook which I still find amusing.

All these spit and polish types, careerists from the Pentagon, pretending to be on top of things. . . . If they only knew! If they only knew what they are about to witness! Their collars would pop, their socks would fall off. The Secretary of Defense seems impatient, almost bored. General Catburd of the Joint Chiefs is wearing his golfing clothes, anxious only to get to the next fairway. They're here because the President asked them to come. The President, to his credit, thinks the Jet Car might have military applications. Wait till the test! He doesn't know the half of it . . . In any case they'll be excellent witnesses for posterity.

One hundred yards away, members of the Banzai team filled the tank of the unusual-looking, asymmetrical car with extremely flammable jet fuel, while others, almost unnoticed, loaded aboard three special liquid helium dewars for super-cooling the magnetic components of the Jet Car. These superconducting magnets were essential for the operation of the OSCILLATION OVERTHRUSTER, a miniature colliding beam accelerator which created intermediate vector bosons from the annihilation of electrons and their antimatter counterparts, positrons. My fellow residents and interns and I saw this being done and crossed our fingers, but I am certain the event went utterly unnoticed by the others in attendance, those representatives of the news media, the military, and the Congress who seemed more concerned with matters on the other side of the globe and the social whirl back in Washington than with anything that might happen on this desolate spot.

The main subject of conversation seemed to be the exact whereabouts of Buckaroo. He had not been seen by anyone, and as Professor Hikita and Perfect Tommy continued to make ready the car, amid television screens and monitoring devices, I found myself stealing a peek at my own watch and overheard General Catburd's aide give him the latest.

"He's not even here," went the conversation.

"Who?"

"Banzai."

"Where the hell is he?"

"At a hospital in El Paso."

"What? Why weren't we informed? What's wrong with him?"

"He was called away to do some surgery."

"I'm supposed to tee off in a couple of hours. I have a golf game."

And so on. Catburd, feeling somehow vindicated by this bit of unexpected news, ambled over to the Secretary of Defense. "Banzai hasn't showed, Mr. Secretary," he said. "Looks like he's got cold feet. I may as well go ahead and lift off."

The Secretary shook his head. "I want you here," he said, frowning at the general's country club golf cap. "I have a hunch Banzai has something up his sleeve."

"Like what?"

Perfect Tommy interrupted my eavesdropping. "Better see what's keeping the boss, Reno," he said.

"Why me?" I replied drily, to get his goat.

" 'Cause I'm busy. And get your clodhoppers off the UNIVAC."

I lowered my feet from the computer console and walked to a less conspicuous part of the room where I used a miniature television transceiver to dial Rawhide's mobile number. It was a quarter of seven, and Buckaroo Banzai had already been up four hours.

4

I HAVE HEARD it said that fame is the sum of misunderstandings that accumulate around a well-known name. If that is so, then B. Banzai is surely the most famous man on earth, as there is so much in error said and written about him. He is called a communist by the right wing and a bourgeois tool by the left. His motives are impugned, his name slandered. Lawsuits are filed against him simply to harass or for the notoriety. I am convinced that if Jesus Christ Himself were to return in this day and age, He would not be crucified but sued unto death.

I have to think that it is simply a case of small mean minds unable to comprehend someone so different from themselves, as B. Banzai is different from any man I have ever met. He is, above all, a man who stands for certain principles, and unfortunately, in our time that elicits only suspicion, so cynical has society become. If one stands for something, if one draws a line and has the audacity to declare one side right and one wrong, he is lambasted by the popular press as being unnecessarily rigid, a throwback. Worse, he is accused of being a hypocrite, a *poseur* interested merely in getting his face on television. With B. Banzai it has always been thus, but he continues to fight for a better world, and there are those of us who choose to fight beside him.

What are these so-called principles of his, these subversive ideas which set so many knees quaking in high places? Every school child who reads the Banzai comic books or listens to his weekly radio broadcast or watches his Saturday morning adventure show knows the principles by heart. They are called the Five Stresses, the Four Beauties, and the Three Loves. The Five Stresses, those things to be stressed, are decorum, courtesy, public health, discipline, and morals. The Four Beauties are the beauties of mind, language, behavior, and environment; and the Three Loves are love of others, love of justice, and love of freedom. Such is the nature of the controversial program set forth by Buckaroo Banzai, whose only desire is to help humankind.

At the moment I called, in fact, B. Banzai was nearly up to his elbows in living brain tissue. Rawhide at once stepped out of the OR into a small anteroom where he produced a microTV transceiver identical to my own, an exclusive patent of the Banzai Institute we call a Go-Phone. "What's up, Reno?" he said into the Go-Phone, as my image appeared on the tiny screen.

"I was about to ask you the same question," I said. "They're getting kind of anxious over here at mission control, yours truly included. How much longer?"

"I'll run it down," said Rawhide, and I experienced with him the sensation of walking back into the operating room where he looked over Buckaroo's shoulder at the open skull of a young man sitting in a chair. Using a laser instead of a scalpel, Buckaroo had plumbed to a depth just behind the youngster's eyeballs, and I could hear the tall, somewhat ungainly surgeon next to him suppress a gasp of apprehension.

"What are you doing now?" asked the young surgeon, who I vaguely recalled as having attended a seminar or two at the Banzai Institute.

Buckaroo took the question in stride without batting an eye, continuing to manipulate the delicate laser beam deep within the brain. "What I'm doing, Sid, as you well remember, is fusing the artificial nerve fiber to the original, bypassing the massive tumor damage. Then we'll implant the subcutaneous computer chip—"

The young surgeon nodded, visibly shrinking before my eyes, as Rawhide cut in. "Sorry, Buckaroo," he said, "but we're running into a problem with scheduling. Any idea as to—?"

"About twenty minutes," Buckaroo said. "You wanna take it from here, Sid?"

"I don't know—I mean—are you sure?" Sid vacillated with the same look of unmitigated terror that I have often seen in the eyes of men about to enter battle. It is nothing more or less than a failure of the will, an assessment Buckaroo was quickly forced to make.

"Maybe forty, forty-five minutes," he said to Rawhide, at the same time growing noticeably exasperated with his surgical colleague, at least noticeable to this observer who has felt the same withering stare of disapproval from that sternest of taskmasters, B. Banzai. "What am I doing now, Sid?" Buckaroo continued. "Why don't you explain to the others?"

By the others, Buckaroo meant the crowd of curious surgeons in the spectators' gallery.

Sid stammered, trying to make points. "You're connecting the computer chip to the subcutaneous microphone which will permit the patient to transmit verbal instructions to his own brain—"

"Such as?" Buckaroo prodded.

"Such as 'raise my left arm' or 'throw the harpoon'— depending on the language and culture, there are different computer chips. This boy's an Eskimo."

Minutes later when the operation was over and B. Banzai and Sid washed up together, Buckaroo did not pull any punches. "You know, Sid—"

"I know, I know." Sid threw up his hands, profusely apologetic.

"I know you know." Buckaroo sighed. "If I wasn't convinced of your talents, I'd haul you before the medical board. That's what's so frustrating."

"Maybe next time I'll—"

"The next time we might lose one, Sid," said Buckaroo. "What if I hadn't happened to be in the neighborhood?"

"I know." Sid wrung his hands, agonizing, as Buckaroo

21

picked up a Nikon camera and walked over to take photographs of his handiwork before the Eskimo's skull could be closed. Sid dutifully followed.

"How long have we known each other?" Buckaroo asked. "Since Columbia P and S, right?"

The motorized Nikon whirred as Sid, whose real name was Sidney Zwibel, nodded. "We met in Thornburg's histology class and then later in enzymology."

"As I recall, you were near the top of your class in every subject," said Buckaroo. "I don't want to belabor the point, but we both know you have the gray matter to be a success in any field of endeavor."

"Then—"

"But gray matter in itself isn't enough. There's a saying, 'Consciousness is the impotent shadow of action.' "

"Meaning?"

"Meaning, maybe you think too much. You've taken my seminar on this operative technique, you've read my paper, but when it comes down to it . . ."

"I just don't seem to have the confidence to try a new procedure."

"Confidence in the procedure or confidence in yourself?"

Sidney slumped against the wall, his face drained of emotion. "Confidence in myself," he said. "I'm filled with doubt, fear."

A notion occurred to Buckaroo. "Have you ever thought of coming aboard?" he asked.

"You mean—?"

"Joining me and my team full time."

"Are you serious? Have you got an opening?"

"Possibly," Buckaroo mulled. "Can you sing?"

Sidney's heart leapt. "A little. I can dance," he said.

5

THE FIRST GLIMPSE of B. Banzai by General Catburd and the other personages in the desert blockhouse caused a wave of excitement to sweep through the room.

"There he is!" someone shouted, at the sight of a figure in a black commando parachute suit carrying a battered brief-case. "He's getting in the Jet Car!"

Crawling in, would be more like it. There was no door, only a window through which he slithered. I looked over at Hikita to see if his pulse had quickened as certainly as had my own. "Inertial control positive," he continued, his throat tightening. "T minus seven zero and resume counting."

The voice of Mission Control, none other than Big Norse, crackled over the loudspeaker. "All systems righteous. We have a driver. Do you read, Buckaroo? Over."

"Roger." Buckaroo was performing a preignition check, going down the list he had rehearsed countless times; and though I am safe in saying that he is a man to whom fear is unknown, he could not have been human without experiencing a momentary twinge of misgiving as he removed from his leather case an odd-looking object the size of his fist and plugged it into a gyro cradle near his head. At the flip of a switch, a light emitting diode on the object came on, and a similar signal was activated on Professor Hikita's private console, causing the cryptic words OSCILLATION OVER-THRUSTER ARMED to flash.

"All systems check," crackled the voice of Buckaroo Banzai.

Mission Control: "We have a definite 'go.' "

Then all was quiet, as only the American prairie can be, the odd gust of wind and the whirring of gnats deafening next to the nothingness that stretched for a hundred miles in every direction.

The tension gave rise to nervous patter among some.

"What's this rust bucket supposed to do anyway?" said General Catburd to Senator Martha Cunningham of the Senate Armed Services Committee.

"Five hundred miles an hour, General," she replied. "That's my information."

"Senator, if you weren't a lady—"

"If I weren't a lady, what?"

"Then you're full of stuff. Five hundred miles an hour?" Catburd scoffed.

"Maybe the lady knows what she's talking about," interjected the Secretary of Defense as he looked out the viewing slot and was amazed to see a sheet of flame twenty-feet-long shoot out the back of the Jet Car like the exhaust of a fighter plane.

Catburd's face twitched, his head suddenly throbbing as it performed mental calculations. "Five hundred miles per?" he said, moving closer for a better look. "In that queer-looking thing?"

Another flame erupted from the rear of the stationary car as Buckaroo stepped on the gas once more and took from his flight suit a ceremonial scarf emblazoned with Chinese ideographs commemorating the failed attempt of his father on these same windblown sands better than thirty years before. "Ready," he said, tying the scarf around his helmet as his hand moved to the four-on-the-floor gearshift.

"Fire when ready, Buckaroo," came the voice of Big Norse.

Buckaroo's hand moved to a final row of controls, the pulsating power of the jet behind him increasing with each successive throw of a switch until at last it seemed the car was a quivering caged beast. To his infinite relief, the vehicle had thus far held together, but he could not be certain until the last switch, which his finger now curled around like a fatal trigger.

He drew a breath deep into his chest, though the air was noxious with the odor of kerosene. So circumstanced, having so long dreamt of being here, for a fleeting instant a ribald song from his days at Merton College, Oxford, came to mind, a song he had once sung to Peggy despite his vociferous protestations.

"I won't sing it," he had said.

"Yes, you will, if I have to wheedle it out of you." She had laughed, tickling him until he surrendered.

"You're crazy."

"Crazy about you, Buckaroo Banzai. Now sing."

He had sung the song, as he sang it now in the Jet Car. How could he not sing it? She had been so lovely, lying by the Thames, wearing a garland of roses he had fashioned for her, and a summer dress. Some young Oxonians, mates of his, had come upon them and raised their draughts of wine in hearty laughter when they heard him singing.

"Who's the bird, Buckaroo?" they had shouted.

"My fiancée," he had replied.

"I didn't know you had a finacée," one of them had said.

"Neither did I," had retorted Peggy, gazing at Buckaroo in an altogether accusing way.

"Will you marry me?" he had proposed on the spot, and the shining tender light in her eyes was the only answer he needed.

"Yes," she had said, not hesitating lest it prove a dream.

Had he looked further, he would have seen the squat furtive shadow of Xan looking down on them. Xan, the renegade and blackguard of the 20th century, whose cowardly plot would soon unfold and deprive B. Banzai of yet another person close to him.

Eyes burning, Buckaroo pressed the final switch and threw the car into gear. To the observer it appeared that the hand of a giant had grabbed hold of the car and flung it as far as one could see in a single second, so fast did it dart toward the horizon.

Perfect Tommy, Rawhide, and I leaned forward, knuckles turning white, watching his progress on the monitor. Nearby, Professor Hikita furrowed his brow in resolute concentration. "Now it's in the lap of the gods," I heard him murmur.

6

TECHNICALLY SPEAKING, ALTHOUGH B. Banzai's surname is Japanese, both he and Xan can trace their ancient lineage back to the steppes of Mongolia, back to that race of aggressive Asiatics who from the fourth to the seventeenth century struck terror in the hearts of Europeans. Hordes of these invaders, one wave after the other, raped and pillaged as far as the Atlantic coast, laying waste to all they encountered. It was they, the Mongol ancestors of B. Banzai and Xan, who overthrew Constantinople in 1453, enslaved Russia for centuries, and extinguished the glory that was Baghdad. It was among these, too, that the hatred between B. Banzai's forbears and those of the savage Xan gave rise to the terrible blood feud of generations to come.

On that morning of the Jet Car test in Texas, halfway around the world at his cave city in Sabah, Xan (or Hanoi Xan as Interpol knows him) practiced his usual deadly arts with his bravos, specially trained killers sworn to obey his every poisonous wish. I know from tales told me by his captured former associates what these daily sessions of grueling combat are like, and I have no reason to doubt them, having met a few of Xan's bravos myself on more than one unpleasant occasion. Pound for pound they are the most lethal fighters in the world, and one of their rites of initiation of which I have heard is rather typical. The young man or woman desirous of becoming a bravo is nailed to a tree by the ear and is sometime later handed a knife to cut himself down. A moment's hesitation or a single scream is sufficient grounds for being shot on the spot. The one-eared survivors are then led away for further training in sabotage and commando tactics. They are immersed in cruelty and learn to view pain and suffering with delight. It can be stated with no exaggeration that they study murder as a discipline, devoting the rest of their lives to what Xan calls "walking in the hidden ways." He is the object of their veneration, unstintingly given, and acts of the grisliest nature are perpetrated in his name as a kind of perverse tribute.

Thus it is that these bravos hold all of Sabah in their bloody grip and do not rest until they find fresh victims. Xan, as the head of this unholy order, has bestowed upon himself the title "His Sublimity the Pivot of Mystery, the Hinge of Fate of all the Asias." Needless to say, the peasants of Sabah bow down to the tyrant rather than dispute him.

On this particular morning, as B. Banzai prepared to race the Jet Car across the no man's land of western Texas, Xan partook of the daily rigors of jujitsu alongside his bravos before retiring early to watch American television through the miracle of satellite communication. In his underground library, its every niche filled with dusty records of torture and mayhem, the lank-haired savage watched as B. Banzai blasted across the wide open spaces, the Jet Car throbbing as its speed approached three hundred and then four hundred miles per hour. Xan leaned forward, his repellent stare fixed on the screen. Something puzzled him, though even with his global web of spies he could not know what. He knew B. Banzai better than perhaps any man, perhaps better than B. Banzai knew himself. A mere world speed record seemed trivial to a man of Banzai's intellect and talents. Xan stared and wondered, disdaining to talk to a swarthy servant who arrived with news.

"The death dwarves have been taken aboard the *Calypso*," announced the servant. "Should we order them to detonate?"

"Not now, confound you," barked Xan. "Out of my sight!"

In the blockhouse in Texas, eyes were similarly glued to the TV monitors, the streaking Jet Car seen from ground cameras and helicopters overhead. It was already forty-five miles downrange, its speed edging toward five hundred miles an hour. In reviewing my notes, it is evident all over again how unprepared were all but a few of us for what was about to happen.

General Catburd: It's fast, I'll give Banzai that, but war ain't Indianapolis. One heat-seeking missile and he's history.

Senator Cunningham: I doubt it, General. All the high-tech hardware in the world just might be useless against one American boy in a fast car. Isn't that right, Rawhide?

Rawhide: You're the ones saying it has military applications. No one at the Banzai Institute has said that.

Secretary of Defense: But surely, man, you must admit—!

Rawhide: The Jet Car is not for sale. Just watch. You might miss something.

(Across the room I observe a female commentator from one of the networks sitting with Perfect Tommy. I will delete her name, for she is well-known. The mercurial Tommy is looking very pleased with himself as the amazing car which he helped design goes ever faster.)

Commentator: Perfect Tommy, how on earth is Buckaroo able to keep that thing on the ground?

(Tommy, who can one moment appear dark and quarrelsome and the next bright as sunshine, does not take his eyes off the monitor as he answers in a calm, even voice.)

Perfect Tommy: She's just one sweet road hugger, lady. Plus the dude can motor. (pause) What are you doing tonight?

Commentator: Flying to Cambodia.

Perfect Tommy: What are you doing before you fly to Cambodia?

(The speed of the Jet Car is approaching six hundred miles an hour when suddenly it happens: The car veers off course sharply, toward the mountains on its right. The room is thrown into panic.)

Professor Hikita: Buckaroo, do you read?

Big Norse: Advise you abort. Over.

Buckaroo Banzai: Sorry, can't oblige.

(The car accelerates, Buckaroo's voice through static and crackle, unintelligible, then a sonic boom. A shot from a helicopter camera reveals that the Jet Car is literally setting the desert on fire, leaving it smoking in its wake.)

Commentator: The Jet Car has left its prescribed course, has broken the sound barrier at a speed in excess of seven hundred miles per hour. Radio contact with Mission Control apparently severed . . . Buckaroo Banazi in possibly serious trouble.

General Catburd: Either that or he's popped his cookies.

Big Norse: Mach one point three. Buckaroo! Do you read? Commence braking procedure. Over.

Secretary of Defense: He's heading for the mountains. Must be a steering malfunction.

Big Norse: Eject, Buckaroo! Eject!

(On the monitors the Jet Car is seen heading directly into a wall of mountain, impact virtually assured.)

General Catburd: Looks like Banzai's finally gonna get more than he bargained for, and take the Friends of the Earth with him.

What to make of this? I include this portion of the transcript only to illustrate what confusion reigned at the precise moment B. Banzai had chosen to turn the laws of physics topsy-turvy. I shall never forget that sweltering blockhouse and the noisome array of witnesses to the incredible event which I am about to describe.

And what did Buckaroo see? Between the hydraulic fluid spurting across his visor from a leak overhead and the side of the mountain closing fast, it is accurate to say that he had barely time to see his life flash in front of his eyes before pressing the button marked OSCILLATION OVER-THRUSTER. In a picosecond, colliding beams of electrons and positrons exploded in a continuous burst of particles, spewing intermediate vector bosons in all directions, power-ful super conducting magnets focusing the bosons at a single point on the side of the mountain, from which point radiated an expanding shock wave of spontaneous symmetry break-ing, leaving in its wake a region in which the increased mass of photons drastically reduced the range of the electromag-netic force. For an instant, solid matter ceased to be solid, every elementary particle of the mountain in rapid motion, and the seven-hundred-mile-per-hour Jet Car slid through it like a hot knife through butter.

Big Norse: It's off my scope!
General Catburd: What the—? What is going on?

With the exception of Tommy, Rawhide, Professor Hikita, and myself, the room was hysterical, for we had *seen* it. The helicopter camera had afforded us a perfect view of the Jet Car 'hitting' the mountain and disappearing within. Minds reeled, even my own, and I had been, as much as one could ever be, braced for it. It was as though slumbering devils had been awakened in all of us. There were screams, horrible laughs, but nothing compared to the torment Buckaroo was going through.

"God in heaven," burst from his lips. Just as the solidity of matter had long since been dissolved into mere mathemat-ical relationships in space, B. Banzai had for some time harbored the revolutionary notion that consciousness was not in the brain of the beholder but in the object itself. Consciousness was an intrinsic mysterious property capable of mathematical measurement, albeit its transmitting agent, as with gravity, was not yet known. It had been B. Banzai's contention, along with Professor Hikita, for at least a decade that consciousness was a particle wave akin to light, and in the manner of a radio transmitter, broadcast on our planet on a single frequency, although it was mathematically probable that the exact frequency would vary throughout the cosmos. The reader will jump ahead to the next conclusion without any prodding from me: namely, that most humans are *aware* of receiving fuzzy signals of alien consciousness from other worlds, other dimensions, but for reasons of psychological resistance or biological limitation, cannot interpret them clearly. Not only until Buckaroo Banzai have we lacked a medical physicist's concept of consciousness, but the probability is that we and *they* broadcast on different spectra. Unfortunately, the human brain, in particular the reticular activating system in the brain stem, localized by B. Banzai as the likely consciousness receptor, is even by our own standards of evolution a quite antiquated contraption. In effect, our so-called sophisticated brains are obsolescent radio sets without tuners. Locked into a single station, we miss the other ninety-nine hundredths of the dial.

There are exceptions, as B. Banzai noted in his last address to the American Psychiatric Association. Valid clairvoyants and schizophrenics, as well as certain "primitive" tribes which use mind-altering drugs, possess wider tuning ranges than the average person; and while these abnormal cases are intriguing in and of themselves, of greater interest to Buckaroo Banzai was the possibility of going to the seat of consciousness itself, within an object. Again to cite our radio analogy, instead of bringing his energies to bear on improving the tuner, he would go to the transmitter. For if consciousness were found to be a force within the atom, like the strong, weak, and electromagnetic forces, as he believed, then in the process of bending these forces with the OSCILLATION OVERTHRUSTER, the entire band-width of consciousness would become clear. It was central to B. Banzai's theory that every object, every molecule, contained the full range of universal consciousness even if it "broadcast" or radiated only a miniscule portion of the spectrum.

At the risk of digressing further, I must say that B. Banzai had empirical evidence supporting his ideas, or I am confident he would never have staked his own life as well as the Banzai Institute's great world renown on the outcome. This evidence derived from an experiment gone awry in the 1930s at Princeton University in New Jersey, during which Professor Hikita and a scientific colleague named Dr. Emilio Lizardo accidentally glimpsed a burst of enhanced consciousness radiation or, put simply, alien life on another dimension. From this void of brilliant colors came the despairing screams of the damned, captive monstrosities that defied belief, much less description. Lizardo had, in fact, for a brief moment that seemed an eternity, been sucked halfway into the void through a supposedly solid wall. Alien hands clutched at him! What further horror he witnessed as a result of the terrifying ordeal was never known, except to say that when he emerged to safety he was plainly mad. His hair had turned to orange, and he fled in terror, almost immediately embarking upon a life of crime. Subsequently he was captured by the authorities and sentenced to an asylum where he never recovered. (More on this shortly.)

Well aware of Lizardo's case, B. Banzai nevertheless undertook the perilous journey to the seat of consciousness, into the mountain, his devouring passion to *know* perhaps even fanned to flame by the prospect of danger. What he saw there has been widely viewed, insofar as the film he brought out with him. One may see the hideous shapes, the hues of unnatural color, the fragments of mysterious light, and the rest of it, along with the voices that still cause my skin to creep with terror; but watching another fall through a trapdoor is not the same as falling through it oneself. Film is not the reality and cannot convey the true *feel* of the place, if *place* is the word. B. Banzai's obsession had become all too real, and he had no way of knowing, once inside, whether he would ever escape.

General Catburd: Where is he? Will somebody tell me?
Rawhide: Sit down, General.
General Catburd: Not until I get an explanation.

"Like a roller coaster ride through a meteor shower," was how Buckaroo would initially describe the experience of traveling through what has come to be called "The Eighth Dimension" by the popular press. The G-force was apparently vastly greater than anything ever experienced on earth. The car's two inch thick windscreen broke as if struck by a sledgehammer, Buckaroo's Plexiglas helmet shattered, and he was hurled back in his seat and riveted there like a helpless doll. Gigantic static electrical charges lit the unfamiliar atmosphere laden with acrid odors. Amid tears and wailing and ferocious stinging pests that managed to penetrate even Buckaroo's flight suit, there were the fearsome yells I have already mentioned. A red viscous stream and its tributaries were encountered, swirling like a great river toward an unknown destination. Sinister shadows with sweat-grimed faces and membraned eyes attempted to grasp hold of the car as it shot past, adopting any such desperate means as might help them escape the dreadful place. One such beast even came face to face with B. Banzai as it fell headlong across the hood of the car and managed to hang on for a moment, its horrible stare and foam-flecked mouth a sight Buckaroo will not soon forget. To the young reader's excited fancy, this may all seem the stuff of romantic adventure, but I must believe Buckaroo Banzai when he tells me that never in his life had he felt such . . . yes, fear was the word he used. These angry demons had a way of infiltrating even the spirit, B. Banzai hearing them jabbering with glee within his brain, experiencing the pulsing exhilaration of pure evil, chaos. "Now I know how Lizardo felt," he remembered thinking. But he was stronger than Lizardo. The psychic attackers could not subjugate him, although if the incredible journey had lasted a moment longer . . .

Of the terrain, I have alluded to the red river. In addition there were vast chasms of hissing swamp and stench, alpine ranges with countless crags, which B. Banzai avoided with difficulty. Spurts of flame issued with volcanic energy from unseen sources, forming huge thunderclouds and gurgling rock formations of fantastic shape. Here and there the topography seemed to fall away altogether, and there were descents into great voids of pandemonium, illuminated by flashes of momentary radiance. These blinding rays would last but for an instant, to be followed by a darkness likened to liquid ebony, total and all-enveloping. At one point, a gasping B. Banzai recalled looking up into a heaven full of stars, only to realize he was upside down and the glowing lights were not stars at all, buy millions of eyes peering up, lost souls in the black mantle of eternity.

As for those of us back in the blockhouse, we held our breath; for although the harrowing passage seemed to last forever, in fact is was mere seconds before the Jet Car blasted out the opposite side of the mountain to our cheers of victory tempered with relief. Like owners of a winning thoroughbred, each of us—Rawhide, Perfect Tommy, Hikita, and myself—felt a part of a glorious moment. (How glorious we could not yet even guess!)

"Banzai!" shouted Hikita, thumping the table with his fist, and I turned, feeling a muscular hand grip my shoulder. It was Rawhide, that quietest of men, dancing a jig and embracing me. To the others, the invited guests, we must have seemed mad, but we didn't care. For once the news media were as good as speechless, confronted with the story of the century.

Commentator: I have seen something strange, something very strange.

General Catburd: Certainly irregular.

(Senator Cunningham jumps a foot into the air, her heart contracted with excitement.)

Senator Cunningham: He's done it! He's gone through the mountain without a scratch! Oh, my God!

Secretary of Defense: Oh, my God!

He *had* done it, but Buckaroo could not relax just yet, having his hands full trying to slow the still-speeding Jet Car, wooing it like a woman. "Easy now. Come on," he cajoled, tugging a switch to release the trailing parachute, but would it be enough in the scant space remaining before the next ring of mountains? There would be no more passing through solid matter today; he was low on liquid helium. The OS-

CILLATION OVERTHRUSTER was of no use. It was strictly man versus machine now. He plunged the brake to the floor and tugged at the wheel. To his dismay the loss of hydraulic brake and steering pressure had been greater than he thought.

A billion or so people awaited the result on television and none with greater anticipation than Xan. His expression no longer so arrogant, permeated by dark depression over the incredible achievement of Buckaroo Banzai, he felt events now crowd in on him with a rush. One hand reached for the telephone as he watched B. Banzai struggle to stop the car. He dialed the number of a home for the criminally insane in Trenton, New Jersey, and requested to talk to Dr. Emilio Lizardo, one of the inmates.

In the same instant he knocked aside a glass with an angry blow. Banzai had stopped the car in the nick of time, as the soulless Xan had expected and perhaps deep down had hoped he would, for it was never fated that Banzai die by accidental means. That happy moment would belong to Xan and his ruffians, if Xan had his way. The joy of driving a dagger through Banzai's heart would be Xan's destiny, and his alone.

"Hello." It was a curious voice at the other end of the phone, a thick Neapolitan accent speaking from a long distance.

"We have a bad connection," said Xan.

"No, I am weak," was Lizardo's reply.

"Are you watching television?"

"No, I've just been drugged."

"You're lucky."

"What's on?"

"Banzai. Turn on your set."

7

No hurried explanation could account for the insane, wild, unkempt figure which Dr. Emilio Lizardo had become. Once handsome and faultlessly groomed, now he was a twisted creature with pendulous cheeks and unsightly paunch, his only solace the treacherous antipsychotic drugs given him daily. So far and so long had he deteriorated that one could faithfully say that the best that could await him now was a painless death. Inflamed eyes beneath a shock of red hair, he was nightmare incarnate, a fitting mate for the devil himself. Trembling in every limb as one crazed, which indeed he was, he dropped the phone and surged for the television with a terrible whoop. Looking neither right nor left, he fell back limp in his armchair and clasped his hands to keep them from flopping. His beloved TV was coming alive; and by turns recoiling and seething like a reptile, he watched as the smoking Jet Car came to rest in a thicket of stump mesquite trees and B. Banzai clambered out the driver's window.

Ah, yes, Banzai . . . convinced somehow by his own dementia that the two were kindred souls, Lizardo had followed B. Banzai's exploits over the years. He had more than once even sent friendly overtures to the Banzai Institute.

37

"How's your work coming, pal?" I recall one such letter. "My suspicion is you need help."

Buckaroo had paid little heed to the message, but I had inquired about the unusual name. It had rather caught my fancy. "Who is this Dr. Lizardo?" I had asked him.

"He's a true tragic figure," Buckaroo had said. "An incalculable loss to science and to those who knew him." He had gone on to relate the circumstances of the experiment gone awry in the '30s, the close friendship that had once existed between Lizardo and Professor Hikita, fellow professors in the Princeton physics department. As for the "other vexatious business," as Buckaroo put it, no one could say. "The whole thing about going into another dimension, another sideband of consciousness, is still so foreign to us that perhaps we won't really understand his case until long after his death." All in all, the entire bizarre tale made a lasting impression on me, arousing more pity than anything else.

"Did you ever meet him?" I asked Buckaroo finally.

"No, I never did," had been his reply. "Hikita-san went to see him once, and Lizardo had to be restrained from attacking him. He's simply not the same man."

Still, though they had never met, to Lizardo it seemed more than coincidental, uncanny almost, how his and B. Banzai's paths had intertwined over the years; how through Banzai's mathematics Lizardo felt he had come to know the man and know him well. To Lizardo, B. Banzai's was the only mind near his equal. They approached problems similarly; they shared the same cosmology. They were the twin jewels of intellect on this planet. Still, there were differences. Banzai was an upstart, a Johnny-come-lately to the field of extra-dimensional physics. He had started with the ground plowed already, plowed by the blood and sweat of the Great Pioneer Emilio Lizardo. Granted, Banzai had inherited his parents' talents and then some, but no one should forget that it was he, *he,* Emilio Lizardo, who as a young man with dreamy eyes and jet-black hair had smashed the never-before-broken dimension barrier. The Greatest and Most Unappreciated Scientist of His Time, who before being framed and unjustly incarcerated for crimes he had no knowledge of, had, in a flash of vision, dared catapult himself through a solid wall before running off terrified into the night.

Why had he run? Who was he? Whorfin? Who was Whorfin? Sometimes in the early morning when the dawn tinged the east and he had just received his antipsychotic dosage, he caught a glimpse of his old self behind the eyes, the eyes of this obviously schizophrenic red-haired old man whom he did not know but had learned to obey. The eyes seemed to scream: Help me. Who am I? What am I doing here?

What was Banzai doing now? Lizardo stalked the TV and crouched. Upon taking inventory of the Jet Car, B. Banzai had discovered two unusual physical specimens which he carefully put into plastic sandwich bags to be labeled although they defied classification. From the wind screen, he removed a handful of foul-smelling gelatinous substance that looked clammy, hot to the touch, at least on TV, and close quarters inspection of the car's undercarriage disclosed a curiously shaped parasite that attached itself to the drive shaft and now resisted attempts to dislodge it. B. Banzai appeared to pick at it with a stick but without much success.

"That sucker's stuck," muttered Lizardo. "What the hell is it?"

His outstretched prehensile hand reached for the phone he had dropped, as he watched Banzai poke at the apparently lifeless object only to have the thing spring at him and go skittering across the desert. Banzai in rapid pursuit. "What am I watching?" demanded Lizardo, finding Xan still there.

"Do you see that mountain in the background?" Xan said.

"Yes."

"Banzai went through it."

There was a moment of silence, Lizardo bereft of movement except for the odd palsy. "He what?"

"He went through the mountain. He drove that car of his through a piece of rock a mile wide."

A creeping awareness of what Xan meant came over Lizardo's unseeing bloodshot eyes. He who had labored day and night these past many decades, whose fierce devouring passion it had been to duplicate that singular moment when he had stepped through a brick wall as if it were slush, had now merely turned on the television to see the usurper Banzai snare his glory.

For some time speech was impossible, but finally he said, "What's it to me?"

"Well, I know you have been interested in this sort of thing," said Xan cagily. "You'll recall you once came to me through my associate in Hong Kong, a chap named Lo Pep, seeking funds for your research in this area."

"I have no recollection of such a thing," said Lizardo, and that much was true. Often just after his medication was administered, his memory became clouded. The staff would tell him things that the redhead had done, and he would try in vain to remember.

"I don't blame you," said Xan. "I laughed in your face. I called you a simpleton, and I found your story about coming from outer space through a brick wall patently absurd."

"I'm sorry, I have no recollection of that."

"That's your problem. There's no doubt in my mind you're exactly where you belong, but that's not why I'm calling. I should have had the good grace to make you feel more welcome in my camp."

"I just have no recollection of any of that. My name is Dr. Emilio Lizardo."

"How are your own calculations coming on your solid-matter-penetrator?"

"Well—" Lizardo feigned indifference, eyeing the spate of mathematical equations scribbled on the wall in his own jerky hand. "Not bad."

"That means you're getting no place. Perhaps you need Banzai's help."

"It could be opportune," Lizardo admitted.

"Very opportune, I would imagine. What would you say if I told you I could spring you out of that institution in a couple of hours?"

"I would say who is this?"

"It's Xan, you fool! Hanoi Xan!"

The name had a certain ring of familiarity, but again Lizardo could not say how he knew it. There was a hollow click at the other end of the line, and Lizardo regarded the call as he would a prank, meanwhile watching the plucky Banzai catch the errant parasite and stuff it into a sandwich bag before heading back to the Jet Car where his radio was crackling.

General Catburd: This his frequency? Nobody's home. Banzai?

Secretary of Defense: Give me the phone. You tell me, Buckaroo, what in tarnation is this going-through-solid-matter-and-rendering-all-existing-conventional-defense-perimeters-useless-overnight-bullcorn?

General Catburd: Buckaroo, Catburd here. I've got egg all over my face—all right, crow feathers, too—but that's okay. No room for egos here. We're all Americans, and I wanna buy that toy of yours. Senator Cunningham here feels the same way—right, Madame Senator?

Senator Cunningham: Don't put words in my mouth, General.

Secretary of Defense: We'll talk turkey later.

Professor Hikita: Not for sale, Mr. Secretary. Jet Car is not for sale.

Secretary of Defense: I wasn't talking to you, little Hikita-san.

(Rawhide and I move closer to the professor, backing him up in the matter.)

Professor Hikita: Buckaroo, did you see them? Did you?

Secretary of Defense: See who?

Buckaroo Banzai: *See* them? They about had me and the whole car for breakfast.

Professor Hikita: They attacked you? They tried to take control of your mind? They exist?

Buckaroo Banzai: With any luck I have the pictures to prove it.

Professor Hikita seized upon the news, clutching it with the relief of a man from whose shoulders had just been lifted a cumbersome weight. For more than forty years he had lived with self-doubt concerning what he had seen the night of the ill-fated experiment at Princeton. Had he actually seen creatures in the other dimension, or had they been figments of the imagination? He was a scientist, an exponent of the scientific method, and the fact that he had been unable to repeat the experiment and ascertain the truth to his satisfaction had come to be an obsession. In hopes of learning more, he had made the painful journey to visit Dr. Lizardo, only to see with his own eyes the abject folly of the enterprise. Emilio Lizardo was gone; he had ceased to exist, his place taken by the raving red-haired apparition who called himself John Whorfin and who babbled endlessly about his empire somewhere on the other side of Saturn.

8

SEVERAL HOURS LATER, after Buckaroo had showered and shaved for the news media with the Banzai Institute's latest invention, a gyroscopic razor that worked on the principle of a spinning top, Lizardo's antipsychotic medication had begun to wear thin and John Whorfin seized control. This coup d'etat was usually accompanied by an irresistible urge to wander. The combination of a starry night and the fascination of travel often sent the two of them, Whorfin and Lizardo, to a comfortable chair by the window where they watched the heavens through the heavy iron grate that sealed them in.

Whorfin would use these occasions to recite a daily menu of gripes, in particular berating Lizardo with accusations of stupidity and sloth, blaming him for a lack of progess in recreating the Princeton experiment. For his part, Lizardo tried to explain that his scientific work had been hampered by Whorfin's presence.

"You dominate my brain," Lizardo would say. "You give me no freedom to think."

"If I didn't dominate you, you wouldn't help me," Whorfin would reply. "You have no loyalty to the cause."

"That isn't true. I want to help you get off planet Earth, because I know I'll never be free as long as you remain."

43

"But you think I'm evil. There is resistance. I can feel it."

And around they would go. Out of this discord between two souls in one body would come nothing constructive, and every day brought more of the same—Lizardo praying for the next dawn and a fresh dose of medication which would bring him at least a few hours free of Whorfin's torment. On this particular day, Whorfin seized control with dramatic suddenness and with a volley of furious curses commanded to see the television.

The two of them were still in front of the set hours later, watching replay upon replay of the amazing Jet Car, when the phone on the wall rang.

"You get it," said Whorfin's pouting lips, and the right hand (that side of the body in which Lizardo seemed to reside) reached for the phone. In his shaking hand he heard the voice of Xan.

"Who is this?" demanded the villain.

"John Whorfin. Who is this?"

"Xan here, Whorfin. I called earlier. I must have reached Lizardo."

"Yes, you probably did. What's on your mind, great Xan?"

"You've seen the news?"

"Banzai? Of course!"

"I have a proposition for you."

"In the past it was always I who made the propositions to you, great Xan. What has changed?"

"Shut up. I made the same offer to Lizardo I'm making to you. I don't which one of you is which—"

"That's our problem."

"That's the way I look at it." Xan paused, perhaps second-guessing himself for ever getting involved with these two. "In case you're interested, I can have you out of that hell hole by tonight. What do you say?"

"I say there's no doubt you can. Who is to stop the great Xan from doing whatever he wishes? But there is no need— my own boys can get me out easily enough."

A peal of irksome laughter came from Xan. "Your boys from outer space? What planet is it you're from again? I forget."

Whorfin quelled his rage and answered calmly. "Planet 10."

"Right . . . Planet 10. Well, they haven't gotten you out so far, have they? How long have you been rotting there?"

"Forty-five years, which is but a day—"

"I know . . . 'which is but a day' on your planet. Maybe you've got the time, but I'm not sure about Lizardo. He's not of your planet, is he?"

Whorfin cocked his head a short distance from the phone. Was Xan only humoring him, only pretending to believe his story about coming from Planet 10? Whorfin had learned many things about human beings (and I include Xan in this category only reluctantly), but he did not possess a sense of humor and hence could not comprehend one, much less one as barbed as Hanoi Xan's.

"You may have a point," Whorfin said, looking at his gnarled hands. "Lizardo is getting old."

"And I'd say perhaps you miscalculated as far as your *boys* are concerned. We both know what loyalty among criminals is worth." With this parry Xan obviously had touched a raw nerve, Whorfin's own paranoia doing the rest. "They've probably got a good thing going on the outside," continued Xan. "Why should they give a damn about getting you out? What do they need you for?"

Whorfin listened and spoke little, the wheels in his mind turning on their own. His latest conversation with his boys *had* made him uneasy. John Bigbooté had sounded evasive, too busy to be bothered. They had had, by Earth standards, a long time to start life anew without him, without the discipline of a strong hand. Perhaps his fears were unfounded, but now was the time. . . . *Banzai had done it! Banzai had succeeded in breaking the dimension barrier! There at last existed the means of going home to Planet 10, if only he could* . . .

"I want you to build me what Banzai's got," Xan said.

"The Jet Car."

"Whatever it takes to go through solid matter," said Xan, practically salivating. "I must have that power!"

On the television, the entry of the Jet Car into the mountain was shown once again, and the attractive network commentator was still sitting next to the fair-haired Perfect Tommy, with Rawhide and myself along for laughs.

Commentator: Here she is, slowed down as far as we can take it. Lookit there . . . slam! Right into the side of that mountain! Perfect Tommy, Rawhide, Reno, you guys are known as the Hong Kong Cavaliers, Buckaroo's most trusted inner circle. So I gotta ask, did it surprise you fellows as much as the rest of us when the HB 88, the experimental jet vehicle, went right off the scope and with the device known as the Oscillation Overthruster vanished inside solid matter?

Perfect Tommy: Nope, not really.

Commentator: Was Buckaroo acting any different this morning? I mean, in terms of other mornings?

Perfect Tommy: I don't know. I was asleep. Rawhide, you saw him.

(The quiet gunsmith Rawhide, uneasy before the cameras, knows only how to speak the truth.)

Rawhide: I don't think he went to bed. Buckaroo normally only sleeps an hour or two a night anyway, ever since—

(Rawhide glances at us, notices our keen scrutiny of what he is about to say, and thankfully neglects to mention the profound change in Buckaroo since the death of his wife Peggy.)

Rawhide: Buckaroo just doesn't sleep much, that's all. Plus, Tommy had a late-night petting party that went on till the wee hours. I doubt he could have gotten much sleep anyway.

(The commentator raises her eyebrows in Tommy's direction, nodding knowingly.)

Commentator: No wonder Tommy looks so awful today.

(Tommy, ever conscious of his physical appearance, turns several shades of crimson.)

"Money is no object," said Xan. "I'll give you a million dollars. Can you build it for a million?"

"I don't see why not," Whorfin said, making other plans even as he spoke.

"You'll report to Lo Pep. He'll be in touch and can give you whatever assistance you require."

"Thank you, mighty Xan."

"Thank you, mighty Whorfin."

Whorfin hung up the phone, gloating, for he had not the slightest intention of upholding his end of the bargain. He would get what Banzai had, this queer device called the OSCILLATION OVERTHRUSTER, but he would not give it to Xan. He would use it himself to free the rest of his army from the Eighth Dimension and take a short cut through the same dimension to Planet 10, where he would scatter his enemies before him and rule mercilessly.

The only obstacle that lay in his path was Buckaroo Banzai, and possibly the Nova Police, if they knew his whereabouts. Hiding in Lizardo's body, it was a risk he was more than willing to take.

9

DEPARTURE TIME FOR the Banzai Institute 727 from the El Paso Airport was two o'clock in the afternoon, which put us into New York around eight where we were met by Pinky Carruthers, an auxiliary guitarist with the band. Pinky, his usual irrepressible self, was always a delight to behold. Fond of sporting pink suits and stating that he knew over forty-seven thousand unknown facts, that day he was giving anyone who would listen an earful of some new philosophy he had embraced only that morning, something called Kashmirian Shavism. (I have no idea as to the spelling, or even whether such a thing exists.) He was, however, quite obviously taken with the subject, or at least taken with hearing himself pontificate on the matter of the Cosmic Dance of Shiva.

"Is it Hindoo?" I asked.

"It's 'undo,' " he said, "I'm learning to undo everything I've learned up to now."

"What about the forty-seven thousand unknown facts?"

"That's trivia compared to this," he said, as we walked toward a waiting limousine dispatched by the Institute. "Everything is part of the harmonic pulsating 'it,' "

"Have you watched television today?" I asked him pointedly.

"No, I've been practicing guitar."

"Why do you think those police were having such a hard time holding back that mob of reporters?" I said, referring to at least several dozen reporters all frantically trying to shout questions at Buckaroo and the rest of us across the tarmac.

"Because we're the Hong Kong Cavaliers," replied Pinky, as though it were the most obvious thing in the world, and in a sense he was right. Buckaroo's blazing artistry, with an able assist from the rest of us, had brought millions of fans to their feet the world over, and the glare of television lights was no stranger to us. But today was different, and the army of reporters, like a pack of dogs, were kept at bay only by the vigorous blows of police truncheons. At last, sensing something unusual in the air, Pinky Carruthers thoughtfully rubbed his nose and asked sheepishly, "What's going on, Reno?"

"Buckaroo went through solid matter," I said.

He was dumbfounded. "Any particular reason?" he said.

I laughed. "You'll have to ask him."

"I wonder if there's a haberdashery around here."

"Why?"

"Won't his head swell?"

I didn't quite see the connection, but it didn't matter. I could always appreciate Pinky's touching honesty. He had been with us not quite a year, but already we had all taken him to our bosom. He played his instrument well and did not tolerate rascals and scoundrels.

"Once you get to know Buckaroo a little better," I said, "you'll see he never changes. But it's a natural question."

"That's a relief," he said, as we reached the waiting limousine just in the nick of time, the police line suddenly having broken, sending reporters and hordes of teenaged girls rushing our way. We were quickly joined inside the car by Buckaroo and Rawhide and all found ourselves asking the same question.

"Where's Perfect Tommy?" said Buckaroo. "Anybody see him?"

"I saw him," said Rawhide. "He was with that reporter from CBS. The blonde."

"Well, he'll have to catch up with us," said Buckaroo. "We can't wait for him."

It was easy to see why not. As the limousine pulled away, I looked out my window and saw the full fury of the reporters as they pounded the glass, shoving one another. My indignation was aroused as threats were heard, but soon it was all left behind like a wild drum roll ringing in our ears, and Buckaroo asked us to join him in a drink of potent *aguardiente* he had picked up in El Paso.

"Anything new from Pecos and the *Calypso?*" he asked, looking at me.

"Not yet." I shook my head. "Still too much signal jamming going on."

"Keep me in the picture," he said.

"The minute I hear," I replied, tipping my glass as Pinky shoved a tape in the cassette player and to an infectious syncopated beat we fell to talking among ourselves of less urgent matters.

As unofficial annalist of the group, I am often asked what such times are like, when we are alone. The truth is neither newsworthy nor particularly out of the ordinary. What do friends do when they are together? What do they talk about? The truth is, of course, nothing and everything. We have no festering feuds or simmering rivalries, though that may disappoint some to hear. On the other hand, neither are we saints. Maudlin with drink, we talk of women, gangster chieftains, music, and weapons with the easy familiarity of men who have gone on stage and gone through battle together. Some cloistered critics have accused us of having a myopic view of the world, living out the sorts of adventures that other men hold only as fantasies. I would retort that it is our view of the world which brought us together in the first place, and whether or not it is a correct view is an issue historians will decide. We prefer to think of ourselves as realists. One cannot always deal gentlemanly with brutes, for as B. Banzai has said, "There are times when verbal ingenuity is not enough."

10

I HAD MY own government consulting business, or "think tank," before accepting a fellowship to the Banzai Institute. Every day in my prior work the most trying problems crossed my desk, and my associates and I would put our heads together and attempt to find solutions. Hopefully, sensible reason would prevail, and we would forward the distillation of our hours (usually weeks) of research and discussion to the appropriate government agency where it would sink into oblivion, along with our follow-up reports and further recommendations. After years of such frustration, despite the pleasant living I was making at the taxpayers' expense, a part of me had had enough. Money could no longer satisfy the strong yearning that had begun to insinuate itself into every pore of my being. I longed to roll up my sleeves and take a course of unabashed action without the usual need of diplomatic niceties, what we in the so-called civilized world have come to acknowledge as accepted behavior. The constraints of having to "go through channels" to put in one's "two cents" while the world burned had suddenly ceased to be a viable option for me. I had heard of Buckaroo Banzai of course; I knew of his work, but I had no idea whether he would reply to the letter I dashed off one evening after a particularly bad day at the office. I have no idea to this day what gave me the audacity to drop it in the mail so airily and then forget all about it until a week later when my secretary buzzed me over the intercom, so excited she could hardly speak.

"Buckaroo Banzai is here to see you!" she ejaculated. "Should I show him in?"

I confess to having taken a quick drop of whiskey to energize myself as I arose unsteadily and went to open my door. I have always found it remarkable how a confident and open person can make a strong lasting impression in the space of a single moment, but that was just what I found to be the case with B. Banzai. A ready smile and a firm handshake attached to a body that seemed to be made entirely of sinew captivated me immediately. I suggested that we walk outside, and he agreed.

In the sunshine his face was smooth, unmarked. A smile played constantly around his lips, but the eyes were deep and thoughtful, of an unusual color I cannot readily describe. Neither can I recall who spoke first, a phenomenon I have found common among others when they have been asked to recall their first encounters with the man. I tend to believe it is the eyes, of such an unusual hue and hypnotic intensity that they could make one believe almost anything. In short, within the first minute of our meeting I believe I had decided to follow him anywhere without the slightest hesitation.

"What sorts of things do you enjoy doing?" I recall him asking.

I described my hobbies such as they were, giving a brief outline of my background and education. Throughout, he looked at me with great attention, giving away not a hint of what he was thinking until I mentioned the subject of music.

"You like music?" he asked.

"I like it very much." I nodded. "Jazz, especially."

"How about syncopated music?"

"I like all kinds, but I prefer to play jazz."

"You do play, then?"

"The saxophone," I said, itching to show my skill. "Would you like to hear me?"

"Of course. You have your sax?"

"I don't live far."

Buckaroo whistled, and as if from out of nowhere two women and a young man appeared. "Bring the car," Buckaroo said to the heavyset youth I later came to know as Rawhide, while the two women, both of whom appeared capable of taking care of themselves in a pinch, looked me over with a scrutiny I did not appreciate. "This is Reno," Buckaroo said to them, the name causing me to look around as it was the first time I had heard it. "He plays sax."

Before I could reply, one of the women stepped forward and introduced herself, her eyes still filled with what I sensed to be secret contempt. "I'm Pecos," said the slightly built female who nonetheless cowed me. "Are you hot?"

"I'm pretty hot," I said, slipping into the argot of musicians.

"We'll see," she said, displaying a smile that made me feel only more intimidated. "We're looking for somebody really hot."

"Good," I said. "You've found him."

She muttered something and stepped aside. I remember thinking at the time that this birdlike creature with the steel grip had it in for me, I could not for the life of me figure out why. I immediately resolved not to like her, a resolution that I soon found myself hard pressed to keep, as regular readers of the series well know.*

I received a cordial welcome from Pecos's blonde companion who introduced herself as Peggy. It occurred to me immediately who she must be, for I had read of her in so many of the popular magazines. She and Buckaroo had set a fall wedding date in New York, and no event in recent memory had so stirred the public imagination. While more than pleasing to the eye, it was not her beauty that impressed me most. More than her feminine charms or even her keen intellect, it was her extraordinary gift of life (a trite expression, I'm well aware) that had drawn Buckaroo to her. Her carefree gaiety could bring sunshine to even the darkest of

---

* In the adventure *Bastardy Proved a Spur,* Pecos and I declare our love for one another and agree to marry at a future date, provided we escape the yak skin in which Xan's cat's-paw, the Pasha of Three Tails, has stitched us. —Reno

days. Her warm smile during our first meeting went a long way toward allaying my silly jitters.

"Do you ride?" she asked.

I had no wish to be considered a milksop, and so I nodded. "Oh, yes, indeed," I blurted out. "I come from some of the best riding stock in Virginia."

Pecos howled to the point of collapse, while Buckaroo and Peggy, controlling their own laughter, gave her scolding looks. I think my eyeballs filled with blood, for I saw only the color red until Rawhide pulled up in the car.

"Did I say something untoward?" I asked Buckaroo.

"Don't worry about it," he said, patting my shoulder. "I haven't seen Pecos laugh since Sluggo died. She likes you."

She had an odd way of showing it, I thought, and it was not until we were halfway to my house that I realized with the force of a revelation what I had said. The whole incident suddenly struck me as uproariously funny, and I could not suppress a chuckle of my own. Pecos, her own amusement now piqued further, could but look at me questioningly.

"I'm glad you liked my little joke," I said, joining in the fun, "even if it was at my own expense."

It dawned on her that perhaps I did know a thing or two, and she begrudged as much. "Then you're a very funny man," she said.

"Only when I'm nervous," I said.

"Why should you be nervous among friends?"

She smiled, this time with a genuineness that was touching. Strange to say, I did feel surprisingly at ease with these four worthies at whose exploits I had long marveled. Buckaroo, like most true geniuses, was utterly without arrogance, a simple man in the best sense of the word. Decency toward others was not something he had to work at; with him it was an involuntary as breathing. On the other hand, I have seen him an hour after killing a man and found him to be perfectly composed. To the Occidental mind this may seem a contradiction; but to the soul of the Mongol, that atavistic side of B. Banzai whose blood flows in a straight line from the Khans, mortal combat is the prime rule of nature. We in the West have largely forgotten this. The Mongol has not.

I have not mentioned the hands of Buckaroo Banzai, the same hands that wield both scalpel and sword with equally dazzling skill. I have seen him make a samurai sword whistle a tune as it cut through the air, just as I have seen him swing the same blade close enough to my cheek to snip my whiskers. I have no doubt that he had he not chosen to be a surgeon and a scientist, he could have easily turned his swordsmanship into a fortune on the variety stages of the world, just as he has done with his music.

Upon reaching my house, I pulled out my saxophone; and with Buckaroo on guitar, Rawhide on piano, and Pecos on harmonica, we played syncopated music until late in the evening. Peggy seated herself in the front row of our little concert and passed to us biscuits of toasted barley flour and a thermos filled with an odd pungent liqueur, which after I had imbibed it, made me feel as though I had devoured a more than ample meal. A strange sense of euphoria swept over me and seemed to improve my playing quite markedly. When I asked the name of the hearty concoction, they would say only that it was a favorite of long-standing with the band but was not necessarily for everyone. After we had emptied the thermos and I still insisted on knowing, Peggy smiled and said, "Very well, Reno. You know Buckaroo is part Mongolian?" I nodded. "Well, it's a Mongolian drink," she said, hesitating. "It's . . . fermented mare's milk."

As you might suspect, on that note the party ended. I have no recollection of anything other than crawling off to the bathroom and hearing Buckaroo's voice sometime later through the door.

"Reno?"

"Yes?" I replied weakly.

'Can I come in?"

"I'd rather you didn't."

"Are you all right?"

"No, but there's nothing anyone can do, not even Buckaroo Banzai."

"We're putting on a syncopated show at the Hollywood Palladium in Los Angeles this coming Saturday. I really enjoy your playing. Can you make it?"

"If I'm better," I said.

"Don't worry. You'll be fine tomorrow. I'll wire you a plane ticket and expense money."

"Does this mean—?" I wasn't quite sure of the correct terminology. "You'll be needing me all the time?"

"I'm offering you an internship to the Banzai Institute," Buckaroo said. "The stipend isn't a lot—only five hundred dollars a month, plus your lodging and meals—but you'll learn to fight, shoot, and handle a lasso. And if you make it to resident, you'll have the full resources of the Institute at your disposal. You can study in depth whatever topic you choose, alongside some of the finest minds in the world."

I balked, momentarily awash in self-pity. "Do you think I can make the grade?" I asked.

"Humanity demands it," he said.

"I'll see you in Los Angeles."

(Backstage in Atlantic City we wait to go on. Buckaroo materializes in his usual hurry, looking for something to eat, trailed by a gang of reporters.)

Buckaroo Banzai: I'm starving. Somebody help.

Rawhide: I've got half a tuna sandwich.

Buckaroo Banzai: Same one you had yesterday? Anybody got any fugu?

(I offer him a sliver of the poisonous Japanese blowfish. Depending on how it is prepared, it is either indescribably delicious or deadly.)

Sitting here, looking at my notes of our performance in Atlantic City, the night of the Jet Car test, the smell of fermented mare's milk evokes a train of memories from the early days to the present. I am immobilized by the image of Rawhide, our dear departed friend, offering Buckaroo a tuna fish sandwich from his hat, a half-eaten mouldy piece of fodder which even the voracious Buckarro tosses back as unfit for human consumption. Nearby sits Professor Hikita, brow furrowed in puzzlement as he studies slides through a spectroscope and tries to concentrate in the noisome room which reeks of stale spirits and concerts past. Fermented mare's milk, coffee, and beer are passed around; gorgeous women flit silently through, ready for instant action, awaiting only a chance word or a curious glance, while outside in the waiting audience young hearts beat fast with anticipation that syncopated music will soon begin.

And it isn't long in coming. Someone shouts, "Perfect Tommy's here," and in pads the culprit, guilt written all over his face. With him is the network commentator, no longer on her way to Cambodia, instead intent on a little spade work where we're concerned. Is it true you're all sharpshooters? she asks. Yes. Like the FBI? Somewhat, although we are not crime solvers in the main. Then what are you? She explains apologetically that she is our biggest fan but has been instructed by her network to ask some "hard" questions. I accordingly refer her to a paper issued by the Banzai Institute which lays out our aims, philosophy, and sources of funding, pointing out that we are a non-profit enterprise in all respects. As for our constitutional powers, I say, we have none, unless you consider the extraordinary rights accorded every U.S. citizen by law, in which case we are amply empowered to go about our business. What is your business? she persists. Adventure, I reply.

My chief calls. "Everybody ready?" says Buckaroo. We assent, with the glorious exception of Tommy who is still furiously tuning his guitars. The owner of the club, Artie, comes in, summoning us to the stage. Full of bluster and loud of voice, he is actually a self-made parody of a hepcat, a necessity in this rough-and-tumble syncopated music club.

"You guys gonna play music or play with your chemistry sets?" he says. We all ignore him, feigning indifference. "I don't care if you drove through a rock this morning. That's Texas! This is New Jersey! I want some music outta you characters!"

Buckaroo observes Tommy through narrow eyes, restraining comment, when suddenly Professor Hikita leaps to his feet, his face deathly pale.

"Look at this, Buckaroo!" he exclaims, bringing over the slides and the spectroscope. "It's growing!"

We crowd around, eagerly wanting to see for ourselves, each with his own theory.

(Buckaroo peers through the spectroscope.)

Buckaroo Banzai: It does seem to be larger. Have you phoned the Institute?

Professor Hikita: I've told them to run immediate tests, measuring its response to electricity.

Perfect Tommy: Electricity? What are you talking about?

Rawhide: Are you tuned up?

Perfect Tommy: I'm ready. What's on the slide, Prof?

Professor Hikita: A smear of the specimen Buckaroo pulled off the Jet Car drive shaft.

Perfect Tommy: You mean the thing he picked up in the other dimension?

Rawhide: Exactly.

(The network commentator, thrilled to hear this . . .)

Commentator: What? You brought something back from the other dimension? Something alive? Where is it?

Professor Hikita: At the Banzai Institute, in an Igloo box, undergoing tests.

Commentator: In quarantine? Then there is possible danger?

Buckaroo Banzai: This will all be explained tomorrow at the press conference.

An explanation I'd like to hear myself, I remember thinking, as at last we head toward the stage, stepping into a small antiquated elevator for the descent. As the somber machinery takes us down, we talk freely among ourselves about what we had seen on the spectroscopic slide.

Perfect Tommy: Is it alive or dead? That would seem to be the key question.

Reno: Obviously it's alive—if it's growing.

Rawhide: Not necessarily. Crystals grow in inorganic chemical reactions. You can't say they're alive.

Reno: You have a point. On the other hand— what is life?

Perfect Tommy:	On the other hand, those were like no crystals I've ever seen on the slide. Without even being able to identify the compound, I'd say this conversation is pointless.
Buckaroo Banzai:	Right, let's keep our minds on music.

Thus, we were left to ponder, with only superficial scrutiny of the strange object which I have called a parasite, its significance. It is no wonder human beings become crazed in the twentieth century with so much to contend with daily. I'm sure it crossed all our minds. What is this strain from a place we cannot even name? What have we unleashed? Is there a chance of its springing upon an unsuspecting world, in the manner of classic science fiction? Of course. There is always a chance, miniscule as we might wish to portray it. Scientific progress is always fraught with unknown risks. In fact, even as we gained the stage, beads of sweat glistening from our faces, we could not know that the real danger to our planet was already poised to strike from another quarter.

11

It is in the nature of the mentally ill to wage acts of war upon themselves, and, as I have said, the gods had not been kind to Dr. Emilio Lizardo. His strength undermined, he passed the years in tedious watching and waiting, living in constant terror of himself, some dread act he might commit. At least this was how he must have seemed to his warders, long since accustomed to hearing his wild tales about some-one named John Whorfin or finding desperate notes in his hand shoved beneath his door. They were short and vague. "Whorfin is a stowaway!" he might write. Or, "This is America!"

Naturally there was no tangible evidence against anyone. Apart from his impassioned entreaties, there was no record of a John Whorfin having existed on this planet. Indeed, such a being in the flesh had not; and yet it was John Whorfin who had pulled Lizardo into the shadows of the underworld and into this manic bin, seeking an ally.

It was the same John Whorfin who often gripped Lizardo's hand as it held a bread knife and thrust the long narrow shaft into an electrical wall socket. While the stricken Lizardo gave hoarse, inarticulate cries, John Whorfin convulsed in ecstasy. For an instant, the brow of the scientist and the eyes of the madman danced violently at odds before the body fell back limp and quivering, Whorfin's ravenous hunger for electricity momentarily sated. After such sessions, he was surly and, quite literally, drunk with power, bubbling over as if a quart of brandy has passed his lips; and this evening was no exception, as he lay back and listened with a snarl to the night guard's key grating in his lock.

"Hello, Jack," Whorfin muttered. "Come to tell me your problems?"

The guard Jack, intoxicated himself, thanks to Xan's doing, gazed around Whorfin's room in despair. In such filthy disarray that it might as well have been lined with straw, the room, in its way, resisted intruders. It would have taken days to search it systematically.

"All right, Doc, I've come for your little TV," said Jack. "You been using too much damn juice. . . . Beats me how one old homicidal loony could use that much power."

Whorfin shrugged, sitting in that part of the room which was a sort of bedroom. "Fine with me. Take it."

"Where is it?"

Whorfin pointed to a spot near his chair where, under a small pile of refuse, the television was still playing, its gleam now catching the guard's eye.

"Take it," Whorfin said, making a theatrical gesture with his right hand, while in his left, prehensile fingers curved more tightly around the knife.

The guard made his way cautiously, flipping on his pocket torch. He was middle-aged and had a round, fleshy face. Involuntarily almost, he came closer, chary of the compelling magnetism of the old man's eyes, his sonorous voice, and air of mystery.

"It's all right," said Whorfin. "I don't need the TV anymore. Do you want to know why?"

"Why?" asked Jack.

Whorfin burst into a roar of laughter which chilled Jack's soul, and yet he came closer, reaching for the television, visibly trembling.

"What's the matter?" said Whorfin.

Jack tried not to meet Whorfin's mocking gaze but found it impossible to look away. "Maybe I'll come back later," he said.

Whorfin smiled an ironical smile. "You know I have some reputation as a seer, Jack," he said.

"You're a deep one, all right," agreed Jack.

"Then come closer. I have something to tell you." Jack crept closer, all his efforts to resist proving unavailing. Inwardly Whorfin was already crouching, ready for violent action. His masterful eyes seemed pleased at the look of alarm on his quarry's face, as it took another step. "What I have to tell you is—"

Jack leaned closer, when suddenly, with no warning, Whorfin's hand flicked out with astonishing strength, driving the knife into Jack's stomach and out between his vertebrae. With an exhalation Jack fell forward, and Whorfin lifted him cleanly off the ground.

"What I have to tell you is—" said Whorfin "—I can't help you."

The shock, so to say, of what he had done made no mark on him whatever, as he greedily snatched his victim's keys and fled. What happened in the following minutes I do not know, although the odor of Xan is unmistakable throughout. What is known for certain is that Whorfin wreaked havoc upon various defenseless fellow inmates and delivered a fearful blow to a video game machine bearing a likeness of Buckaroo Banzai before fleeing in a sports car belonging to one of the staff physicians. Who assisted him in his getaway I am not prepared to say, but it is demonstrable fact that neither Whorfin nor Lizardo could drive, in which case the accusing finger would seem to point to Xan's toady Lo Pep, a shady figure with New York and Hong Kong connections who disappeared that night and has not been seen since. It does not strain credibility to think that he may have relaxed his vigilance in Whorfin's presence and ended up the poorer for it, perhaps floating face down in some New Jersey marsh.

At all events, Whorfin was free, and our own problems were just beginning.

12

IT WAS PAST midnight, we were well into our second set of songs, when the girl known as Penny Priddy entered our lives. As far as I am able to reconstruct, no one noticed her come into the crowded club, penniless and alone, carrying the bulk of her possessions with her. She apparently found a table near the back of the room and sat for a time, inoffensive and quiet, replying only in monosyllables to the waitresses who sought to serve her. No one guessed that she was awaiting an opportune moment to end her life.

I have, over the years, seen Buckaroo Banzai do many uncanny things, even mysterious things. That is not to say that I believe in the preternatural, for I believe quite the contrary—namely, that there is no such thing as the preternatural. Let me explain. Some centuries ago static electricity was unknown—or was it? Of course it *existed*—sparks did leap from fingertip to doorknob under the right conditions—but, as electricity was then unknown, there was no frame of reference in which the phenomenon could be understood. It was thus deemed to be of the preternatural realm of things. A century or two later, science having done its duty, static electricity became merely another part of nature in all her moods. People could discuss it without invoking the spirits and could well ridicule the superstitions of their forebears. It is the same, I'm sure, for every generation, each attributing to itself an intelligence out of all proportion to what posterity will afford it.

My point is this: The preternatural of today is the science of tomorrow. Mysteries will be solved, the proper adjustments made, and humankind will go on to new discoveries. This is the bracing challenge at every stage of human history.

Having said that, let me qualify it. Although not a believer in the so-called preternatural, I do believe in unseen powers, causal relationships of whose secrets I am in utter ignorance and yet cannot dismiss, for I have lived too long and have seen too much empirical evidence to the contrary. The intelligence of our species is of a narrower compass than any of us cares to think, and that there are things and processes beyond its pale is but a daily fact of life.

I think of this when I think of Penny Priddy, the young girl whose mysterious glamour would soon woo B. Banzai. As I have said, none of us had the slightest intimation that something extraordinary, bordering on the incredible, was about to occur. We were simply musicians plying our trade, engrossed in the untrammeled, primitive joy of loud syncopated music, in full swing when suddenly Buckaroo stopped and signaled the rest of us to do likewise. Above the decibels of the music, he had, in a flash of intuition, heard something which bothered him. For a moment the rest of us stared at one another in bewilderment, Buckaroo having us all at a disadvantage.

"Excuse me," he said into the microphone, trying to quiet the audience. "Excuse me, but somebody here is not having a good time."

Coming from a mouth other than his, such words would have produced laughter, but in this case the room grew still, heads turning to see what could have so galvanized their hero.

He repeated, "Somebody here is not having a good time. Is someone out there crying in the darkness?"

Like the rest of us, he squinted to descry a waif of vivid good looks lounging at a table by the entrance, smoking nervously, self-pity welling like a poisoned stream from her lips. "Leave me alone," she said, spitting curses. "Can't you just leave me alone, you half-breed?"

The crowd hissed, but Buckaroo hushed them again to silence, saying, "That's all right. I am a half-breed. This great country is full of us."

His measured words only slightly tempered her anger. "What do you care?" she demanded. "What do you care who I am, or what happens to me?"

"I care," he replied. "What's your name?"

"Peggy."

Feigning exhaustion, I think I nearly fell over. I could see the blood racing to Buckaroo's temples, as Rawhide stepped up to succor him. If it was the girl's idea of a joke, it was an outrage.

"Did you say . . . Peggy?" Buckaroo said.

"Penny," was her response, her voice this time heard more clearly, and we all breathed more easily. "My name is Penny. Penny Priddy. What's in a name? It doesn't mean anything to you or anybody else. Please, get on with the show. I'm just a nobody."

"Nobody is a nobody," Buckaroo said. "Everyone has something to offer."

"Save the speech," she cried. "I don't need it."

"Then why are you crying?"

"I'm not crying," she scoffed, as one hand slipped unobtrusively into her plastic purse and felt the welcome barrel of a small-caliber pistol. The thought of death made her strong. Life was a hell, but there was hope! She realized the longed-for-moment had arrived and felt the weapon coldly, examining its joints. She would shoot herself on these premises, would cut once and for all the ropes which bound her fate to Buckaroo Banzai. "It's like this guy said," she added, in a kind of trance, no longer even caring whether anyone heard her. "The guy in the employment office . . . he said, as long as there's a sidewalk, I'll always have a job. So how can I complain? I think he was trying to be nice."

Nothing yet had happened, except that she had knocked over a glass on the table. Those around her snickered insensitively before B. Banzai chastened them. "Don't be mean," he said. "The fates are cruel enough. Remember: No matter where you go, there you are."

She saw only a blur as he went to the piano. Memories floated across her mind, most of them unpleasant. Shortly they would all disappear. She would die and be reborn, perhaps go to that other dimension B. Banzai had discovered only this morning. There was more than this life—that much was now known. The thought of erasing the past, starting again with a clean slate and no memories—how alluring it seemed!

"This song's for Peggy, and anybody else a little down on their luck," announced Buckaroo at the piano.

"The name's Penny." She heaved a sigh. "But who cares?"

Earlier in her nocturnal expedition she had accepted an offer of drinks from the first stranger who had made a momentary impression. In a cracked and pitted booth she had sat with him, enduring his filthy hands and coarse attentions while waiting for the liquor to blot out every feeling. Then he had offered her stimulants to go to his room and had attempted to bar her way when she refused. Only her little handgun had saved her, and now it would save her forever from men of his stamp. She would put a bullet through her aching brain.

She knew there was no drawing back. At the threshold now, she cocked the hammer. Soon, she thought, I'll be steeped in blood . . . white-hot, then cold.

Now began a dreadful scene. In my shorthand notes of the affair I have described what happened next.

(Buckaroo takes a seat at the piano and begins to play. This in itself is rather unusual, for despite his many other natural gifts, he is a fledgling pianist at best and is ordinarily loathe to play in public. On this night, however, he seems to have forgotten where he is. His face is brooding, his eyes far away as he inflicts upon us the first chords of a song we have not performed since Peggy died. For a moment the rest of us stand irresolute, confused. Is he actually going to play it? Does he want us to accompany him? The others are as uncertain as I. The song had been Peggy's favorite. It frightens us to hear it. There is something intangible, abnormal in the air as he begins to sing the sad lyric of unrequited love. Then suddenly . . . the sound of a shot! We whip out sidearms, join forces around our leader. Is there a plot afoot? Club security men dive for Penny Priddy, struggling to disarm her, when a second shot is fired harmlessly into the ceiling. The club is a screaming melee, as they drag her toward the door.)

Penny Priddy: Let me go! Let me go, you creeps!

Buckaroo Banzai: Let's have calm. Calm down, everybody. Everybody okay? Anybody hurt? Anyone in need of a doctor?

(The house lights come on, as we holster our weapons, and for an unobstructed moment gain a clear view of Penny Priddy. Almost as one, we gasp. What intended treachery is this? She is amazingly the mirror image of our dead Peggy!)

My eyes immediately darted to Buckaroo, the poor devil. What must he think? A queer look on his face, he was in immediate consultation with Rawhide, who quickly left the hall to pursue the secret of the girl.

"Did you see her?" he asked us.

I consequently shrugged, not wanting to believe what I had seen with my own eyes. It was the same with the others, the shock to our nerves leaving us spellbound and speechless. After all, the very idea was incomprehensible. We must have been seeing things. I myself suspected at once the malevolent genuis of Xan somehow in this but said instead, "Your piano playing gets them every time, Buckaroo."

He nodded, stabbing thoughts testing his sanity. "I heard someone crying. I must have had a premonition," he said.

"Must have." I nodded. "I don't know what else it could've been."

A numb feeling tugged at my heart. Either someone had embarked upon a hellish scheme against our chief, or cruel Fate had made him its sport. Either way he would have no surcease of bitter memories for sleepless nights to come.

13

FOLLOWING THE DISCOVERY of the night guard's body and the disappearance of the inmate known as Dr. Emilio Lizardo, a furious hunt for the callous criminal was immediately organized. Airports and train stations were watched, roadblocks erected; but in vain. Although the stolen sports car was found in a rural county of the state wrapped around an electriclight standard, it seemed that death would have none of Whorfin. He had walked away from the violent collision and headed straight to a telephone.

"Operator," he shouted. "I want to place a person-to-person call, collect, to John Bigbooté, Yoyodyne Propulsion Systems, Grover's Mills, New Jersey. Tell him it's John Whorfin calling, from the *outside*. W-H-O-R-F-I-N. Got that?"

He had to wait several minutes, as his party, the alien Lectroid called John Bigbooté, had to be found and roused from sleep, a circumstance which only confirmed in Whorfin's mind the timeliness, nay the necessity, of his escape. Clearly his fighters, once fearsome to behold, had grown enfeebled. It pained him to think it, but even the cold mouth of the grave, even the hideous Eighth Dimension (its Planet 10 name) was preferable to the bourgeois life of ease. Nothing good could come of years of peace—muscles atrophied, the will failed. Soldiers who had once fought back-to-back fell to bickering among themselves amid the creature comforts. No, it was best he had arrived. He would make inquiries, establish the iron discipline needed. He would make examples! Yes, there was much to be done and little time.

The groggy voice of John Bigbooté came on the line, almost whining, it seemed to John Whorfin. "What's the matter, John Bigbooté?" he said tersely. "Did I take you from something important?"

"No, I was just getting some snooze."

"What kind of language is that?" Whorfin screamed. "Snap to attention when I talk to you! I'll have your head! Prepare for my return!"

Bigbooté seemed to revive, understanding that this was not a mere social call. Far from his original muttering tone of voice, he now began to purr. "Lord Whorfin, my liege, this is the happiest night of my life," he sputtered. "Where are you?"

"Camped by the side of the road," rejoined Whorfin. "You'll send a car."

"Yes, of course, but—"

"What?"

"Isn't there danger? I am concerned about your safety."

"Be concerned about your own. Things had better be in order."

"Of course. I'll be right there."

Whorfin gave him the location and hung up the phone, rubbing his hands together. He had thinking to do, plans to create. There was a saying on Planet 10, "No positive edifice can be built on a negative foundation." First he had to get Banzai's OSCILLATION OVERTHRUSTER and then work his Lectroids into a fury to complete the Panther Ship being built secretly at Yoyodyne. By morning, he would be at his place, back where he belonged at the head of his paltry band of fighters on this worthless blue planet named Earth. What had to follow would not be easy. He did not underestimate his formidable array of adversaries who would do all they could to thwart him, once his plans became known. Secrecy must be the foremost consideration. Accordingly, he stepped away from the deserted country road for the cover of a tree. The night was clear, the location of Planet 10, his home, hidden by the bright edge of the moon. Somewhere up there as well, his hated nemesis, the Nova Police, were on constant patrol. How much did they know? he wondered. Had they been alerted to his presence on Earth? God, how he hated this place! Better to die fighting, to be torn to pieces and scattered like cosmic dust throughout the universe than to be standing here under a tree in New Jersey.

A thought came to mind. It was Lizardo's thought, wild and beautiful as it was. Something about the little Jap, Hikita. Whorfin laughed, his cackle echoing in the stillness, as he siezed upon the idea before Lizardo could take it back. "Too late, Lizardo," he gloated. "Good idea."

In the chaos of the escape, he had nearly forgotten about Lizardo; now, his fancy excited, he probed the disorder of the old man's mind. "So you think the little Jap Hikita might be able to get me the Overthruster? I hadn't thought of that. In turn, he could be my key to getting off this rock. Is that what you're thinking? Nice work. That means I'd be leaving you, and you could get on with your life."

"What life?" snorted Lizardo. "You've taken my life, you indolent maggot! You parasite!"

"But you'd be your old self again. You'd have your old body . . . er, young body back again."

Poor Lizardo's lip trembled. "What do you mean?"

"Why, I mean in the Eighth Dimension your body's just where you left it—young, just as it was that day in '38. How old were you then?"

Lizardo's mind was reeling. For half a minute he could not think or speak. "Twenty-five," he said.

"Then that's how old you'd be again. Twenty-five . . . your whole life ahead of you. Vibrant and young! You could marry, have children, gain the fame that rightfully should be yours."

"More probably than not you're lying."

"Help me prove it, Emilio." Lizardo wished at all costs to believe such a thing but could not, trying desperately to pull away as Whorfin reached around their body to clasp hands. "Help me return to the Eighth Dimension with the Overthruster. You have knowledge you've never given me. I know it! Why resist me when youth and boundless energy await you?"

"What is this talk? A trick?" exclaimed the besieged Lizardo, who with a sudden cry grabbed a stick and struck himself a feeble blow to the head. "I'll kill myself and take you with me—rid creation of you once and for all!"

Whorfin, much the dominant one, easily dealt him a disabling blow. "You're too late," he sneered. "You should have thought of that sooner. Without the medication I am in control all the time. There can be no deliverance for you now, not even an hour a day. You have plighted your troth to me for the rest of your miserable life, unless I get that Overthruster and return to my natural body in the Eighth Dimension!"

Lizardo despaired anew, trying to draw the materials to defy him, but it was hopeless. He was in the villain's embrace and knew the power of the bear hug.

14

NOR HAD THE long night ended where we were concerned. At the Banzai Institute, the lights were burning into the early morning hours when Rawhide arrived and Perfect Tommy and I cornered him.

"What did you find out?" we demanded to know.

"Where's Buckaroo?" said Rawhide.

"Upstairs. Did you see the girl?"

Rawhide nodded. "It wasn't difficult. She's in the hoosegow."

We waited for more. "Well?"

"Well, what?"

"What does she look like?"

Rawhide paused. He could be exasperating at times! "Well—"

"Out with it, great fellow!" I blurted, unable to contain my curiosity.

"She looks like Peggy."

"How much like her?"

With a grave face, he pushed up the brim of his hat. "Exactly like her," he said. "Bewitchingly so."

The three of us traded looks, making no pretense of the fact that we were worried. I had captured only a glimpse of her in the club, and had thus been able to delude myself into thinking that I was mistaken, and the others, probably including Buckaroo, had done the same. But now there was more, as wildly far-fetched as the idea seemed, for Rawhide was not given to exaggeration.

"How close did you get to her?" asked Tommy.

"As close as I am to you."

"Then we'll have to put the comb through her," I said. "We must find out what she is."

"Her name is Penny Priddy," said Rawhide. "She's from Wyoming, thirty years old. I got her vital statistics from her driver's license."

Then we should run her through Interpol at once to be sure it isn't a trap," proposed Tommy.

We agreed hard routine inquiry would be the order of business. Tommy suggested we involve Mrs. Johnson in the case at once, as well as our team of computer sleuths headed by Billy Travers. If there was going to be an error of judgment on our part, it was to be on the side of caution. If the girl was shamming her identity, we would know soon enough and could take the appropriate countermeasures.

In the meantime there was the matter of Buckaroo. "What are you going to tell the chief?" I asked Rawhide.

"The truth," he replied.

We all agreed it was as good a plan as any.

15

In the adventure *Extradition from Hell,* I apply myself to the evidence in Peggy's murder. Although the case received front-page play, for those coming to the Banzai series for the first time, I shall attempt to recapitulate the facts as briefly as possible. Half an hour after her marriage to B. Banzai, Peggy Banzai, nee Simpson, was discovered dead in a changing room just off the sacristy in the Church of St. John the Divine in New York City. She had entered the room quickly to undress following the ceremony, and despite the presence of sentries outside (who neither saw nor heard anything suspicious), minutes later she was found lifeless and prone on the floor, still in her wedding dress. The postmortem performed by the coroner found the cause of death to be poisoning by cyanide gas, the source of which was discovered in one of the many floral arrangements sent by well-wishers. A small metal cylinder of cyanide dropped in a flower vase filled with sulfuric acid and yellow roses had done the trick. As she bent over to smell the roses, one whiff of the deadly gas had extinguished her life instantly. Such were the meager facts of the case.

As for the culprit or culprits, none was visible; and the praiseworthy efforts of the authorities produced none, save for the ghostly curate rumoured to haunt said church. He, or it, had been seen in an acute state of agitation by several of the wedding guests and by Captain Happen and Pecos who actually conversed soberly with the black-robed shade! In the way of mortal suspects, however, the trail had run cold. The European manufacturer of the cyanide cylinder and the Brooklyn florist through whom the roses had been ordered could provide little information of value, and that is where the investigation had foundered when B. Banzai decided to engage the services of a well-known psychic, Georgiana Albricht of the Duke University Department of Parapsychology, whom he had tested in the past. A series of séances took place subsequently, the first in the Church of St. John the Divine, followed by several more at the Banzai Institute, held under controlled scientific conditions. I reproduce here edited excerpts from the last one, dated 5 November 1981. The reader will note the presence of Captain Happen in the room, something Buckaroo had insisted upon, aware of Captain Happen's great interest in the paranormal.

(G. Albricht changes moods, the sound of footsteps arousing her to a highly wrought state of tension, as a shiver comes over us all . . . the footsteps descending, as though on an invisible stairway in the ice cold room. G. Albricht begins to write in her folio volume, murmuring as in a deep sleep, her cheeks flushed.)

G. Albricht: I have before me a lost spirit with a trouble and anxiety which prevent it from taking its heavenward flight. What is your mortal name, spirit?

(A terrible female chuckle is heard.)

G. Albricht: Speak, spirit, unless your misery be unutterable. What is your name?

Spirit Voice: Peggy Banzai.

(Captain Happen appears agitated, jumps up from his seat.)

Captain Happen: That's a lie! This wizard's a phony!

Buckaroo Banzai: Sit down, Captain.

Captain Happen: I'm leaving.

Buckaroo Banzai: I'd rather you stayed. No one leaves.

(Pecos and I bar the door; Captain Happen refuses to return to his seat, paces nervously.)

G. Albricht: Spirit, will you emerge into view?

(At the back of the room, all of us detect a growing obstrusive fragrance.)

Rawhide: Smell it? It's Peggy's perfume.

Captain Happen: It's impossible. It smells more like cyanide!

Pecos: My God, it's her! There she is!

(Where the musty scent has emanated, a pale light now appears, in the midst of which stands a female figure in Peggy's shimmering white wedding dress, her bridal veil draping her face, a bouquet of withered flowers in her grasp! We all shrink from the unearthly visage, but in particular Captain Happen, who, as someone whose secret of sin has just been uncovered, cries out like a fiend.)

Captain Happen: It's not real! It's some magician's trick! Buckaroo—

(The bride of death now produces a gleaming dagger from the withered bouquet and begins to move toward us.)

G. Albricht: Spirit, you would do violence to those who love you?

Spirit Voice: One does not love me. I would fain have my revenge.

Captain Happen: No! It's not Peggy! Peggy's alive! They've foxed me! I can't breathe!

(With those cryptic words, he makes a run for the door, Pecos and I leveling our pistols to stop him, when suddenly the young man's mind snaps before our eyes and he hurls himself out the window instead, breaking his neck on the sidewalk three floors below. Buckaroo comes over, looks out the window grimly, as Pecos rushes down the stairs and confirms the lifeless attitude of the body.)

Reno: On his belly like a reptile, where he belongs.

Pecos: He's dead.

(Buckaroo himself turns on the lights and thanks the participants in our little midnight charade: Georgina Albricht, who is as accomplished an actress as she is a medium, and of course the unhappy shade in white, who, upon raising her bridal veil and removing her wig, turns out to be none other than our own Mrs. Johnson.)

Mrs. Johnson: I don't mind telling you, this thing gave me the creeps.

As I have said, the seance was carried out under *controlled* scientific conditions . . . controlled to our advantage. The autopsy performed on Captain Happen revealed a miniature radio receiver implanted surgically in his brain, through which he got his orders, almost certainly from Xan, as the same principle—that of converting man into puppet through a similar device—was to be employed with continued devastating success in his infamous death dwarves. And what of Captain Happen's astonishing statement that Peggy was alive? Permission was promptly obtained from the necessary authorities to exhume the body of Peggy from the Banzai family plot in Texas, and on a windy day several of us stood at the grave as the casket, bare of ornamentation, was brought up and the simple lid opened to allow the escape of gasses and to disclose . . . nothing! The cavity was empty! It seemed we had buried a phantom.

It was against this inexplicable backdrop that the remarkable discovery of Penny Priddy must be seen. She had, wittingly or unwittingly, reopened that vacant crypt beneath the clods and with it raised the bare thought: Had Peggy returned?

There was still a quenchless gleam in B. Banzai's eyes, though since the departure (a word I prefer) of Peggy, his affairs had become more disordered. For weeks following the black events of New York and their bizarre aftermath, I would find him, a miserable object, in the dark receptacle of his study. Wearing his spectacles, hunched over some recondite volume, he gave the appearance of an infirm old man, a pale imitation of himself that no mediocre actor could have improved upon. With a constant fixed gaze, he seemed unconscious of all but his innermost soul.

True, of late, we had become reassured that his former aspect had returned—but now this. It was no wonder that with this twist of fate we feared that all of our brightening prospects were in jeopardy.

Buckaroo stood in his small, almost bare cell at the upper rear of our transmuted Greyhound Scenicruiser bus as we made our way to the jail the morning after. It was there he was to meet the fair maid Penny Priddy and we were to rendezvous with a potential new recruit—not necessarily one and the same, I remember hoping. There was still nothing from Pecos and the Seminole Kid, all our efforts to get through still stymied by radio interference. Perhaps they were merely lost, or lost in more ways than one. The concern on my face must have been evident, for a sad quiet smile flitted across Perfect Tommy's lips.

"Thinking about Pecos?" he asked.

"Thinking about all of them," I replied.

"But particularly Pecos?"

"Maybe."

We were sorting the 35mm slides taken by Buckaroo in the other dimension, making a new world unto ourselves. "Whadda you think of this one?" "Nah, this one's better." "Let's use this one." "What's wrong with this one?" And on it went, the two of us in effect providing our interpretation of the boldest exploit in human history.

Behind us the stern-faced Buckaroo was doing his mental exercises with his sword, mental exercises which required of him strength of hand, and of us, stoutness of heart, as he brandished the razor-sharp blade dangerously near our heads in the cramped cubicle. It had something to do with absorbing energy, the Oriental yin and the yang. Why it had to be done in a tiny room on a moving bus doubtless has implications in physics that exceed my love of science; at all events he performed always without the semblance of a flaw and held sway in so doing over certain inharmonious spiritual elements. While one who rides with B. Banzai learns quickly to expect at any moment to die in the middle of a breath, there is nothing quite like the whistle of a blade above one's head to bring into focus one's own mortality.

We had already awakened with a start to find a blurry picture of Penny Priddy in the morning paper, which showed us little that we did not already know. Taken during the excitement of the night before, without the repose essential to a good photograph, her image was as confoundingly elusive as had been the subject herself. Buckaroo, however, had cast his eyes upon it and after examining it with a peculiar expression at the breakfast table had set it near his bathroom mirror. He inspected it at greater length while shaving with his cordless gyroscope. Such was its effect upon him that whatever presentiment any of us had hitherto felt regarding the girl could not, in the spirit of good fellowship, be spoken.

Also discussed at the breakfast table (all manner of things were discussed daily at that appointed hour) was the news of Dr. Lizardo's escape and, among other items of business, a letter, and an extraordinary demo tape from a stateless Armenian seeking entry to this country in order to join our group. Of the former, we could only conjecture what must be going through Lizardo's bewildered brain, but found the timing of the escape intriguing. It was very neat, to say the least.

"He must have had help," said Perfect Tommy. "A seventy-year-old man who has been locked up forty-five years doesn't just go crazy one day and kill his guard, walk out the door, and conveniently steal a sports car."

"Correction: he didn't *go* crazy. He *is* crazy," said Rawhide.

79

"Yeah, but he can't drive," retorted Tommy. "Isn't that right, Professor Hikita?"

Professor Hikita, indubitably the man who best knew fact from legend in Lizardo's case, nodded. "I never knew him to drive," he said. "What kind of car was it?"

"A Maserati," said Tommy.

"I know he never drove a Maserati."

The professor's words inspired us to laugh, though he himself wore a quite opposite expression as he craftily lit his pipe. The professor enjoyed making phrases but seldom provided unambiguous answers.

"Who would have helped him?" pondered Rawhide aloud.

"He had his votaries," said Buckaroo. "I seem to recall that in his later crimes he had a number of accomplices who were never caught."

"This was after his hair turned orange?" I asked.

Hikita nodded. "Long after. He was not himself. It is no small thing to take a man's life."

"He threatened your life, didn't he, Hikita-san?" I recalled.

"That was years ago," the professor said, raising his eyebrows to simulate surprise. "We had rough words, but I doubt him capable. I know too well the limitations of his age."

"Don't be so sure," said Buckaroo. "That guard he killed was younger than you. Pinky, put the Institute staff on heightened alert until further notice."

"Right," said Pinky, by all appreciable signs his inflamed eyes only half-awake after some nocturnal ramble. "I'll pass the word."

"In the meantime the rest of us had better head for the press conference," Buckaroo said.

"I thought it wasn't till noon," questioned Perfect Tommy.

Ill-concealing his restlessness or the newspaper under his arm, Buckaroo strode for the door. "We have something to do first," he answered.

I glanced sidelong at Rawhide and met his eyes as he

entered the upstairs cubicle with the emotions proper to a man who had news to tell.

"What is it, Rawhide?" I said.

"A report just came in."

"What kind of report?" Now it was Buckaroo speaking, superbly naked save for his breeches. Having smitten his last invisible enemy, he sat on his haunches astride his sword, breathing heavily. An agreeable light fell from the window across the coconut matting on the floor, as Rawhide brought us up to speed.

"The state police found the doctor's Maserati that Lizardo stole," he said. "And they lifted a set of prints. You'll never guess whose."

"Then why guess," Buckaroo said. "Especially when you're going to tell us yourself."

"Lo Pep!" exclaimed Rawhide.

Our attitude of dismay was unanimous. I can't remember which of us it was—perhaps Perfect Tommy—who spoke to the serious and deplorable consequences. "Xan's lieutenant?" he said. "So there is an external force at work here after all . . . an external evil! If he helped Lizardo escape, then Xan must want—"

"The Oscillation Overthruster," put in Rawhide.

"We should make a special investigation at once," I said "We're the only ones in a position to know what's happening."

"No sign of Lo Pep or Lizardo, I take it?" said Buckaroo.

Rawhide shook his head. "The car was wrecked. There were no eyewitnesses, apparently."

"Get an exact location of the site of the wreck," said Buckaroo. "After the press conference, perhaps we can drive over to the asylum and retrace their route. Someone may have seen something. Do we have a recent picture of Lizardo?" None of us was certain. "Maybe you can draw one, Reno," he said to me. "Professor Hikita can direct you."

"I'll get right to it," I nodded. "What about Lo Pep?"

"Lizardo is of more concern," said Buckaroo. "Lo Pep is a mere hireling."

I stood to leave at once, but Rawhide demurred, having one further detail. "There's something else," he said in a puzzled way. "I was talking with Big Norse, and—"

"And—?" Buckaroo said.

We smiled, Rawhide's enthusiasm for Big Norse being common knowledge. Not unreasonably, he resented our teasing and on another occasion might have reacted—for he could breathe steam at the mere suggestion that he fancied her—but not today. He was deliberate and to the point.

"She says this whole atmospheric disturbance thing is very curious," he said. "It seems to be following us."

"Following us?" Buckaroo asked. "Sounds more like a problem with the equipment."

"It's not the equipment. The equipment's been checked," said Rawhide. "It's something else—a heavy electromagnetic pulse, strictly localized, that must have followed us from Texas."

"More in the nature of jamming, then?" asked Buckaroo.

"Not exactly. More like extremely powerful eavesdropping."

"On all frequencies?"

"Yes."

This was a stupefying premise in the sober light of day, a plot of unaccountable proportions which in all our minds brought the vicious rogue Xan into sharp relief. Was he saying that our nemesis was upon us at all times?

"And the source?" inquired Buckaroo. "Where does Big Norse think this listening receiver is?"

Rawhide opened the door, and Big Norse's tip-tilted nose and golden hair poked around the corner. Her sturdy bearing, unselfconscious and dignified, bespoke her Viking heritage, as she scanned our faces.

"It seems we have a mysterious pursuer," Buckaroo said to her.

"That's my opinion," she said. "It's not unheard of."

"It's nothing aboard the bus?"

"I'm positive," she said. "I've checked it thoroughly

myself with the usual debugging devices and have found nothing. Anyway, it isn't that. It's something . . . colossal. I think I've located the source of the signal."

"Where is it?"

She searched for a way of saying it, then pointed at the ceiling.

"A helicopter?" said Buckaroo.

She kept pointing up.

"A satellite?" he asked.

She intimated that was not the case and kept pointing, her shoulders beginning to sag in desperation. "Deeper in space," she said. "I've got my calculations if you'd like to see them."

"Yes, very much," said Buckaroo, not quite sure what to make of this young female mathematician, liveried in a Banzai T-shirt and dungarees, whose record was thus far the most outstanding of all the active interns. "Name of God, yes! Save them for me. I'll be right there."

She nodded, and Buckaroo responded in kind; whereupon she left, unaware, I'm convinced, of the extraordinary nature of the encounter to which we had all just been privy. Had she really intended to make such a claim? If she were correct, I was in awe and admiration. But if she were wrong, what an intrepid spirit! Her remarks were simply amazing. (Remember, reader, we had not the benefit of hindsight that you enjoy.)

To his credit, B. Banzai seemed to take her incredible story somewhat seriously. After our initial buzz of conversation following her leave-taking, Buckaroo stiffened as if thinking out his line of action. Somewhere, in the black and cold, a million miles from our position, an unknown race was monitoring us. Nothing seemed more fantastic than that, and yet that was what was allegedly happening. Unconsciously, I had supposed we were famous, but I would never have been so gullible as to believe that even on other worlds we were known. The assertion, made even now, seems impudent, and yet we know it to have been exactly the case. However, I'm pushing hither and thither, getting ahead of myself.

"What if they can hear our conversations in this very room?" Perfect Tommy said. "Should we whisper?"

"Not unless you want to," said Buckaroo, beginning to get dressed. "If they're millions of miles away, they won't hear you for several minutes even if you scream."

"Buckaroo, I was thinking," I said. "Granted, we don't yet know where all this will lead, even if in fact whether there's anything to it—"

"Go on," he said, then startled me by asking: "Do you believe in the evil eye?"

"What?" I said.

"The Italians have a word for it—the *iettatura*. The evil eye. Do you put any credence in it?"

"No," I replied. "It's just superstition, *non è vero?*"

"I'm inclined to feel the same way," he said, then continued dressing. What had led him to raise the issue was left hanging, but it is my theory that it had to do with the girl Penny Priddy, because in the next breath he said, "Too bad the photograph wasn't clearer."

"Of the girl?"

"Yes," he said, coming out of his reverie with an almost audible snap. "I'm sorry, you were about to say something."

I sensed the time still not right to express my misgivings about the girl—Billy had as yet learned nothing incriminatory about her—and so I continued with my train of thought as we walked out of the room together. "I was just thinking, as I said, that perhaps this electronic signal could be some sort of homing beacon for the extraterrestrials."

At that moment his eyes fell on me and looked long as if at some fearsome vision. "Firing from the hip, aren't you?" he said.

"Maybe."

"Big Norse says they're up there, and now you say they're coming here?"

"It's crazy, I know."

"You know what such a visit could mean?"

His words shot me through the heart. No, I had denied vehemently to myself just what it could mean. The entire defense forces of Earth might have to be mobilized. Already horror-stricken, I trembled, instinctively knowing that something catastrophic was very likely to happen if I were right.

"I'm sure I'm mistaken," I said.

But the sheer enormity of what I had so offhandedly suggested had struck me with an impact that was almost physical. Like a change in air pressure, I felt a tremendous lethargy and an inability to wrest myself free from its grip. We are in for it, I thought, when after Buckaroo had carefully vetted Big Norse's calculations, he spoke the incomprehensible. "I think you may have something," he said to her.

There was complete silence. It was still early in the day, and yet I had the sensation of being in a Turkish bath. Perspiration was flowing off me freely. For several moments Buckaroo's entire being had centered on the hieroglyphics of Big Norse's formulae and figures, and he had now pronounced them accurate.

"It's coming closer?" he asked, estimating from her figures.

"Yes, although it seemed to appear out of nowhere yesterday morning," Big Norse replied.

"Over Texas."

"That's right."

I still had not recovered the power of respiration as Buckaroo put on her headset and listened to the noises. There were apparently twin rays of a singular mind, reaching Earth at two points, (viz.) our bus, and the Institute. The Institute had begun to experience a similar disruptive phenomenon with its worldwide communications even before we did; and by comparing their data with our own, Big Norse had by triangulation located the source of the signal and suceeded further in plotting its course and speed. It was a sizeable achievement, and I used the opportunity to tell her so.

"Thank you," she said, rather complacently. "Anyone could have done it." *I* couldn't have done it, but my want of breath prevented me from contradicting her. "Mathematics comes easy for me," she continued. "I wish it were the same with music."

She had been a girl of whom much was expected. By the time she reached twelve in Denmark, she had entered the university, and as a result, grew further estranged each year from the general populace. Her sole concern became the symbols of abstract mathematics, and although an arresting girl to this observer's eye, she had always felt vexed with boys and even unwell in their company. I daresay she had never even been kissed before accepting a fellowship to the Banzai Institute to study experimental physics.

Her musicianship was the only constituent of her repertoire of talents needing improvement in order for her to "make" residency and join our lively group, and it seemed to her paradoxical that musical composition, so neat on the page and so mathematical in form, should so seek to involve the emotions in its performance. Her problem, I suspected, was not a poor ear, or a lack of facility with her hands, but an overabundance of earnestness.

"How are your piano lessons with Rawhide coming?" I asked.

"Not as well as I would like," she said earnestly. "We don't seem to accomplish as much as we should."

I felt for the first time in several minutes the urge to smile but did not, the increasing severity of B. Banzai's facial expression overshadowing our idle intercourse, as he perseveringly dotted the reverse of her page of calculations with strange formations of figures.

"It increases and diminishes almost at regular intervals," he said to Big Norse. "Have you managed to find a pattern?"

"You mean a code?" I queried.

"Exactly."

She shook her head. "It rather seemed like a greeting to me when I first isolated the major features," she said. "I overlaid it with several code wheels, but none of them applied. Any suggestions?"

He held up his hand for quiet, listening. "There's something about it that I perceive to be familiar—why? It booms and then lapses into silence."

Buckaroo then lapsed back into silence himself, anxiously scribbling with pad and pencil; and for the historical record, if nothing else, I inquired of Big Norse her thoughts at this moment.

Her words were well-chosen. "It means there is intelligent life in the universe other than ourselves," she said.

"And they're headed this-a-way."

"They're a long way off. They may even be lost, or friendly. There's nothing to be gained by worrying about it until we're sure."

I then posed the question I had resisted asking precisely because it so clearly marked the place to which we had come, but now this waggery of fate demanded it. It was perhaps the commonest line of science fiction. "If they continue at present speed and course, when would they reach Earth?" I asked.

"Sometime early tomorrow," she replied.

I felt the rush of blood drumming in my ears once more and excused myself to go in search of Professor Hikita so that I might execute the drawing of Dr. Lizardo, never dreaming that out of this boiling confusion would soon crystallize a thousand-year-web of sanguinary encounters between Lizardo's occupant Whorfin and the space voyeurs above us. I departed with something of anticipation, however.

16

SINCE WELDING MY modest physical and intellectual resources to those of B. Banzai, I have traveled the world over, from horizon to distant horizon, in every mode of conveyance known to man. I have seen parts of the globe that remain veritable mysteries, places where—tired as it sounds—few men have ever set foot. Engendered by a hunger for discovery and adventure, I have surveyed the inertness of the desert, the teeming life of the sea, and the two poles, as well as the loftiest heights and loneliest valleys of this planet; but none of that prepared me sufficiently for the sight that greeted us upon our arrival at the police station where Buckaroo Banzai was to meet Penny Priddy face-to-face, and we were to collect a new recruit.

Standing outside the building—sitting actually, although he appeared to be standing (such was his height)—wearing such a collision of colors that his face appeared animated even when it was not, was the splendid figure of Sidney Zwibel, Buckaroo's self-doubting medical school colleague. Scarcely within the limits of the probable, he was, as they say, "decked out" like a cowboy in red shirt and bandana, tight-fitting black pantaloons and pinto chaps, and a sublime ten-gallon hat of the sort featured in early Hollywood Westerns. I am tempted to add, Where else?, because I am certain that such an outfit until that moment had never been worn anywhere in the real world. Add a pair of four-inch-high ruby-red cowboy boots, and you will understand why our bus nearly tipped over from the shifting weight of our collective troupe endeavouring to swipe a look at him. I do not stray far from the truth when I say that when he inevitably stood to stretch and rose higher and higher, his luster challenged the permanent brilliance of the sun. Thus did we lay eyes upon our "new recruit."

He did have pluck; I had to give him that. It required more courage than I possess to wear such garb on a public street, and he did it with an undeniable style. What else could be said about a man who in addition to the items of wardrobe I have already mentioned carried a large stereophonic portable radio and wore a wampum belt around his middle. Clearly, events in his life had led him to a fork in the road, and he, like the rest of us, had chosen the diverging path.

At the very least, he gave us all a needed respite. Buckaroo peered out my window and flinched at his friend's gross breach of good taste, ordering our driver Louie and the rest of us not to open the door, so that when Sidney took several steps toward the bus it quickly became apparent that no one was going to step out to meet him. For an awkward second, Sidney's long shadow seemed to quiver, unsure whether to go forward or retreat in this humiliating condition. It was, I suspect, both a joke and a little test, for B. Banzai has a way of getting the whole sum out of his men. In all events, Sidney responded gallantly, overcoming whatever misgivings he must have had and knocking on the bus door. Needless to say, this time Buckaroo ordered it opened, and we all shared a laugh.

"Fellows, this is Sid Zwibel," said Buckaroo. "He'll be riding with us as an observer for a few days, so give him the treatment."

"Don't worry. We will," said Tommy.

"The treatment?" asked Sid, quailing.

"Where do you hail from, Doc?" I asked.

"Fort Lee," he said. "New Jersey." And from that moment he was "New Jersey" to us. "You'd be Pecos," he said, extending a hand toward me. "I've heard a lot about you."

"Nope. Reno," I replied. "Where's your spurs, New Jersey?"

He knitted his brow. "You making fun of me?" He grinned, and in that approximate instant I knew we were friends. There followed the usual flourishes of boisterous banter, although compared to other occasions, it was relatively artificial for reasons I have cited. Having no way of knowing it, Sidney had joined us at a troubled hour, a fact he may have divined when halfway through his offer of congratulations to Buckaroo Banzai for accomplishing the apparently impossible, i.e., traveling through solid matter, B. Banzai excused himself suddenly as if a precipitant pain were felt and walked toward the police station with Perfect Tommy.

For what occurred within the building before I belatedly arrived, I have to rely upon the recollection of Perfect Tommy, who accompanied Buckaroo and a female jailer to the cell where the pitiable girl sat with her back turned to all who might enter, her indescribable solitude seeming less a function of the steel and mortar that enclosed her than the anticipated futility of life. She was certainly not the proverbial little bird in a gilded cage. She was not so congenial as that.

Even when the jailer announced to her that she had a visitor, her head did not turn. There was, however, a humble vanity mirror in one corner of the chamber, and it was this that B. Banzai ingeniously used to step into her line of sight. Positioning himself so that she might see him in the glass, he began to talk as to an old friend, of subjects ranging from the commonplace to the recent coronation of a Nepalese monarch at which he had been in attendance. By dint of persistence, he succeeded in irritating her to such a degree that she sprang up full and shouted with a sneer on her face, "What are you doing here? Whadda you want?"

It was his first unencumbered look at her, and it staggered him. He flushed to the temples. True to Rawhide's words she was inexplicably the very reincarnation of Peggy—a perfect stranger, and yet someone he had loved and loved again the moment he saw her. Those were the irreconcilable facts. Perfect Tommy, like the rest of us, a doubting Thomas who wished not even to consider the existence of such a girl, lest she might somehow supplant the memory of our Peggy, had managed indifference to this point. But now . . . he stood gazing on her as in a profound sleep, unable to utter a sound. In those first seconds of close quarters with her, he later told me, he felt a recurrence of the same arctic frigidity he had experienced the night of the final seance when Mrs. Johnson had charaded as Peggy's ghost. But the woman standing before him now was no mechanical contrivance of hooks and wires illuminated by the moon. She was, how else to put it?, the reincarnation of our slain sister, the same creature, the same particulars down to the minutest corner of her face. If it were a guise, some trick of surgery that had transformed her thus, the shadowy supposition was that the Creator, Himself, must have been in envy of the hand that had wielded the scalpel. It was no wonder Perfect Tommy thrilled in silence.

Of Buckaroo, himself, what words of this or any writer could give a fair accounting of the exquisite agony he must have felt? His feelings beyond register, his doubts at once long passed and only beginning, he was in too sorry a state to speak. Noting their extreme reaction for as long as she lingered upon their vision, Penny Priddy must have been moved to curiosity herself and at some length asked: "Will somebody tell me what the hell's going on?"

"Suppose you tell us," said Tommy. "Who are you?"

"Penny Priddy. You're Perfect Tommy."

"That's right."

"In the company of Buckaroo Banzai," she said, moving closer to the steel bars which separated them. Buckaroo withdrew slightly as she advanced, a small triumph she did not fail to notice and which in an ironic way rather raised her spirits. She threw her head back fancifully, and Perfect Tommy viewed her aslant from a new perspective, as if examining a fetching but unfathomable work of sculpture. Up close she was even more beautiful—no, beautiful is not the word. There was about her something wayward and dangerous. Lips slightly parted, tawny hair uncombed as if she had not attended to her toilette for days, she held that remarkable power common to certain Gypsy women I have known: the ability to arouse both repulsion and desire with a single look. Her hypnotic eyes fastened on our chief, who already adored her. I am convinced she could have asked him to go in search of the gold of El Dorado or the vineyards of the North Pole, and he would at the very least have called a council to discuss whether the notion appeared practicable.

Thankfully, she did not ask. No doubt contented with the surprising discovery that he found her attractive, she was of a mind to be generous.

"Getting an eyeful?" she said, the line eliciting screams of delight from various of the other female prisoners whom I have not had occasion to mention, but who at intervals made public their riotous feelings.

"Remove your coat, please," said Buckaroo, outwardly calm once again.

"My coat?"

"Yes."

"How much will you give me?"

"Five dollars," he said, reaching into his pocket. "Do you want more?"

She looked steadily at him, unpenitent. "No, five will do." she said and began to remove her coat.

"Who were you trying to shoot last night?" he asked.

"You," she said. "I wanted to make the papers, and I did, didn't I?"

"To be from Wyoming, you're not much of a shot."

She shrugged, at first making no remark, and then, "I'm glad I missed."

"Are you?" He believed she had tried to take her own life, and he now was intent on knowing the aftermath.

"Yes, I'm glad. Otherwise, one of us wouldn't be here, would he?"

Buckaroo did not at once respond, as she threw aside the coat to reveal her splendid form and, what was more, a scar on her upper arm that disappeared beneath her shirt. He bade Tommy and me to look away (I having just arrived) and asked her, "Would you do me the favor of taking off your shirt?"

It was clear early on that no request could shock her, and

she took no exception to this, merely offering wearily, "For five dollars more, I'll show you my secrets."

"The shirt will be enough," he returned. "A woman should always guard her secrets."

"Even from her doctor?" She gave a light laugh like chimes.

"Turn around," he said. "Let me see your back."

Although curiosity seized me, I continued to avert my eyes from the girl, even as a visible shudder ran down B. Banzai's frame. "Where did you get such a terrible scar?" he asked.

"In a fire when I was little," she said.

"A fire? Was anyone with you?"

"My sister."

"Your sister, was she your twin?"

"How did you know?" she asked, slumping on her bunk, once again the vision of hopelessness borne down with sorrows as she pulled her clothes around her in a gesture intended to shut out the world. "You've had your fun. Why don't you be the gentleman you're supposed to be and go now?"

The sulky indifference upon her face led Buckaroo to play his trump card. "I promised to pay you," he said. "Here's a shiny gold sovereign."

Trembling, she gazed at the coin in his hand. By the glow in her eyes I knew the riddle was solved and her aching ordeal, if not over, would soon be, all being quiet and hush as she came forward to claim the sovereign.

"My coin!" she said breathlessly. "Where did you get it?"

"*Your* coin?" Buckaroo said. "Your father gave it to you?" She nodded vigorously. "And one to your sister?" Again she assented, as he pressed the coin into her eager palm.

"Thank you!" she rejoiced. "I lost it. Where did you get it?"

"From your sister," he replied. "The one they told you died in the fire with your parents."

Wiping away tears, she did not comprehend a word he was saying. It flew in the face of a lifetime of belief, but there would be time later for protracted explanations. What was plain was that B. Banzai had once again carried all before him and, not to rhapsodize unduly, had saved her life as he had rescued untold others. Under one pretense or another, her release from the authorities was won by him, and she clambered aboard our bus with wide-eyed exuberance, neither knowing nor bothering to ask into what vortex she might be heading.

17

BEFORE MOVING ON to the press conference where it is well known B. Banzai glimpsed the extraterrestrials for the first time, I would be remiss if I did not resume the account of Whorfin. Having begun his work with a phone call to Yoyodyne, it fell fittingly upon a company wrecking truck to transport him to the company site outside Grover's Mills, where he found his worst suspicions confirmed. The morale of his troops was lamentable, and far from receiving a hero's welcome, Whorfin was met with disbelief and even a certain scorn, as though hs Lectroids blamed him for their condition of exile instead of being grateful for their survival. There was every kind of wailing and woe imaginable; and although a few of the heartier fellows (officers, in the main) greeted him with their usual tremendous shrieks, the compound as a whole had become a den of debauchery, given over freely to every sort of Earthly vice and idleness.

His face contracting with rage and eyes narrowing ominously everywhere he looked, Whorfin sallied forth among them, bringing home his rash message of impending doom unless the Panther ship was finished and the OVERTHRUSTER obtained from the Banzai project. Only the state of emergency, "the anxiety of the hour" as he put it, imposed upon him certain restraints and prevented him from ordering indiscriminate executions. Still, certain offenders cried out to be punished in what can only be characterized as a flagellantic ritual peculiar to that race of warriors. Whatever their motive, whether to prove their slavish devotion to their master Whorfin or to demonstrate their capacity to endure torture, these Lectroids would one after the other step forward to recite litanies of self-accusations and to pronounce themselves deserving of the most inhuman cruelties for their crimes. That they did so of their own volition (it was confirmed by the Nova Police and the captured grimy documents at hand) is in no way explained by the simplistic dictum, "They weren't human," for in combat it was later seen, and I can attest to the fact, that they felt pain as fully as our own kind. But, apparently their fanaticism overrode what little reason dwelt behind their bulging foreheads, and in repeated displays of this abject worship of power they would, after prostrating themselves before John Whorfin, readily suggest specific tortures appropriate to their misdeeds—unfailingly such exquisite methods of slow and agonizing destruction that the mind is moved to anguish to think of any living thing subjected to them, much less wittingly volunteer.

At the head of their list of transgressions was not, as we humans might expect it to be, bloodshed; bloodshed, even murder, was of no consequence to them one way or the other unless it imperiled the group as a whole. Numerous recorded cases of homicide and assault against humans have since been found in the Yoyodyne archives. Highway robbery, especially in the early fledgling days of the company, was even encouraged as a means of garnering precious working capital. Frolicsome violence—instances whereby the Lectroids' presence on this planet might be made known—were judged more harshly, but even in this, the passage of decades without discovery had lulled the creatures into a sense of security. It would delight me to add the qualifier "false," but the facts of the matter are otherwise. Had two certain events not happened, the Nova Police would not have undertaken to alert us as they did, and in all likelihood the aliens would be among us still, living unnoticed. I refer of course to the momentous experiment in Texas and the subsequent escape of the scourge Whorfin from the mental asylum.

So what were these crimes for which several of the self-confessed perpetrators paid by being beheaded in reverse order, i.e., from the feet up? Foremost among their fatal offenses were those activities which fell loosely into the category of decadent living. Vegetarianism, art collecting, bathing, consorting with the "daughters of men"—all were forbidden and equally odious in Whorfin's eyes because they sapped the fighting spirit of his minions and made their habitation on this planet more palatable, which in turn could only detract from his stated goal of returning to Planet 10 and seizing power. Besides this practical consideration, there was old-fashioned bigotry at work as well, to which he appealed at every opportunity. Earth has, it irks me to say, an apparent reputation throughout the universe as a planet of devils, and the impotence of human knowledge is much derided. Whorfin often spoke pointedly to this prejudice among his followers when condemning the "unnatural" practices I have noted above.

I have before me a collection of Whorfin's speeches and writings from prison which were delivered faithfully in his name to John Bigbooté over the years of his leader's absence. They provided an illuminating look at the Lectroid mind, the most significant aspects of which I shall attempt to summarize before moving on.

The typical Lectroid is above all in awe of power. Power for its own sake in his *raison d'être,* and he is obsessed with its attainment and exercise. To his underlings he is devoid of mercy, indeed has no sense of such a concept, whereas to his superiors, i.e., those holding power over him, he is obeisant and servile to the point of eagerly sacrificing his own life, as we have seen. The Lectroid does not thirst for knowledge or beauty, has no record of intellectual attainment, has never produced a single notable figure in any area of endeavour, save one: the field of battle. His attitude toward such things as history and culture, even his own, which he does not bother chronicling, is one of the utmost indifference. All that matters in his scheme is lust for power, his single-minded will to possess a thing by destroying it.

Insofar as his personal habits, the Lectroid is filthy by preference, it being common for him to bathe but twice in a lifetime, (viz.) at birth and after his wedding night. It is evidently a belief of theirs that washing shortens one's life and is "unmanly," and having encountered many of them in close combat, I can vouch from firsthand experience that both as a tenet of faith and as a practical matter there is much to be said in favor of their squalid appearance. With a heavy coat of decorative grease paint on top of layer upon layer of encrusted dirt thick enough to be spooned out of their palms, added to their already thick hides, they are able to withstand all but the most powerful blows and projectiles.

They have apparently but a single fear, and that is the fear of ridicule. They lack the most elementary sense of humor and are, unless of a mood to fight, quite reserved, even somnolent. For this latter trait, I am most grateful; otherwise, having not caught many of them napping, the scales of our engagement might not have tipped so propitiously in our favor.

By and large carnivorous, they are wont to supplement their intake of smoked meat with large doses of electrical current, although the years on our planet has seen them grow to rely increasingly on what is called "junk food," many of them foregoing their traditional diet entirely in favor of sweet cakes and candy bars in bright cellophane. As a result, they were by this time mired in lethargy which, compounded by the gravity problem, had caused their normally robust physiques to deteriorate to an appalling degree. Although, in this also we were fortunate.

For physiologic reasons I will avoid harrowing the reader with, sexual coupling with beings other than their own kind is an impossibility for them. But that is not to say that they do not enter into a kind of sexual frenzy in the presence of pain and death, whether it be their own or another's. To the Lectroid, sex derives its value merely from its relation to power, and cases of them abducting human "brides," both male and female, for sado-masochistic purposes are now known to abound, as the ever-growing cache of hacked bones exumed from the damp tunnels of Yoyodyne amply bears out. It is as if within these creatures' extraordinary propensity for inflicting and suffering cruelty there had to be developed the whole range of our emotions. Within the bounds of their cruelty is both pain and pleasure, love and hate, and even something hideously resembling art.

The same metaphor of destruction as a form of possession, which I have mentioned, could be seen repeated in the condition of their private compound. Away from the public portion of the Yoyodyne plant, in that secret hangar where the Panther ship was being constructed, valuable machinery lay broken and helpless, seemingly vandalized in orgiastic fits of fury, vilely humiliated so as to confirm who was master. In a safer time, such profligacy would have been of less concern, but now it could easily spell the difference between success and failure; and failure meant—

"Failure means death!" shouted Whorfin, haranguing them in their native tongue with that strange Italian accent he could not avoid. Dreadful to behold when he was in such turmoil, he paced to the right and the left, making a spring like a great cat now and again to recapture the attention of his corpselike audience. "How could you take vengeance on machines?" he railed. "Are they your enemy? What have these low objects done to you, except in your pitiful imaginations?"

Neither was he averse to flinging himself down upon the floor to implore them. "Because you have done this, we have lost precious hours! Days! Above us, the Nova Police! You hide, they seek! History is made tonight. Character is what you are in the dark! I should slay a score of you, nay, two score; the sight of your heads rolling would give me comfort! But in your heads is where your vital essence lives! I need that essence to fulfill my desire. Without your companionship, I am but a poor old dreamer, more dead than alive, trapped in this miserable three-brained being's feeble body, led on only by irrational hope. No power of mine can get us off this rock! I freely admit it, and yet the appointed time has come! I have cast the die! And yet you gibe and mock me. I came here expecting to find the great ship finished. Instead I find the equipment turned on its side." He sighed, gauging their expressions. "Is it payment you want? Booty? It's waiting for you on Planet 10! The dusky ones have your payment! So do their dusky wenches! Payment of another kind, the Nova Police will surely give ye!" Now he was giving them the medicine. They were with him now, their hard eyes brightening. "My wisdom can err! My knowledge is small compared to the Flying Fish." (The god they idolized–Reno) "But the Flying Fish is never wrong, and the substantial terrors of my mind are laid to rest when he speaks to me, as he has. Gather closer, closer." The beasts came nearer so that he could lay his hands upon them with a certain tenderness. "I have a message from the Flying Fish." His face torn with passion, he resorted to the time-honored debating trick of taking a piece of paper from his pocket and pretending to read from it. "He addresses us: 'Mighty soldiers of Whorfin, ignorant fools, listen to Whorfin when he tells you that the time has come to reclaim your planet. A thousand years of waiting has culminated in this moment of great importance. You must finish the Panther ship in these short hairs remaining!'" An obvious slip of the tongue engineered by the accursed Lizardo, Whorfin quickly shaking his head violently and correcting himself: "'In these short hours remaining, you must succeed because you labor within the very jaws of death! For the sake of cruelty if nothing else, murder those who have brought you to this desolation! Listen a second time! Murder those who have brought you to this desolation!'" So choked with emotion and theatrics had his voice become that huddled figures long thought dead were beginning to emerge from the shadowy tunnels of Yoyodyne, more Lectroids coming forward, drawn by his inhuman oratorical powers. "'There is no time to be lost. In the space of waiting, all may be lost! No more beheadings, no more volunteers. Show your unconquerable strength by getting to work, using every resource to finish the craft and stealing Buckaroo Banzai's Oscillation Overthruster!'" He crumpled the paper, concluding by saying, "I need three volunteers."

Every arm in the place shot up, but Whorfin's gaze had already settled upon three of his most capable lieutenants— the aforementioned John Bigbooté, Chief Executive Officer of Yoyodyne Propulsion Systems; John O'Connor, Vice-President, Research and Development; and John Gomez,

Vice-President, Controller. They would be the ones, chosen over all their companions, for this mission so glorious and decisive to their race, and it was they who appeared as an unlikely trio at the press conference wearing forged credentials.

Before I proceed, the reader may wonder about their appellations, in particular their common "Christian" name "John," this latter being no coincidence but rather an approximation of the sound they call one another in their own language. With the exception of Whorfin and Bigbooté, which are their true names rendered phonetically, the other Lectroids in the main carry legal surnames chosen at random from a Manhattan telephone directory found in the Grover's Mills social security office where they originally applied for identity papers after entering our dimension during the so-called Halloween hoax broadcast by Orson Welles on that fateful day in 1938. I will come back to this later; suffice it to say that all Lectroids have two names, just as Yoyodyne had two sets of books, one for Earthly consumption and the other for themselves.

I wish I could say that something about these three individuals—Bigbooté, O'Connor, and Gomez—attracted our keen scrutiny in that hotel ballroom we had hurriedly booked to disseminate the facts of B. Banzai's latest astounding feat to a breathlessly waiting international press corps. But, it would be simply that, wishful thinking. On the other hand, I doubt our knuckles deserve rapping. There was, other than a certain reluctance to come forward atypical of most newsfolk, nothing about them to set them apart in any way. Perfect Tommy has since told me that he thought them immediately suspicious-looking by the way they lurked near the coffee urn and peered cautiously from side to side while filling their cups with enormous spoonfuls of sugar. The little good service his suspicion does us at present is obvious, so there is scant cause for raising it except for these annals, where the question, Did Tommy have a leg up on all of us?, may or may not join the many interesting disputes in the world today.

At all events, it is a matter of public record that the press conference was easily half an hour underway before the grim adventure began in earnest. Up until the supposed phone call from the President of the United States, independent of all modes and customs, there was not a hint that soon to come, was the most bizarre introduction to a case we have ever had.

I will set the scene. Buckaroo and Professor Hikita were fielding diverse questions from the media. Seated at the dais under the bright television lights, besides myself and the two scientific stalwarts to whom I have just alluded, were Rawhide, Perfect Tommy, the Secretary of Defense, Senator Cunningham, and the two fellow travelers we had only minutes before taken aboard . . . the studious, medicinal New Jersey, who had already found a place in our hearts, and the troubled Penny Priddy, who I'm sorry to say had not. Still in the bus, very much in the middle of things thanks to the wonders of modern electronics, was Big Norse and her team of technicians.

Buckaroo had already given a brief history of the OSCILLATION OVERTHRUSTER concept, from the ill-fated Hikita-Lizardo experiment at Princeton in the '30s to the mortal accident involving his own parents on the arid Texas prairie. He had explained, as well as it could be explained, the amazing notion of matter going through matter, not in a ballistic sense but in the sense of two objects occupying a single space. He touched upon that revolutionary thesis which had sprung from his own fertile head, the theory of consciousness as the fifth basic force governing all matter in the universe*: and had made veiled reference to that which we saw, and found, in the other dimension.

He had at one point tapped the table in front of him to make a point. I quote excerpts from the transcript.

> (He demonstrates by picking up his plastic water glass and dropping it, splashing water as the container naturally bounces off the table.)

---

* The other four being the so-called strong force, or nuclear force, which holds the atomic nucleus together; the weak force, which governs particle decay; the electromagnetic force, which binds electrons to the atomic nucleus; and gravity.

Buckaroo Banzai: This table I'm sitting behind, it appears to be solid matter, right?

(A collective murmur of assent.)

But in point of fact, the solid parts of this table . . . the quarks which are the elementary building blocks of neutrons and protons, along with leptons . . . comprise only a quadrillionth of its total volume. What is the rest, I wonder?

(Since no one else answers, I volunteer.)

Reno: Nothingness.

Buckaroo Banzai: Nothingness? You mean the Great Void?

(I refuse to be tripped on this point, having sat in on a physics seminar or two.)

Reno: Chang Tsai said that when one knows the Great Void is full of ch'i one realizes there is no such thing as nothingness.

Buckaroo Banzai: Then what is ch'i?

Reno: It is a force. Like alaya consciousness.

Buckaroo Banzai: Like—?

Reno: *Alaya* consciousness, the conscious ness which is never extinguished, which flows eternally in order to make the world exist. It is the universal force that transcends the centripetal force of the so-called ego-consciousness.

Buckaroo Banzai: It is the true consciousness in every object, in every empty space, between all particles?

Reno: (Unhesitatingly) Yes.

(Out of the corner of my eye, I can observe Rawhide getting a message over his Go-Phone from Big Norse in World Watch. From the look of him, it is something important.)

Buckaroo Banzai: It is different from sentiency, that is,

103

what we individuals mean when we say we are conscious?

Reno: I would say so. We are sentient receptors of consciousness, even receptacles of it, as the memory can be said to retain bits of consciousness in the way a computer retains information. The conceit is to think consciousness resides, or originates, in the brain. The effect of a beautiful melody, for example, is felt even by lower organisms who cannot possibly be said to be "conscious" as the term is generally understood.

Perfect Tommy: Even plants. I once had a science fair project—

Reno: Exactly. An organism need not even be a sentient being, as the term is generally understood, to receive conscious "radiation," for lack of a better term. Nature is full of examples.

Buckaroo Banzai: Perhaps one need not even be "alive," for lack of a better term.

(In this I was somewhat nonplussed, feeling suddenly out of my league. I must remind the reader none of our exchange was rehearsed, although such see-sawing dialogues are an everyday occurrence at the Banzai Institute, Buckaroo being of the Socratic school.)

Reno: Perhaps.

Buckaroo Banzai: Is the glass I dropped conscious of the table?

Reno: If it wasn't, it is now.

(Buckaroo laughs, along with the news media, as Rawhide now steps over, whispers in his ear.)

"Buckaroo, the President's calling you," was what I subsequently learned Rawhide had whispered, a statement sufficiently vague to warrant Buckaroo's counter.

"Which President?" Buckaroo asked.

"The President of the United States."

"Is he having trouble?"

Now it is I who should explain. Besides being a friend of the President entrusted with certain details of State and the odd mission owing to his unique versatility, B. Banzai had recently attended the President in his capacity as physician. Upon examination, surgery of a minor nature had been recommended and performed by B. Banzai himself at Walter Reed. It was to the still tender condition of his patient that he now referred.

"I don't know," said Rawhide. "Big Norse has jacked the signal way up, but it's still pretty fuzzy. She patched him through to the pay phone down the hall."

In such an inauspicious way did our series of mischances begin, Buckaroo arising slowly from his chair and telling Professor Hikita to go ahead and begin the slide presentation which Tommy and I had arranged. "I'll be right back," I overheard him say.

Naturally, his departure attracted the attention of every eye in the room, including my own, and under ordinary circumstances I would have followed to investigate, but in this particular case there were other considerations. An audience of some billions was watching on television, and it would have been, I think, abnormal ugliness for us all to have gotten up to leave the room. Thus, despite my intellectual deficiencies, I remained to assist Professor Hikita in explaining to the world in allegorical terms that which B. Banzai had done.

I recall making some failed attempt at levity and instructed the first slide to be shown. The old adage of a picture, even a poor one, being worth a thousand words was again brought home to me as the haunting face of a young United States sailor appeared upon the screen. Comely and spruce and yet with the stamp of horror upon him, he flies out at me even now as I reperuse that distressing moment in my memory. Tommy and I had examined the slides on a light box, but that had been at a single sitting, and the full impact of what we were seeing had not truly sunk in until now, when I felt at once overwhelmed.

"This slide was taken yesterday in the other dimension," I announced and then, ignoring the frenzied hands of the journalists, said, "Next slide, please."

The details around the sailor had been obscured by shadow and a curious electrical fog, so that now when the second slide appeared, it produced a very odd effect upon the nerves, as I had intended it. It was the image of a United States naval vessel, the boyish sailor being but one of many visible upon her decks, all wearing the same ghastly expression of disbelief and helplessness, jaws ajar, eyes dilated and fastened on some nameless unholy terror.

To say that the exposure created a stir among those present would be understating the obvious. Exclamations of surprise echoed through the hall as I ceded the microphone to Professor Hikita, and it occurred to me how preposterous was our hope of laying forth the cold facts in any kind of objective way. Already, reporters were storming the exits for the telephones, more interested in getting a scoop than in getting it right. If this was how they reacted to the tamest of our disclosures, what would be their reaction, I wondered, to the handful of shocking creatures glimpsed in the other slides? Or to the foul parasite in the Igloo ice chest resting at the far end of the table? Something in the air boded ill. I feared outright hysteria at any second, as Professor Hikita called for order and spoke coolly.

"In 1942," he began, "a U.S. Navy frigate, number 754, disappeared on a clear day in the North Atlantic. Long thought to have been the victim of a U-boat, it apparently entered the other dimension through a process we do not yet understand."

I noticed the Secretary of Defense, his face the color of clay, as he jumped from his chair. A wild yell pealed from him, his breath coming in gasps. "Now wait a minute here! That's my department! You mean to tell me—?"

"Next slide, please," said Professor Hikita. "We have a lot of ground to cover."

Outside in the hallway, equally dramatic events were unfolding, already conspiring against the ends of evil. Buckaroo had stepped into a telephone booth expecting to talk to the President only to find no one apparently on the line.

"Big Norse said it was a bad connection," Rawhide said. "But they used the Elephant-Bravo code."

"Mr. President—? Anybody there?" Buckaroo held the phone slightly away from his ear, enabling Rawhide to hear the odd-sounding computer switching equipment in the distance, through a hail of interference.

"Maybe just a prankster?" suggested Rawhide. "One of these computer hackers like Billy?"

"Then our codes need updating. I'm not going to stand here and fence with them, whoever it is. See if Big Norse can get us a clean line through to the President—"

"Right."

Rawhide got on the Go-Phone at once, alerting Big Norse to the state of things, when abruptly it seemed that all the devils in hell had broken out of their holes as one to torment us. The telephone began emitting a high-pitched whine, and the air, of a sudden oppressive like a torpor or a strange dream, gave Buckaroo and Rawhide the queer feeling that their very souls had at once been laid bare. Buckaroo, in attempting to hang up the phone, felt something compelling him to do quite the opposite, to bring the phone once again to his ear and to listen to those mysterious noises. The sight of his face, the fact that it was trembling and twitching, prompted faithful Rawhide to try and rush to his chief's aid, only to be obstructed by the inexplicable slamming of the telephone booth's glass door. No agent had touched it, and yet it closed hurriedly, as if sentient. Such was the freakishness of the events taken as a whole that Rawhide's typical calm deserted him. He began frantically to whack on the glass and watched impotently as the pages of the telephone directory inside the booth began to turn, again with no perceptible cause, flipping faster and faster, as Buckaroo held the phone to his ear, his elbow locked in the characteristic rigidity of tetanus. Suddenly an electrical jolt jumped from the phone to his ear, a shock of such magnitude that his hair literally stood on end and his body bent like a bow. His every sense heightened tenfold, his brain cudgeled to its limit, he gave a wild agonized moan as the lights now began to flash, and he reached into his pocket for a ballpoint pen with which he feverishly wrote certain mathematical formulae on the palm of his hand. These numbers and symbols evidently came to him in a kind of trance induced by the electrical impulse to his ear, as he scribbled them without volition or awareness. When he had finished, he dropped the phone, and the electrical phenomena I have mentioned completely ceased.

Rawhide could at last open the glass door and attempt to take Buckaroo in his arms, finding him disheveled and deadly pale and in a terrible state of agitation. He implored Buckaroo to sit and rest a moment while he administered a restorative, but Buckaroo curtly pushed him aside. "There isn't a moment to be lost," he said cryptically. "The world's in mortal danger."

Relating to how B. Banzai was seized with this sudden intuition was the fact that his body still exuded a formidable electrical charge, which Rawhide learned to his intense discomfort when he sought to grasp him. Meanwhile, Buckaroo had started off for the hotel ballroom, and Rawhide, thoroughly frightened now, followed closely behind.

Speaking for myself, Professor Hikita and I had found an unexpected repository of scientific information in the person of Penny Priddy. For some inexplicable reason, she had without warning opened her mouth and, as much to her own surprise as ours, had begun to speak in the most learned terms about the theory of consciousness radiation and her own "pet hypothesis" that said radiation, or the universal force known as ch'i, was in fact not merely the Clairvoyant Reality popularized by certain exponents of the pseudopsychic, but was nothing less than a new grand unified theory. B. Banzai had resplit the atom into many dimensions, exploding four coordinate space and time. After listening to her for several minutes, far from being annoyed, I was rather in awe and thrilled to the fact that she was suddenly one of our party, even the cynical news media having fallen under the charm of her intelligent personality.

"Of course information comes through the senses," she interposed between statements of Professor Hikita. "No one here is suggesting otherwise. The way an object smells or looks—these are its physical properties—but it has, in addition, an essence, its unitary identity, which is communicated through consciousness radiation. To use the famous apocryphal story of Newton's encounter with the apple, Newton was correct insofar as his mathematically accurate theory of gravity went, but he did not go far enough in his *Principia*. He failed to see consciousness as a fundamental force. The perfect example of the falling apple as manifest consciousness escaped him entirely, even when it struck him on the head. In everyday terms, using the analogy of a baseball pitch, consciousness is neither the pitcher nor the catcher—it is the moving ball. In music, neither the violinist nor the spectator—it is the melody that floats from the strings, millions of vibrating molecules. It is The Thing Which Makes Itself Known; it is Newton's apple, a particle closely related to the graviton and gravitino hitherto unincorporated in any unification theory. I believe Buckaroo has called it somewhere in his writings 'The Door That Opens You,' meaning we need not seek other levels of consciousness but be neutral and free of psychic obstructions. Consciousness is neither sought nor seeks; it radiates everywhere."

At that moment, as I hung on her every word, the door through which Buckaroo and Rawhide had left was suddenly flung open, and in amazement I saw Buckaroo, seemingly possessed of a form of madness, pointing with trembling hand at someone across the room. "Stop them!" he screamed. "They're Evil from the other dimension!"

In a flash he was after them, the Lectroids who have since come to be identified as John O'Connor and John Gomez, the two of them making ungainly leaps for the nearest exit, bounding like human kangaroos with Buckaroo and Rawhide in pursuit. In the same instant, their comrade John Bigbooté appeared unexpectedly at our rear, having stepped through the curtain behind the dais and grabbing Professor Hikita while pressing a pistol to his throat. In a loud shrieklike voice he cried out, "Anybody moves, the Prof gets it through the esophagus!" (The throat area, we came to learn, was their own mortal spot, their heads being thickly plated.)

The effect of his dramatic announcement was to freeze those of us near him and to cause Buckaroo and Rawhide to lose valuable steps in their race for the main doors. Those of us on the dais could but attempt to collect our wits and appraise the situation that was unfolding with lightning rapidity. (Remember, reader, we had not heard of such a thing as a Lectroid, and to everyone except Buckaroo they still appeared as normal, if somewhat awkward, human beings.)

It was at some point in the confusion that I saw Bigbooté's eyes shift away from me and made the instinctive play to go for my gun. It turned out to be a mistake, which in hindsight I readily admit, as Bigbooté's reactions proved faster than I had anticipated and he nailed me with a single shot, his bullet striking me in the shoulder area and knocking me backwards over the table. Another inch and it would have pierced a lung, New Jersey later told me. Three more inches, and it would have been my heart, although I wasn't thinking of any of that then, as I watched Bigbooté jerk the professor through the curtains and disappear. Tommy immediately followed, only to find the door through which they must have gone somehow firmly shut. At all events, he could not budge it open and so was forced to run to another exit, losing crucial seconds in the process.

In the meantime, New Jersey was bending over me and attending my wound, his voice hoarse with emotion when I vainly tried to rise. "Just lie still," he said. "You're not going anywhere."

"It's not that," I muttered. "The Overthruster—"

Then it was the voice of Penny, as pretty as an angel in that moment, holding something small and shiny in one hand. "I've got it," she said. "Buckaroo handed it to me when he left the room. He said, 'Hold my thruster,' and I said I would."

At least that was something, I thought. I only hoped the professor would come to no harm. That was the last thing I remembered for some time, feeling the onrush of a faraway dreamy feeling, as New Jersey pulled a needle from my arm. (His wampum belt we had so derided held his medical supplies, as it turned out.)

I will now relate, as it has been related to me, what happened in my absence. Buckaroo and Rawhide had gone after the Lectroid duo, O'Connor and Gómez, in different directions only to run into one another again at the conclusion of their respective chases in the hotel parking garage, where O'Connor and Gomez, reunited with Bigbooté, were seen loading a crate roughly the size of Professor Hikita into a Yoyodyne van. From across the garage, Buckaroo and Rawhide both raised their pistols and ordered them to stop, and when they did not, Buckaroo fired, the gun discharging without any discernible result other than the sight of a slightly affronted John Bigbooté rubbing his head as if he had been tweaked by a mosquito. When Buckaroo attempted to fire again, Rawhide, still thinking the targets human and his chief momentarily under great stress, deflected Buckaroo's barrel, much to the latter's irritation. "It doesn't matter!" Buckaroo yelled. "Let me put it plainly! They're devils!"

In the meantime the three Lectroids had scrambled into their van and raced up the exit ramp; and when Buckaroo identified himself to a passing motorcyclist, the chase was resumed in earnest, B. Banzai riding in tandem with the cyclist who quickly showed himself to be quite fearless and also bitterly drunk to the point that he would not have hesitated to die for the cause in any number of deadly maneuvers. Even Buckaroo, who had just traveled faster than the speed of sound through a mountain and a man to whom I have said fear was a stranger, had at last met that stranger. Within several blocks of the hotel, his hand was already turning the nonexistent door-handle to jump for it when the cyclist uttered a wild scream and Buckaroo ordered him to pull over to the curb before he hurt someone. For whatever reason, the man surprisingly complied and Buckaroo was truly glad.

"I'll have this returned to you," Buckaroo said, and the man, giving him a queer intent look, waved as Buckaroo sped away on his machine.

"You're Buckaroo Banzai!" the poor receding figure was heard to exclaim.

When Buckaroo related the story to us much later, we all laughed uproariously, although at the time the events occurred, Buckaroo was anything but amused. In the jumble of the chase, he had lost sight of the Yoyodyne van and now scrambled madly to catch up, threading recklessly through traffic and at last espying the vehicle near the outskirts of town.

If anything, falling far behind the vehicle for a time now proved advantageous to B. Banzai, as it appeared to the Lectroids (if such things occurred to them at all) that they were suddenly out of danger. Buckaroo was astute enough to surmise the same, and thus was able to trail them easily by keeping his distance.

This situation continued for the better part of an hour, during which time he communicated to us over his Go-Phone, updating us at intervals and again illustrating the versatility of the cellular radio*, an invention of the Banzai Institute and one which already gave promise of revolutionizing worldwide communications.

Informed of my condition (he had not known I was wounded), he insisted on knowing what had been done for me and dispatched us all to the Institute where we were to begin investigating at once the shadowy company known as Yoyodyne Propulsion Systems. Even in my dazed state, the name struck a chord, although I could not say why.

"How about you, Buckaroo?" Rawhide asked.

"I have a hunch that's where I'm going," he said. "I'm switching on my locator just in case."

(His "locator," a cellular emergency beacon, would allow us to know his location within fifty feet at all times.)

Despite the fact that we itched to know more, we accepted his instructions without question and prepared to move on them, but there was one matter he had not thought to address; this was the issue of Penny Priddy. Had we been soulless, we could have easily left her behind. Speaking for us all, I think we still had our doubts about her, this business of identical twins leaving us shaking our heads, and now this sudden and unexplained outburst of hers at the press confer-

---

* Cellular radio, or simply "cellular," is a fairly recent technological breakthrough of the Banzai Institute enabling persons with small units the size of a cigarette lighter or a wristwatch to telephone from anywhere in the world. It interfaces with all existing telecommunications networks, including satellites, can receive and transmit video, can communicate with any computer, and can even navigate electronically, as airplanes do. Cellular, in short, represents a total communications system without wires.

A rare family portrait circa 1955: Sandra Banzai, Masado Banzai, and the young Buckaroo. Taken in Texas (probably by Professor Hikita) on property owned by the Texas School of Mines.

The wondrous, elusive Buckaroo Banzai . . . neurosurgeon . . . cosmologist . . . high-speed racer . . . snapped here on stage at Artie's Artery in New Brunswick, New Jersey.

Reno . . . moody and dangerous . . . real name unknown . . . possessing an easy grin, a quirky artistic streak . . . saxophonist and official chronicler of the exploits of Buckaroo Banzai and his fellow Hong Kong Cavaliers.

Rawhide . . . Buckaroo's most trusted Hong Kong Cavalier . . . real name unknown . . . holds several advanced degrees in psychology, anthropology and entomology.

Perfect Tommy . . . an enigma . . . real name unknown . . . designer of the Jet Car's extraordinary suspension system . . . vain, pleasure-loving, heartless, sordid, callous, sentimental . . . a chameleon.

New Jersey . . . medical colleague of Buckaroo's from Columbia's College of Physicians and Surgeons . . . real name Sidney Zwibel . . . the newest Hong Kong Cavalier . . . plays a mean piano.

The 1984 Banzai/Hikita Jet Car on its history-making charge through solid matter!

Penny Priddy, down to her last nickel, prepares to end it all as Buckaroo Banzai serenades her from the stage of Artie's infamous Artery.

As evil as they come ... Lord John Whorfin from Planet 10 poses with his two most trusted comrades in their earthling disguises, John O'Connor and John Bigbooté.

Appearing as a human being, John Bigbooté kidnaps Professor Hikita right from the press conference!

Scooter Lindley, Junior Blue Blaze Irregular 41½, receives a coded transmission from Perfect Tommy in World Watch One . . . Buckaroo's in trouble!

John Emdall, Chief Executive of the black Lectroids on Planet 10, transmits herself by way of mysterious record directly into Buckaroo Banzai's study.

Casper and Scooter Lindley, courageous Blue Blaze Irregulars, join Buckaroo Banzai and the Hong Kong Cavaliers in their daring assault on Yoyodyne Propulsion Systems.

A rare photo of a red Lectroid guard napping with his Dream Goggles on.

"Te, te, te!" shouts a frustrated, terrified John Bigbooté from his flight jacket, daring to correct Lord Whorfin's mispronunciation of his name one last time before blast-off for The Eighth Dimension.

Seat belts fastened, Lord John Whorfin gives the final thumbs-up signal from the cockpit of his ramshackle Panther ship. "Let'sa go home!"

ence! What to make of such a girl? The night before she had seemingly taken a shot at us, and now here she was nursing me, taking my head in her lap, and sponging my forehead with a cool cloth whilst saying the most soothing words. The night before, and this morning at the jail, she had appeared as but an unassuming unlettered vagrant, a *gamine*, who we now learned possessed an astonishing familiarity with B. Banzai's theories and with even a few of her own! And yet in the next breath, when pressed by Tommy, she disclaimed any knowledge of such things, saying she had "no idea" what came over her, disavowing the very erudition with which she had just mesmerized us. Again, as I have said, *who is she?*

Still, we couldn't abandon her. Buckaroo would have had our skins had we tried, and, truth to tell, she was not unpleasant to be around. Given enough idle theorizing, anyone can sooner or later be painted in the worst lights, and in person there was certainly nothing sinister about her. If she had long carried a torch for B. Banzai, then so had many women. There was no crime in that, nor in her plaintive condition, nor least of all in her poverty. As I reminded Tommy, we are not members of a secret society, charged as judge and executioner. We are, hopefully, good citizens bearing the unmistakable hallmark of decent people everywhere—a willingness to help our fellows. I said to Tommy, "If she portends bad things, do we have the right to commit minor crimes against her because she might do worse to us?"

"Don't try to talk like Buckaroo," he said.

"Isn't that what Buckaroo would say?" I replied.

"I don't know."

"Then why don't you wait and ask him?"

He looked at me silently, then said, "All right, she comes with us. But I don't like it. I want to go on record."

And so he did. His objection is here duly noted, as is the fact that she did accompany us on the bus back to the Institute, indeed sitting beside me, where she continued to concern herself with my comfort. (Luckily, the bullet had only cut flesh, but the soreness was not insignificant.)

As she leaned across me to pull aside the curtains covering my window, I inhaled a faint breath of the most unusual perfume I had ever encountered and complimented her on it.

"It's Chinese," she said.

"Chinese," I pondered aloud. "It's very different. What's it called?"

"It's called I Don't Remember," she said.

"Interesting name."

"Well, you know the Chinese."

"Not really."

I did not really mean to fence with her, but now she had me. I was intrigued. All the old questions, my doubts about her, came back, and I queried her stonily.

"Where did you buy it?" I asked. "I'd like to get some for my friend."

"What's her name?"

"Pecos."

The name made her smile, but only for a moment. Perhaps my stare disconcerted her, or perhaps it was something else which caused her to look away, the colored radiance having left her cheeks. I sensed I had gained the advantage. (How mistaken I was!) I also confess to having searched her face, now more revealed amid the sunlight, for any surgical marks. Although I could see none—in fact I was struck most by her expression of gentleness—she was clearly restive under my gaze.

"What is it?" she said, impatiently.

"It's that sweet odor," I said. I'd give anything to know where you got it."

"I promise to get you some. I really don't know where I got it. It must have been a present from someone. Anyway," she said, "that's not what you were really thinking."

"No?"

"Tell me your private mind, Reno."

Again, I inhaled that rare fragrance, scarcely perceptible and yet exquisite, as though it were her very breath, my flesh at once burning feverishly as if by the urgency of some torrid blaze. I felt a surge of fear, that the lock on my inner door was giving way, my immortal soul fleeing in horror from those latent abysmal instincts she had awakened within me. Suddenly the thought of death gave me no pain. This life was a mystery I despaired of ever solving, and I had perforce to be content with leaving it, my brain beginning to swim as if some occult change in the atmosphere had summoned the most weird nonsense, the strangest fantasies, and bade them to dance as airy figures before me. With each successive whiff I grew dizzier, my hold on reality more tenuous. A dull red crept to my temples, a shimmering phoenix took flight, and just then the timely voice of New Jersey pulled me back from that remarkable intoxication.

"Get me a wet towel," he shouted.

"I think he's delirious," I heard Penny say, as I felt the coolness of water.

"What happened?" I asked.

"You're suffering from ague," New Jersey said. "Are you all right?"

"Her perfume—"

"Her perfume?" New Jersey sniffed. "What's that got to do with anything? You two take it easy—we'll be at the Institute in a few minutes. Reno, you're going straight to the infirmary."

"I'm all right," I protested and saw Tommy dimly across the aisle, a gleam of "I told you so" in his eyes, looking down on me in more ways than one.

"I'll be around if you need me," New Jersey said, rising to leave.

"I'll take care of him," Penny replied.

Once more "alone," the circuit of my riotous thoughts broken, she remained to stroke my hair with graceful gestures and stare at me, almost hypnotically. I would like to say her smile gladdened my heart, but I cannot. When she leaned close, I could still smell that most subtle of lures, and I was more convinced than ever that the evasive scent was not a perfume at all. It was her breath, it was she!

As we neared the Institute, I wished to test my theory by bringing matters to a head. After some preliminary conversation about her past—the death of her parents and her identical twin sister in that terrible fire, about which she was confused by recent events; followed by her adoption by a distant relative out west in Wyoming; her flight from home as a troubled adolescent; a brief time as a *religieuse* in a convent; her adventures as a world traveler; her failures in various careers—the talk turned to me.

"You're the writer, Reno," she said. I did not deny it. "You write the Buckaroo adventure books."

"I take notes and report what I see."

"What did you do before you joined the outfit?"

"We in the 'outfit,' " I said, "don't ask one another such personal questions, but since you didn't know better, I'll tell you. I had my own think tank, but I got tired of thinking—I wanted some action."

"What are you working on now?" she asked. "Or should I say what new adventure are you taking notes for?"

"I don't know yet," I said. "But I am reminded of a story from classical antiquity, in which an Indian prince sent a beautiful girl to Alexander the Great as a gift. Naturally, the young conqueror was smitten by her loveliness, but what was more amazing about the girl, what set her apart from every other of her sex, was the strange delectable perfume on her breath, sweeter than any flower. It was this seductive scent which covered her terrible secret."

"Which was—?"

"That all her life she had been raised on poisons, nurtured by them, fed them from her birth, so that the deadliest toxins became her element, as natural to her as water and the air we breathe, and in time she became poisonous herself . . . lethally so. Her embrace was literally the kiss of death."

Like an owl, Penny watched me, her rapt attention attending every word of my tale, dwelling on every line of it. It was not the reaction I had expected but one I was happy to note. "So that's how Alexander died?" she said. "He kissed her?"

"No," I replied. "One of his soldiers saw through her and stole a kiss himself."

"Or perhaps he did not see through her," she parried. "Perhaps he only wanted a kiss before Alexander got there."

"In any case, her plan was foiled. The end, when it came for her, must have been a blessed relief. It couldn't have been pretty."

"For her or the soldier who kissed her," she pointed out.

"Oh, he died instantly. Her kiss was painless."

She smiled at me rakishly, saying, "That's the most roundabout proposition I've ever heard. Do you want a kiss, Reno?"

"It might ease my mind." I said, whereupon she put her lips to my own and kissed me like a pagan. When she withdrew and I took a breath, no harm having come to me, I apologized at once. "I was wrong about you," I said. "Please forgive me."

(Bear in mind, reader, I was delirious with fever.)

18

WE HAD NOT yet begun to worry unduly about Buckaroo Banzai. His locator put him on the road to Grover's Mills, and at last report he was still following the Yoyodyne van, presumably at a sensible distance. Were life to mirror our intentions, however, it would be nowhere near as entertaining. B. Banzai may or may not have realized from the curious "phone call" that he had an appointment with destiny, but I am certain he could not see the serpentine road by which he would arrive; else he would have taken greater precautions. But how can one anticipate the behavior of extraterrestrials, friend or foe? They were the great unknown factor, the jokers in the deck, which in turn meant a new set of rules.

We have but conjecture to rely upon as to why the Yoyodyne van suddenly veered sharply into the ditch by the side of the road and reversed its course, nearly running down B. Banzai in the process. The most probable explanation is that the three Lectroids inside received a radio message from home base, informing them of the downed thermopod. Essentially a life craft dispatched by the Nova Police father ship to find Buckaroo Banzai, it was shot down by those now-famous duck hunters whose posthumous pictures have appeared in so much of the media.

The details of the incident are well-known but merit repeating for the record: Two duck hunters on a weekend outing north of Grover's Mills fire into what they think is a phalanx of mallards. The mallards turn out to be electronic camouflage for a bizarre UFO approximately the shape and outer texture of a tangerine. (How this electronic camouflage is done by both the Nova Police and the Lectroids themselves I will come to later.) The UFO crashes into the upper branches of a tree; the terrified duck hunters observe what seems to be a dread-locked Jamaican emerge from the craft in a silver Nova Police spacesuit; the "Jamaican" loses his footing and crashes to the ground—upon his death turning into a hideous thing from another world, that species which on Planet 10 is called an "Adder," a sleeker, less brawny sort of creature than the Lectroid and of a darker color, thus giving rise to the racial epithets heaped upon them by Whorfin and his followers.

By this time one can imagine the panic of the duck hunters, gazing in disbelief at the dead Adder on the ground, when a second "Jamaican" manages to scramble down the tree and with a graceful gait makes a run for it, carrying some kind of package under his arm. Despite being pursued by the duck hunters' spaniel, he reaches safety, delivers his "present" to us, and thereby becomes a linchpin in our story. In person, full-limbed and wonderful-looking in human camouflage, he is the redoubtable John Parker, whose indispensable help in saving our world has earned him the undying gratitude of peoples and nations everywhere.

Upon seeing John Parker come out of the craft, the duck hunters hasten their retreat to the CB radio in their car. Having no idea how many such beings might be found inside the space pod, they decide to summon help. A state police car receives their SOS and is there within minutes, setting the scene for the arrival of John Bigbooté and company.

What thoughts must have gone through the three Lectroid minds when the news of the downed Adder craft was radioed to them? It must have hit like a bombshell. It could not be an accident, a mere coincidence that it crashed within miles of Yoyodyne, the Lectroids' last refuge. The universe was too large, the chance too small of such a thing happening at random. It could only mean that their colony had been discovered, or had been monitored for some time. Perhaps always, thought John Bigbooté. Once an avid believer in the tenets and leadership of John Whorfin, Bigbooté now harbored considerable doubts. In Whorfin's absence, Bigooté had, in a sense, become his "own man." He had taken over the reins of Yoyodyne in 1939, shortly after he and Whorfin had founded the company with the proceeds from Whorfin's criminal escapades. Whorfin-as-Lizardo, already a wanted man, was soon arrested by Hoover's G–men, but the fledgling new armaments company continued, its survival assured by the coming World War and cold war era. Under Bigooté, the company had grown into the nation's largest privately held defense manufacturer; and as its "innovative CEO," as *Forbes* magazine had called him, Bigooté hobnobbed with bureaucrats and captains of industry. Under his stewardship, company earnings had soared, key defense contracts had been bidded for and won, and there had been plans for expanding the company's share of the ever-growing international arms trade by opening a branch in London. Toward that end a piece of property on West India Dock Road, in the heart of Limehouse, had been bought, and an artist's conception of a new facility lay at that very moment on his desk back at Yoyodyne. Of course he had told John Whorfin nothing of this. All John Whorfin was good for was carping. He, John Bigooté, had built Yoyodyne into all that it was today despite the constant interference and meddling of John Whorfin. Once before, Bigooté had raised the question of the company's growth and the inevitable prospect of hiring humans, and Whorfin had berated him loudly over the phone, threatening his life. Whorfin was an imbecile, Bigooté was convinced, and the same was doubly true, unfortunately, of his own subordinates. The other two members of this management troika so highly regarded by business publications, John O'Connor and John Gomez, were irretrievable losses. Both careless simpletons, he dared not trust them with anything of importance, certainly not his true opinion of John Whorfin. No, for better or worse, he, John Bigooté, was an unusual Lectroid, unique even. He had original thoughts, a rudimentary knowledge of Earth history, and even a lot of money. He was almost cultured.

The only cloud on the horizon, until now, had been the disagreeable affair of the Navy's top secret Truncheon subkiller, a carrier-launched plane with advanced sonar and highly sophisticated solid-state hydrophones designed to recognize the "signatures" of Soviet Delta class submarines and identify them by name, from up to a distance of several hundred miles. By Planet 10 standards, the technology was fairly primitive, the job definitely 'doable' within the billion dollar budget allotted. The problem, as usual, had been Whorfin, and his insistence on diverting massive resources from the Truncheon program to the accelerated development of the secret Panther ship, that huge craft intended to enter the Eighth Dimension and collect the remnants of the Lectroid army and carry them home to ultimate victory over the Adders. As a result of this ongoing misappropriation of colossal amounts of funds, work on the plane had fallen far behind schedule. A congressional committee had interested itself in the matter, and he, John Bigbooté, had been subpoenaed to testify on the Hill. He had defended the company staunchly and vigorously. In the opinion of the company lawyers, the congressional questioners "hadn't laid a glove" on him, to use their parlance. But the investigation was not over and showed no sign of going away. Worse, he feared that the reputation of the company had been permanently damaged. There was even some talk of an "on site factfinding tour," an inspection! The very thought made him tremble . . . hordes of media gadflies and snoop-types from the General Services Administration poking their noses into every corner of Yoyodyne. Such a visit would require a huge generated field of electronic camouflage, and what if there were not ample time to prepare? What if something went wrong? They would find the Panther ship! How would he explain that away? Damn John Whorfin! It was perhaps a blasphemous notion full of bravado, but for some time now John Bigbooté had mulled the possibility of killing John Whorfin and eating his brain. Under happier circumstances, Whorfin had been like a father to him; but that was all remote now, those blissful bygone days spent shuttered from the cold and darkness without, wrapped in the company of trysting, writhing Lectroids and the frigid gray of Planet 10.

No, the more he thought on it, the more compelling the idea seemed. For the sake of the greater family of Lectroids and the aerospace company he had built into a thriving concern, it had to be done. By eating Whorfin's brain, he, John Bigfooté, by law would become Lectroid Leader. There would be no one to dispute him, no one to whom he must report every purchasing order like a measly errand boy, no imperious sufferer of flatulence in whose eyes he must continually strive to pass muster. At the thought of killing, the old excitement returned. His eyes were lit with an icy shine, his stomach taut. It was a Lectroid tenet that the greatest deeds were possible to a murderous mood. The severity of the act must be indescribable, an attack so vicious that it would cause the entire universe to take notice, and other murderous betrayals to seem but trifles in comparison. He recalled once enjoying *Julius Caesar* some years ago in his "reading period" and resolved to look at the play again. How many blows had been delivered Caesar? He would stab Whorfin twelve times that number! It would be so easy! John Whorfin in that ridiculous Three Brained Being's body! By the Oath of the Flying Fish, that bloodthirsty winged beast, he would have Whorfin's three brains!

He dared tell none of this to anyone, nor invite coconspirators. He must choose his moment carefully and act alone, he thought as he caught sight of the state police car parked by the side of the road up ahead, and John O'Connor tapped him on the shoulder.

"That's it," said John O'Connor. "These are the coordinates."

Bigbooté slowed the car and shook his head in response to an offer of a dry-cell battery from John Gomez. "No, thanks," he said. "I'm trying to quit."

John Gomez shrugged and raised the battery to his mouth, touching both poles with his tongue. His eyes rolled up with pleasure, and there was the faint odor of burning carbon.

"There it is!" exclaimed John O'Connor, having caught

sight of the pod in the tree. "It's the Nova Police, all right! Look—human hunters."

"We'll have to kill them," said Bigbooté, parking the van behind the state police car. "We'll have to kill them all."

"No survivors," seconded John O'Connor.

After a quick check of the crate containing Professor Hikita in the rear of the van, they got out of the vehicle and walked toward the space pod despite the warnings of the state trooper to stay back. Bigbooté, his murderous confidence growing, merely produced his Yoyodyne ID card.

"Yoyodyne, officer," he said jauntily, to gain the poor fellow's trust. "I think she's one of our birds."

The officer approached skeptically until he saw Bigbooté's identification. "Bigboote?" he said, pronouncing it Big Booty.

"Bigbooté," Bigbooté corrected. "Chief Executive Officer, Yoyodyne Propulsion. And these are my assistants, John O'Connor and John Gomez. What happened here?"

Behind the lawman, the Lectroids could see the hunters still in a state of shock, standing near the grotesque body of the Adder. Gomez decided to walk over to look for himself.

"The duck hunters evidently shot the thing down," the officer said, again glancing at the plastic ID cards. "Yoyodyne, huh? That big aerospace outfit?"

Bigbooté nodded. "Yeah, we were doing a little testing of a sensitive nature—I can't tell you exactly what—there must have been trouble with the guidance system. Sorry for the inconvenience."

"It inconvenienced that fellow," said the officer, indicating the dead Adder who at that precise moment was being kicked ruthlessly by John Gomez. Caught in the act, Gomez backed off. "What do you think you're doing?" the officer shouted at him.

Bigbooté caught Gomez's attention and gave him a signal as evanescent as lightning. "It's okay, officer, it's just one of our 'droids. We have some tools in the truck. We'll chop down that tree and get everything out of here right away. John Gomez, why don't you go back to the van and notify headquarters that the situation is under control—?"

The officer, by now totally off balance despite beginning to sense the menace of the three so-called business executives, protested feebly that nothing should be touched, but was outnumbered, as John Gomez went briefly back to the van and returned with a power saw. In the meantime, Bigbooté had called the hunters over on the pretense of questioning them so that they stood with the patrolman, Bigbooté and John O'Connor flanking them. None apparently had any idea of the peril they were in, Bigbooté's mirthfulness having its desired effect in disarming them.

"Yeah, that's one of our 'droids," Bigbooté joked. "Must have been flying north for the winter."

"You mean south," replied one of the hunters.

"South," laughed Bigbooté, his fearsome stare lingering on the quaintly dressed hunter who had caught his small mistake. "That's why it was lost."

"Looks like no 'droid I've ever seen," said the hunter. "The other one ran so fast my dog couldn't catch him."

This was the first Bigbooté had heard of a second Adder, and it betokened trouble. By some odd conceit it had not occurred to him that a second Adder might have evacuated the craft. It was unlike Adders to move on foot. He conferred quickly with John O'Connor and dispatched him to scout the area. Where would a single Adder go? he wondered. Why were they out here in the middle of nowhere in the first place?

What he could not know, of course, was that the thermopod had been on its way to Buckaroo Banzai, following the azimuthal beam from the father ship detected earlier by Big Norse. What he also could not know was that my gallant chief B. Banzai was at that instant less than fifty yards from him, observing events from inside the van, where he had already freed Professor Hikita from the crate and informed him of the strange phone call enabling him to see Lectroids in their true form.

In addition, he had shown Professor Hikita the odd markings he had written in ink on the palm of his hand, as the phone call had "dictated" them to him. He had had no time to analyze them, did not even understand why he had scribbled them, except that in some manner or other they represented something of staggering importance. Having no time to copy them, he moistened his hand and pressed his palm to Hikita's forehead, leaving behind an electrical shock and the symbols intact and legible, albeit reversed.

"There's a motocycle behind those bushes," Buckaroo said. "Ride it to the Institute and get busy on these formulae. For some reason I feel we haven't much time."

"But what will you do?"

"I'll be there as soon as I can," Buckaroo replied. "I'd like to get a peek at Yoyodyne and see what we're up against."

"What do you mean, Buckaroo?"

"There isn't time to explain. Just go . . . quietly."

Without delay the professor slipped from the van to the bushes where the motorcycle was hidden, raising the heavy machine and pushing it some distance down the road before starting it. Buckaroo Banzai meanwhile worked his way closer to the thermopod in the tree. To say that he had never seen anything like it is tautological. Striving for a better look at it and the dead Adder, he circumambulated the field before finding a shallow pit ideal for his purposes. There, slightly below the general level of the ground and hidden by a copse of small cedars, he was afforded a straightaway look at all that was about to happen. Unfortunately for the hunters and the state policeman, however, his presence could not bias events. I will give the gruesome particulars.

While John Gomez pulled the crank on the gasoline-powered saw and prepared to cut down the tree holding the thermopod, the patrolman took it upon himself to intervene. Aware that state police reinforcements had been radioed for and believing John Gomez in fact to be a sensible corporate executive, the officer did not realize until too late that he was in mortal danger. Holding up his hands as if to say "that's enough," he stepped toward John Gomez and was quickly sliced in half by the marauder's power saw.

At this, the hunters ejaculated in horror and were just as rapidly slain by John Bigbooté's Herculean bare hands, as he banged their skulls together with a sickening thud. An attitude of professional and utter cold-bloodedness attended the entire operation, which took less than five seconds *in toto.* In that interval, three innocent men had been executed, and John Gomez turned matter-of-factly to saw the tree.

From behind his hillock, if I may call it that, B. Banzai gaped punily, for that was all he could do, given the speed of events. He lay in this state of great churning agitation, his chest heaving with thoughts of revenge, when he heard a sound behind him.

Nimbly reaching for his pistol and turning in one move, he found himself confronted by the snide smile of John O'Connor, the Lectroid which Buckaroo had lost track of, O'Connor having been sent to prowl the woods in search of the Adder John Parker. If the sight of the drawn pistol was intended to frighten O'Connor, it did not. (The Lectroid has no such reasoning. They are bred as fighters pure and simple, like the pit bulldog.) He merely looked at B. Banzai as if much acquaintance already existed between them and said, "Buckaroo Banzai. I can't think of a fitter moment to kill you."

And then he at once proceeded to attempt to make good his words, lunging powerfully but clumsily in Buckaroo's direction, Buckaroo deftly sidestepping him and then planting a swift northeast foot in his groin. The kick was not without effect, momentarily doubling O'Connor over, although it would have put any "normal" man, i.e., a human being, in a hospital for a week. Still, the consequence of the blow was to provide Buckaroo an avenue of escape past the confounded beast who for a period of seconds could only shriek at a fraction of his normal volume. "Buckaroo Banzai!" he screamed, his usual basso profundo a profound treble.

Bigbooté and Gomez, of course, came running to join in pursuit of the hero with singleness of heart. Like canines, there was a plainness and simplicity to their thinking which permitted them to tear a man limb from limb in one breath and go romping off merrily like children in the next. Naturally, this was no consolation to B. Banzai at that moment, the Lectroids' grunts and heavy tread so close behind; the fact that they would kill him in good fun detracted not at all from his dilemma.

As he ran, he urgently searched his pockets for his Go-Phone. I should add "with vigor" since the ungainly creatures, like heavy trucks, tended to be tireless and not at all slow once they had gathered momentum. Their kangaroolike jumping ability in addition enabled them to hurdle minor barriers that a man would run around, thus shortening B. Banzai's already slim lead. Still patting his pockets, feeling every ply and folding of his jacket, still emptyhanded, he reached another road—or perhaps the same, he couldn't be sure—just in time to see a truck lumbering toward him. Outstretching his arms, B. Banzai charged the vehicle, thinking it might prove his deliverance when in reality it came exceedingly close to doing him in; sufficient reason for this could be drawn from the fact that the driver of the truck was Lectroid and "YOYODYNE" was emblazoned across the cab. Nearly too late did Buckaroo dodge the onrushing tons of steel and leap for the ditch, and by then the trio of Lectroids on foot were almost upon him.

With difficulty he picked himself up and continued running, but the Lectroids only redoubled their effort. They were clearly superior to any human, physically speaking, and there was no telling whether they were tiring in the slightest. What was evident was that B. Banzai was running out of time. There are a pair of maxims often heard at the Banzai Institute which come to mind here just as they doubtless occurred to Buckaroo in those last tense moments: "A thousand pities cannot undo one thoughtless act." and "A fool can throw a stone into the water which ten wise men cannot recover." I mention these here not to moralize but simply to illustrate that B. Banzai is merely human like the rest of us and fully capable of carelessness. In this case, losing his Go-Phone could have proven costly in the extreme. Were it not for organizational safeguards designed for just this sort of emergency, the world might have lost Buckaroo Banzai and in the greater sweep of things lost itself shortly thereafter, as I will show.

Out of breath, out of hope, having sprinted by now the greater part of a mile, B. Banzai determined to stand and fight. He withdrew his pistol, and as the three monstrous

Lectroids came closer, he began to squeeze off shots, finding his mark repeatedly, and yet barely slowing them. Shots to the head fazed them apparently not in the least, likewise shots to the abdominal area. They kept coming, now joined by the truck, which had turned around.

Now out of bullets as well as the two commodities I have just cited above, B. Banzai prepared to defend himself barehanded. But if bullets had been of such little use, of what good were fists and kicks against these insensible brutes? If Buckaroo Banzai had ofttimes whistled at death, he now heard it laughing back and drawing nearer. And yet greatness in a man can be in some way measured by how little alteration the approach of death makes in him. B. Banzai took a slight step back to plant his feet more firmly and assumed a fighting crouch, when suddenly . . . How many times do we humble journalists employ that word and others as dismally frayed—"suddenly," "without warning," "all of a sudden"? How many times do we insert them to bestow drama upon the undramatic, excitement to the ordinary? But in this instance, the circumstances warrant them all, and more, for B. Banzai stood in the jaws of death, the Devil's own breath upon him, no guardian angel, friendly spirit, or agent of nature apparently able to save him now . . . when all of a sudden, without warning, suddenly a ladder fell from heaven and snatched him from his enemies' midst! Buckaroo himself could not conceive of it, having no time even to utter an exclamation of surprise at it, as Jacob's ladder lifted him skyward and the noise of the helicopter directly above could now begin to be heard over the roar of the truck.

On the ground the Lectroids cursed in frustration (and they would curse again when they returned to the van to find their human cargo missing) at the sight of Buckaroo Banzai reaching the top of the ladder and being pulled aboard the chopper by a nine-year-old black youth wearing the familiar uniform of the Blue Blaze irregulars, that scourge upon evildoers everywhere.

"Welcome aboard," the youth said, helping B. Banzai into the rescue craft. "Scooter Lindley reporting as ordered, Buckaroo. Pleased to meet you."

For one of the few times in his life, I think Buckaroo must have been speechless. Anything would I have given for the pleasure of seeing his face, that huge smile of his that is so affecting at such moments, especially upon the young, who adore him.

"Very well, Scooter," he must have said, or something of the kind, as he shook the lad's hand. "The pleasure is mine, believe me. And who is this?"

He referred to the pilot of the craft, a handsome black helicopter jockey wearing the uniform of a gas station worker and a Blue Blaze baseball cap.

"That's my dad," Scooter stated proudly.

"Nice to see you again, Buckaroo," the man said. "Remember me?"

Buckaroo, who I daresay has never forgotten a single face of the millions he has known, assented instantly. "Of course," he replied. "Last year at the desert survival school." The man nodded. "Your name . . . don't tell me. It's something unusual," Buckaroo said, and after a moment he remembered. "Casper?"

"Casper Lindley," said the man, astounded at Buckaroo's memory. "That's amazing."

"Why?" Buckaroo asked simply. "You remembered me."

That is the kind of man B. Banzai is. If Casper had not reported to me their exchange, I am certain Buckaroo would not have seen fit to mention it to me because he would have not thought the recollection of a man's name at all remarkable. Never mind for a moment the fact there were at last count better than six thousand Blue Blaze irregulars world wide—men, women, and children who subscribe to the Blue Blaze newsletter; who attend selected symposia at the Banzia Institute, who submit their bodies periodically to rugged physical training at such places as the desert survival school in Nevada, the mountaineering school in Alaska, and a half dozen others around the globe; who are required yearly to make certain educational advancements; who are "on call" twenty-four hours a day to help B. Banzai in a pinch, or their neighbors in a natural disaster—it was only to be expected, B. Banzai would tell you, that he had committed to memory most, if not all, of their names. Blue Blazes were, after all, ordinary and yet extraordinary people.

As B. Banzai used the copter's radio to relay the welcome news to us that he was safe and en route to the Institute to check what progress we had made in our investigation of Yoyodyne Propulsion Systems, it perhaps behooves us to backtrack slightly and note how that helicopter came to be there when Buckaroo needed it.

19

"THE BANZAI INSTITUTE, an independent, non-profit, research organization of ranking scientists, is located an hour from New York City in Holland Township, New Jersey. Overlooking a truely panoramic expanse of the Delaware River Valley, it is a one-hundred-and-twelve-acre haven for scholars of all disciplines, but the sciences in particular." I am reading from the Institute's brochure. Those of us who live there know it as something much livelier than it sounds, but for a general description of the Institute's history and function, the literature suffices. I will continue. "Founded in 1972 to fulfill a need of the scholarly community for greater continuity of research . . . " In civilian language I will interpret, taking the above phrase to mean that most researchers live and die by the government grant. When the government in its often capricious way loses interest in a given subject, it stops sending money for its study. This stop-and-go process is destructive and wasteful on at least two counts (viz.) the government seldom understands just what it is funding to begin with and therefore is uncannily apt to cut off funds at the precise moment that real progress begins to be made, and the researcher is continually distracted from the greater purpose of his work in order to "show" the government "hard results" so as not to lose his funding. There is, in other words, the constant worry over

131

money in the back of the researcher's mind, costing him time and energy and, most importantly, independent initiative. For when quick results begin to outweight long-range possibilities, experimentation is the first casualty, experimentation by definition being unpredictable. It was this vicious cycle of reliance on the National Science Foundation that the Banzai Institute sought to change at its inception in 1972. Promising researchers would be given the time and freedom to focus their full energies on their topics of interest without the necessity of championing themselves in their roles as fund-raisers. It was believed, and has been demonstrated, that the Institute could be self-supporting if both researchers and staff lived frugally and in a familial atmosphere, donating a percentage of their royalties from any commercial applications and patents which might arise from their work within its walls. This is not to say that remunerative considerations are the paramount criterion by which proposals for funding are judged—far from it, as there exist no criteria at all and no proposals! At the Banzai Institute, it is the candidate who is appraised and not the proposal. As a scientific sleuth himself, B. Banzai knows the impossibility of predicting in advance where one's nose will lead, as well as the exhilaration when one experiences a "sudden flash" from out of the clear blue, as it were. There is a term sometimes used at the Institute: the three Bs, meaning the Bus, the Bath, and the Bed. That is where the greatest discoveries are made in science. When one is at his most relaxed, his most receptive, that is when a foreign consciousness, a "stray bullet" as B. Banzai calls it, may pop into one's head. B. Banzai himself has had so many of his greatest ideas while shaving that he finally has been forced to abandon his father's straight razor in favor of the gyroscopic shaver I have mentioned, so often has he cut himself when seized by sudden revelations.

Again quoting from the brochure, I read: "If a candidate is approved by the board—" (that twenty member group composed of B. Banzai and the representatives from various walks of life who serve without pay) "—he is given a key, a small monthly stipend, and a Spartan cell without electricity or running water, where he sleeps on a straw mat atop a wooden bunk. He arises at 4 A.M., washes in cold water—" I needn't go on, the brochure amply makes its point. It is not the sort of place for everyone, and yet hundreds more apply to enter than are accepted, among them some of the finest minds in the world. If one is tempted to ask why—and many are, at such places as the Rand Corporation, Lawrence Livermore, Los Alamos, Hudson, Sandia, Brookings, and all the other intellectual watering troughs—the answer is predictable—Buckaroo Banzai. His message is simple and direct, the same to everyone, regardless of position: greatness is attainable only when it is not sought. When this paradox is understood, we are great.

"A scientist, like a warrior, must cherish no view," he has written. "A 'view' is the outcome of intellectual processes, whereas creativity, like swordsmanship, requires not neutrality, or indifference, but to be of no mind whatever."

To this end, the famous games and thought experiments so central to the Institute's program have been designed. I will not attempt to describe these games of which so much has been written, other than to say that they employ the full complement of game elements: choice, interdependence, imperfect information, and chance. Sets of partners act as single players, and the stakes are theoretically life and death. Are these games dangerous? Detractors never tire of asking. I would answer by saying that it is the awareness of death that makes life precious, and that which heightens the awareness of death enhances the quality of life. Only a few hairbreadths mark the difference between life and death at any moment; when this is fully understood, life can only be the sweeter. Furthermore, one only learns to win (to live) by being prepared to lose (to die); for this reason if no other, games of high risk are essential to the soul.

Games such as "Airplane and Submarine," "Silent Guns," and others developed by the Banzai Institute have been adopted for use by the militaries of a number of countries in their training and have even found their way into the popular culture, especially what is called "pop psychology," as evidenced by the success of a recent best-selling book which counseled its readers to "cure the anxiety by curing the love". In his foreword to the computer game version of "Silent Guns" (in which a player cannot know when his adversary has fired since he does not know which guns, if any, are silent), B. Banzai states: "The player, emptied of all thoughts, all desire to win, will be the winner. The hand on the joy stick must move independent of intellect and emotion."

Forgive me, reader, if I am obstinate in continuing to digress, but there are things I must say. I am reminded of so many things from my own past history, my own days at the Institute, that I cannot quite end the tune just yet. I am reminded of certain extraordinary successes naturally, the scientific breakthroughs in which I took part as a member, however indirectly, of the team: the OSCILLATION OVERTHRUSTER, cellular radio, the development of the drug Interferon, the computer program later adopted by NASA for assessing survival probabilities of its missions,* the Numerical Aerodynamic Simulator, the invention of Kevlar (five times the strength to weight of steel), DATA-SAT, the first data of steel, transfer satellite (capable of carrying the entire contents of the Library of Congress into space, to be accessed by any home computer), and many more, from robotics to gene technology. But I am also just as proud of those rather quixotic and yet strangely sensible projects which flourish within the portals of the Banzai Institute; ideas, or "moonbeams" as we call them, which would almost certainly only draw quizzical stares and ridicule from other, more staid institutions. I'm thinking of Pecos, my dear Pecos, and her preoccupation with the skyhook concept, a notion best characterized as a space elevator. Briefly, a cable would be strung from a geostationary satellite to the ground and people and cargo would be hauled up, reminiscent of Jack and the beanstalk. Then there was Rawhide and his quest to develop a high-protein livestock feed out of houseflies; and Perfect Tommy, who burst in on us one day and claimed with a totally straight face to have discovered a hitherto undiscovered layer of atmosphere shrouding the Earth. Judging from his excitement,

---

* The survival probability for Buckaroo Banzai in his attempt to pilot the Jet Car through solid matter? Only 52%.

we were excited also. "It's dense," he said, "and getting denser every day. I call it the Flatusphere, formed by all the methane gas from bullsh——s like me!"

Tommy could fill a chapter all by himself, which he does in *Bastardy Proved a Spur*. His testimony before Congress on limiting the nuclear arms race contained the following scheme, which I reproduce here from the Congressional Record:

Senator Nunn of Georgia: You would not then be favorably disposed to the MX dense-pack concept, Perfect Tommy?

Perfect Tommy: As I have indicated in my opening remarks, Senator, I believe it to be a colossal waste of sorely needed resources and one which we need not incur in light of the Bluff Concept developed by the Banzai Institute in the study report now before the committee.

Senator Nunn: Could you describe in layman's terms, without the mathematic notation, how the Bluff Concept works?

Perfect Tommy: Senator, it is predicated upon the fact that nuclear intimidation—the real game we and the Russians play—is a game in the classic sense, in that the outcome is dependent upon the moves of the participants, neither of whom has perfect information about the other; also going on the assumption that each side seeks gain but is also rational—

Senator Nunn:	The "We're both sane men" theory—
Perfect Tommy:	The alternative does not compute, Senator.
Senator Nunn:	Agreed. How do we bluff the Soviets?
Perfect Tommy:	Our concept of bluff comes into play only assuming we have an already credible hand, Senator—an already formidable nuclear deterrent which in fact exists. On the other hand, we would be remiss if we did not analyze the game carefully to derive maximum advantage with a minimum of risk to ourselves. It is this analysis of the parameters of the game that we have undertaken at the Banzai Institute, the result being what you have at your fingertips, Senator. It is our finding that the element of bluff—that side using it—is strongly favored by the peculiar nature of the game: namely, that it is a game of stalemate, the stakes being so high that the degree of risk-taking affordable by either player is quite small, certainly nowhere near the level of calculated risk required to "win" the game. Indeed, the concept of "winning" is limited entirely to the area of intimidation. All of this works in favor of the Bluff Concept, which I will state in practical terms:

since neither side can for the foreseeable future be protected on a maximum basis from nuclear missiles, and using game theory elements developed by the Banzai Institute, we advocate that instead of deploying the one hundred MX missiles presently proposed, we employ a much smaller classified number—roughly ten to twenty, for the sake of discussion—and build ten times that number of dummy missiles. Since the Soviet cannot know which or how many missiles constitute genuine threats, they must assume they all do and will be forced to modify their own game plane accordingly, spending huge resources to match us. In any case, we will have achieved our objective, the effect of our bluff being exactly the same as if we had deployed one hundred MX missiles at a cost of several hundred billion dollars. If the Soviets seek to go ahead in the game, at our much smaller cost we can continue our mixture of real missiles and dummies ad infinitum, staying easily ahead of them while they spend their economy into ruin.

(The Senator hearing room falls almost eerily quiet for a moment, as Senators lean back from their microphones to confer with aides. An initial buzz in the spectators' gallery turns quickly to applause before the Chairman can sound his gavel.)

Senator Tower of Texas:	What if the Russians start to dummy missiles?
Perfect Tommy:	I would answer, Senator, by asking you a question: How do you know they haven't already?
	(followed by a pause)
	I rest my case.

I was in the gallery that day and, as I told Perfect Tommy later, felt it to be the singular most important piece of testimony given before the Senate committee in my lifetime. Without exaggeration it was Perfect Tommy's hour, surpassing even that time we found him singing and clapping for himself—both in his sleep; I only regret that our recommendations have not been acted upon.

And inasmuch as I have been speaking my own sentiments on something as altogether wondrous as the Institute, perhaps I should conclude with something applicable to the subject stated by B. Banzai himself, the following delivered by him to a recent graduating class at the Harvard School of Business:

Not only is the business executive naturally uncertain about the future, but, in addition, rumor (i.e., all the news which he obtains from outposts, through spies, or through the grapevine) exaggerates problems on the horizon. The majority of people are timid by nature, and that is why they constantly exaggerate danger. All influences on the executive, therefore, combine to give him a pessimistic impression of things, and from this arises a new source of indecision. Thus, excessive intellection can easily become irrationality, as the executive *begins to desire to make the right choice at all costs*. To *desire* to make the correct choice is the beginning of the end for any leader. The successful executive is he who grows accustomed to living dangerously day after day and grows the thick skin of a fatalist. He can drop off to sleep with a gun pointed to his head and can enjoy his dinner while a lynch mob prepares his execution all around him. Those of you who learn to step over this threshold, I congratulate you, for that is what we teach at the Banzai Institute.

"A man should be a man," Penny said, her cheeks still showing traces of our recent adventure. "That's what they teach at the Banzai Institute."

"I'll tell you what the Banzai Institute is to me, Penny," I said. "We have a habit at the Institute of debating important questions twice, once over drinks and once sober—over drinks for enthusiasm, and sober for discretion. Some of the finest evenings of my life have been spent drinking in the company of my closest friends and discussing some startling new thought experiment."

"Such as—?"

She listened with composed intelligence as I mentioned to her a thought experiment put forward recently by Professor Hikita, involving the hypothetical particle, the tachyon, which has the amazing property that it can only travel faster as it loses energy, and slows as it gains energy. It can never go slow enough to reach the speed of light! I asked her what would happen to the tachyons unleashed in the Big Bang that created the universe. She promised to think about it as I got up to stretch my legs despite my doctor's advice.

"Reno, I don't think you should be walking around," New Jersey said.

"I was getting stiff."

"In that case maybe you should walk around," he said. "Did you hear what's going on with Buckaroo?"

I shook my head. "Where is he?"

Excitement swam in New Jersey's eyes as he gave me the scuttlebutt about Buckaroo's locator having gone out. "Rawhide and Perfect Tommy got on the radio right away and sent out some kind of call to I don't know who—"

"Blue Blazes?"

"Yeah. That's it. What does it mean?"

Apparently the worried look on my face answered him more loudly than could any words. "Where are they?" I said.

"Rawhide and Perfect Tommy? They're upstairs in World Watch One."

I communed with Perfect Tommy and Rawhide, though was able to make little of the discourse with them, since they knew as little as I. A Blue Blaze helicopter pilot and son had been dispatched to find Buckaroo, and at the moment were nearing his last known location some seventy-five miles away, but as of yet there was no news. Rawhide was taking longer-than-usual strides in pacing back and forth, and it seemed uncertain whether we should proceed to the Institute.

"Maybe he's in trouble," Rawhide was saying.

"What were his last orders?" I asked.

"Don't say 'last,' " Rawhide retorted, his unfeigned conviction clearly being on the side of turning the bus around.

"You know very well what I mean," I said.

"He told us to go to the Institute and research Yoyodyne."

"Then that's what we should do," I said. "Knowing Buckaroo, the locator fell out of his pocket."

(Notice how prescient I am, reader.)

Rawhide continued his dissertation on why we should never have allowed Buckaroo to go off by himself after the "things, whatever the hell they were" from Yoyodyne. This of retrograde aliens from space being an entire other subject deserving greater discussion than we had time for, Tommy and I persuaded Rawhide, technically in command in Buckaroo's absence, not to undertake any rash moves until we heard something from Casper and his son aboard the chopper. We were aided in this by the sensible counsel of New Jersey, who listened much but said little that was not to the point.

"We have to go on the assumption that even though something strange may be going on, Buckaroo knows what he's doing," he said. "Right or wrong?"

We all nodded, though Rawhide with some clear degree of uneasiness which was not lessened when Big Norse suddenly took her phones off and said, "You know something? I've been picking up communications of some kind the last half hour—a mechanical signal, like a beacon."

Rawhide, fingers in belt loops, looked at her impatiently. "So?" he said. "You mean his locator."

"No, I don't mean his locator, Rawhide. Another signal, emanating from almost the same spot, however—only this one has just been answered." Again he stared at her, waiting for her to go further. "It's been answered by that same high-energy source that has been tracking us."

"Outer space?" I said.

She nodded, and no one uttered a word, as we all felt the same chilling presentiment: that our chief and Professor Hikita might even at that very instant be circling the Earth, or worse.

"How far to the Institute?" Perfect Tommy finally said.

"About twenty minutes," she replied.

"Then let's stick to our plan," he said. "Big Norse, radio ahead to Billy and tell him we're coming in and we want to see everything he can dig up on Yoyodyne."

"I think he's still working on Penny Priddy," Rawhide said.

"This is more important," Tommy said. "Anyway, Reno's probing Penny on his own. Isn't that right, Reno?"

At a less-tormented time, I might have laughed in the spirit in which his remark was intended, but at this juncture I thought it humorless and told him so. With New Jersey at my side pestering me with questions about this or that, wanting to be brought up to date on the space signal monitoring us, and on everything we knew or didn't know about it, I returned downstairs to my seat beside Penny.

Everything all right?" she said. I said of course it was. "You look depressed." Now it was she who was pestering me.

"I've been shot," I said. "Weren't you there?"

"Is it Buckaroo?"

In three seconds I had told her everything, and she tried to be reassuring, although I was not deceived by false appearance. Fetching a sigh from the bottom of her heart, she sought to cover her apprehension by mentioning Professor Hikita's thought-experiment.

"I may have something," she said. "Listen to this. See if it makes any sense."

20

FOLLOWING THEIR DISMAL discovery that not only had they allowed Buckaroo Banzai to be snatched to safety from under their very noses but that Professor Hikita had also escaped, the three Lectroids turned their fury on the Adder Thermopod and the helpless remaining crewman inside.

From information provided by the Nova Police, we now know his name to have been John Gant, the pilot and commander of the three-Adder craft. As the angry Lectroids first chopped down the tree and then attacked the pod itself with the chain saw, Gant signaled the father ship (still several hundred thousand miles from Earth at this point) to let them know of the mission's status.

"John Valuk is dead," he said. "He fell on his head. Perhaps John Parker will get through to Buckaroo Banzai. As for me, my most profuse apologies to my homeland and loved ones for my failure."

Aboard the father ship, the Adder fleet commander John Penworthy listened along with his Number One as Gant's message from the thermopod abruptly ceased, to be quickly replaced by Lectroid insults and obscenities.

"John Gant and John Valuk—both dead," said the Number One. "Perhaps we should launch another Thermopod immediately. What if John Parker is also dead?"

John Penworthy examined the situation, turning off his receiver sadly. "I'm afraid there is no time," he said. "We have our orders from Queen John Emdall."

21

"IMAGINE THE BIG BANG," Penny was telling me, as we turned off the highway onto the sepentine tree-canopied road leading to the Institute. "The tachyons traveled outward, speeding through space faster than light and losing energy as the universe expands. Remember, tachyons go faster as they lose energy." I nodded, quite dispassionate in what she was saying. "But there comes a time," she said, "when they are going so fast, at what is for all intents and purposes an infinite speed, that they reach a minimum energy state, like a normal particle at rest. They can't speed up, and yet the universe is still expanding, so that our little tachyon begins to move backward in time, ending up eventually back where it started, at the origin of the universe, but a long way off! What do you think of that?"

Very serious and determined, I said, "Tell me what the tachyon sees on its way back."

"Who knows," she said, "but it must be amusing. It would see all things reversed in time, like watching a movie backwards. It would see dead men rise from the grave, for instance."

"Amazing," I said. "I guess nothing is truly impossible. The dead could rise from the grave under the right circumstances."

I don't know if what I said struck her in any significant way; she did not strive to avert my glance. She said merely, "It is that way with everything. Nothing stays, nothing passes that does not return. It all depends on one's perspective because of the interconnection of time with light."

"Yes, I suppose." I sighed, quite relieved, to be honest, that our little ride together was coming to an end—not that I had not enjoyed her company, but I didn't want to think about her anymore. Despite her best efforts and scintillating intelligence, I still could not get over the feeling in her presence that I was communing somehow with the dead.

Thus, odd as it may sound, I found myself looking forward to the rest of the adventure that was afoot. Whatever it was descending upon us, space beings with three heads or a virus from Mars, I longed for the simplicity of the contest, ourselves against whomever. Thinking of Penny now, I was tired of problems with subtle forms.

Meanwhile, the bus came down the hill toward the Institute, and I could see her gate already, that orifice which had offered me and countless others gentle sanctuary. A small crowd of tourists, music fans, and paparazzi had gathered there as usual—a recurrent difficulty we were powerless to stop—and upon seeing our bus, they became rather riotous. I confess at times to being exasperated by many people's want of pride when it comes to public behavior, especially when they become possessed of the notion of being in the presence of the so-called "famous." Their unchivalrous behavior does everyone, most of all themselves, a great unfairness.

"What do they want?" Penny asked, referring to the somewhat minatory faces at our windows with their cameras and children hoisted high to glimpse us better.

"They want to see us, Penny. Wave to them."

"Me?"

I nodded. "Some of them have driven a thousand miles."

She gamely moved her hand to the glass with a certain awkwardness, genuinely astonished at the excitant effect she had upon the curious, as the gate finally opened and Pinky Carruthers emerged on horseback to shoo back the crowd. Then just as we were through the gate, I heard a giant whoop of delight from Tommy as he practically stumbled down the stairs.

"Buckaroo's all right!" he shouted. "He's on a helicopter, and he'll be here any minute!"

That was great news. I turned to Penny, expecting her to say something, but all she could say was, "I feel like I know this place already."

"Perhaps you came through on one of the tours."

"No," she said at length. "I must have just read about it."

"What an awful feeling," I said, "to feel you've been somewhere before and not be able to explain it."

"Yes," she replied. "It's a feeling I've had all my life, as if I were living in the pages of someone else's life story."

"Perhaps you should write your own," I offered.

"I'd like to—" She smiled rather painfully. "—But nothing has happened yet."

"Well, that's all about to change," I said. "A lot happens at the Institute."

Mrs. Johnson met us at the door and, knowing nothing about Penny, nearly collapsed. "Peggy—!" she gasped.

Rawhide caught her. "No, Mrs. Johnson, it's not Peggy," he said. "But there's no time to explain."

Mrs. Johnson, her thoughts doubtless alighting on that night of the historic séance when she had herself masqueraded as the dead Peggy returned from the grave, attempted to recollect her wits. "Of course not," she said. "How could she be Peggy?"

"The name's Penny," Penny said, extending a hand of friendship. "Penny Priddy, Mrs. Johnson."

"How do you know me?" retorted Mrs. Johnson, still not quite recovered from her initial shock.

"Rawhide called you Mrs. Johnson," Penny said.

"Oh, yes. Sorry if I—it's just that the past conditions one," Mrs. Johnson said.

"Yes, I know," Penny said. "So it is with our mistakes."

A thorough good sport, Mrs. Johnson smiled and took Penny's hand, at the same time looking askance at Rawhide as if to say "What do I do with her now?"

"She'll be staying with us a while," Rawhide said. "At least until Buckaroo gets back."

I thought the thrust of Rawhide's last remark unkind and uncalled for, but now was not the time to debate the point. Perfect Tommy and New Jersey had already headed up the stairs to the computer room, and now it was our turn to follow. I nudged him, and we went, leaving the women to their own devices.

"Come on, I'll show you around," Mrs. Johnson said to our mysterious guest. "It's quite a place, especially for a woman."

"Yes, I know," said Penny. "I mean, I can tell it is."

A half-glimpsed grin escaped Billy's lips. Eighteen years old, our resident computer whiz, he had already established for himself a legendary reputation among fellow hackers when he showed up at the Banzai Institute unannounced one day and presented his credentials: a mountain of super secret data culled by him and his Atari 800 personal computer from electronic data-processing (EDP) facilities of the Pentagon, the National Security Administration, and the CIA, among others. According to him, and I have no reason to doubt it, the NSA at one point offered him a job at the age of fourteen. He was, as one might expect, not the modest and withdrawn type, and quickly finagled his way into our compound, where he has been ever since, usually in the computer room, creating new computer simulations for all sorts of things, based on the theory of games pioneered by the Institute.

His old hacking instincts had never really left him, however, and when Rawhide and I arrived on the scene, he had already accessed the Yoyodyne EDP bank.

"A piece of cake." He smiled. "But it's pretty strange."

Perfect Tommy and New Jersey were already studying the hard copy of the material Billy had provided them—personnel files, financial reports, the usual corporate records—when Tommy was heard to mutter animatedly: "Holy cow, look at this!"

"What is it?" I said.

"Billy, could you put page two of the personnel file up on the viewer?" Tommy said.

Billy nodded. "Coming right up."

"This is incredible," said Tommy, and in a moment we saw what he meant: a list of names of its employees, a hundred or more, all with the first name "John" and beside the names their social security numbers.

"All with the same first name," New Jersey said, articulating the immediate first impression of us all. "Not a single woman."

"Unless she's named John," Rawhide said.

"There must be another page," I said.

"Nope," said Billy. "That's it."

Tommy chewed his gum faster. "What are the odds of a hundred guys working for the same company with the same first name?" he asked.

"I could get you the exact odds in a second," Billy said, "but I'll tell you this—it's more than a few million to one."

"And look at the last names," I pointed out. "Those aren't all your everyday names."

Some were, and some weren't. As I have stated before, some Lectroids carried regular last names taken at random from a Manhattan telephone book, whereas others, those names which now drew our eyes, were evidently translations of Lectroid pictographs, their primitive form of writing.

(To clarify a point, all inhabitants of Planet 10, Lectroids and Adders alike, for the purpose of this book have the first name "John," although it is to them less a name than a form of greeting, comparable to the use of "che" in the Argentine or, to a lesser extent, our own "hey.")

There, interspersed among such ordinary names as Jones or Smith, were such queer ones as these:

John Icicle Boy	John Small Berries
John Repeat Dance	John Ya Ya
John Careful Walker	John Take Cover
John Thorny Stick	John Many Jars
John Mud Head	John Ready to Fly

"Look at this," Tommy laughed. "What is that? They have a lot of Indians working for them?"

"Not that I know of," I said. "This is crazy. Maybe this isn't their real file. It must be some kind of joke . . . a dummy file."

"Trust me," said Billy convincingly. "It's their real file."

None of us knew what to say to shed any light on the matter, and so we all quietly meditated. New Jersey meanwhile, that fresh spirit among us, had been gazing quietly at the screen all along and formulating a question of his own. "Look at the social security numbers," he said.

In the excitement about the names, we had overlooked the numbers; yet in their own way, they were just as astounding. They followed a sequential pattern discernable to the human eye. "What are the odds of this?" I must have muttered aloud, for Billy promptly replied.

"About ten billion to one," he said.

"How difficult is it to access the Social Security Administration's files?" Rawhide asked him.

"It'll just take a second."

While Billy went off to pull wires, the rest of us conjectured about what the strange data could mean. "It's like the song of an unknown bird," said Rawhide. "I know I've never heard it before. I just wish I knew what kind of bird it was. Buckaroo was muttering something about Planet 10."

"It's the planet I postulated as existing years ago," said Tommy, "due to the irregular orbit of Pluto. It might be a planet, it might be a moon."

"Buckaroo said it was a planet," said Rawhide. Tommy shrugged. "But how would people travel from there to here?" Rawhide wanted to know.

"People?" I asked.

"Whatever we're talking about," he said.

"I don't think there's any such thing," I said flatly.

"Any such thing as what? Extraterrestrials?" Tommy said.

I dug in my heels. "Exactly," I said. "Until I see one, there's no proof—just a string of circumstantial evidence. This supposed signal from space that Big Norse picks up, the weird phone call to Buckaroo, after which he starts seeing things, and now this whole Yoyodyne connection. I admit it looks weird but,—"

"You have to admit it's quite a coincidence," said Tommy.

"Definitely," I said. "But nothing more at this point. As a scientist, I'm not prepared to leap to a conclusion."

Nor was anyone else, it appeared; complete bafflement being our shared predicament for the moment, as Rawhide once more posed his question: "How *would* people, or other beings, travel between here and there? Assuming the Planet 10 we're talking about is a part of our solar system, which it may not be—it's not as though it's the most unique name around—it would still require years to make the trip, unless we're talking about the speed of light, a spacecraft simulating a photon. But nothing I know of prepares me to accept that possibility."

I nodded in agreement, doing some quick mental arithmetic. "How far is Pluto? About 30 AU*? That's nearly three billion miles."

"At the speed of light about a four-hour trip," said Tommy.

"Right. At the speed of light," I said.

"It took Marco Polo twenty-four years to make his round trip from Venice to China," interposed New Jersey.

"So?" I said.

"So, nothing," the rangy doctor replied. "There's no law that says trips can't take a long time, that's all."

Perfect Tommy was quick to concur, though adding, "I don't think they would have even had to come through this dimension the whole way."

"You mean the Oscillation Overthruster?" Rawhide said.

"That's one way," said Tommy. "Or they might have gone through a rotating black hole, traveled spirally, reversed direction and passed into another space-time world—another dimension. It's possible they have maps of such things and could take a short cut by simply leaping forward whatever amount of time the trip would have taken, using an Oscillation Overthruster or some such device to reappear wherever they wanted back in this dimension."

"In which case they would not even have had to come

---

* 1 AU = approximately ninety-three million miles, the mean distance from the earth to the sun.

from our solar system," Rawhide said. "They could be from anywhere."

"Exactly," said Tommy. "It's hard to imagine there being any kind of life on Planet 10. If it's like Pluto and the other outer planets, only more so; it has extremely low density and is probably composed mainly of methane ice."

If there were any clue couched in our conversation as to what we were up against, we overlooked it, and so were reduced to sparring about vortices in nature and the like, until Billy enthusiastically called us over to his desk near his beloved IBM 370 to show us what he had come up with. I gathered that our collective look of incredulity amused him, as we stared at the information on the screen.

"Is that some kind of joke, Billy?" Rawhide said.

"The joke's on somebody," Billy retorted. "Look at those dates."

He was of course referring to the dates on which the Yoyodyne employees had first applied for their social security numbers. As it happened, they had all applied on the same day—November 1, 1938—and in the same town—Grover's Mills, New Jersey!

"I can't believe this," said Rawhide.

"There must be a simple sufficient explanation," someone else said.

"Does this mean they've worked for Yoyodyne their whole lives? All of them?"

"Most likely."

"That's more than forty-five years. They must all be old men!"

We all stood there, restless with the inadequacy of our brains to fathom what could possibly lay at the core of the mystery, when New Jersey, who for several moments had sat idly swinging his feet over the edge of Billy's desk, abruptly snapped his fingers as if struck by a furious flash of intuition and began to chatter: "The first day of November 1938 . . . Grover's Mills, New Jersey . . . why does this seem so familiar to me? I wasn't even born yet . . . but something about it . . . Grover's Mills . . ."

"Yeah . . . Grover's Mills," I seconded. "Where have I heard that before?"

"It's where Yoyodyne is," said Tommy innocently.

"Besides that," I said. "There's something else—"

New Jersey was already ahead of me, his mind harking back for some reason to that little mnemonic rhyme we all learned as schoolboys: " 'Thirty days has September, April, June, and November, but when short February's done, all the rest have thirty-one' . . . thirty-one, October, Halloween, 1938 . . ." Then with a tremendous volcanic vitality of which I would never have guessed him capable, he jumped to his feet, exclaiming, "Halloween, 1938 . . . Grover's Mills, New Jersey! Don't you get it?"

"I think so," I said.

I wanted to say "yes" at all costs, such was his high pitch of nervous excitement, but the puzzle still did not come together for me until he said, "Orson Welles!"

At once I knew what he meant. With a smile and a flash of his teeth, he was on the verge of dancing. "Orson Welles!" I said. "That's it!"

"That's what?" said Tommy and Rawhide, still not guessing what had so set our nerves atingle.

"Orson Welles's famous radio broadcast of 1938!" spurted New Jersey. "His Halloween broadcast of Martians landing in Grover's Mills!"

"The famous hoax," Tommy replied.

"Not necessarily," said New Jersey.

Tommy looked at him, it suddenly dawning on him what New Jersey meant. "Nah," he groaned, unwilling even to consider such a thing.

"Everyone thought it was real," New Jersey said, "because it *was* real!"

Oppressed by a strange foreboding, Rawhide's face was deeply furrowed. He did not dismiss the idea out of hand, but . . . "How?" he asked. "You're saying real aliens landed, and Orson Welles covered it up?"

"Maybe," New Jersey said. "Maybe they paid him."

"Don't be ridiculous," said Tommy. "Orson Welles is a great artist."

Billy, by far our junior, had been quiet but now could not resist asking. "Orson Welles? The guy in the old wine commercials? The guy is a master salesman. He could sell anything—"

"Including a landing of space aliens as a giant hoax," I said, hardly believing my own ears.

"But how?" again stressed Rawhide. "If people saw them—"

"Maybe they 'saw' them only in a cinematographic sense," said New Jersey.

"What do you mean?" asked Rawhide.

"What I mean," said New Jersey, as I marveled at the clarity of thought of this stranger among us, "is that as in a movie, people saw the beings and yet did not see them, some sort of camouflage being used. Did any of you notice an inexplicable level of anxiety among those in attendance at the press conference today, or was it just me?"

On thinking back, I was forced to admit he had touched upon something. There had been an almost palpable apprehension in the room, frayed nerves and a general agitation of mind that had seemed almost contagious and which I had at the time attributed merely to the momentous occasion. I, myself, had felt the onset of a headache shortly after entering the room; and although I had at the time thought nothing of it, when I mentioned it now, the others spoke of having experienced similar symptoms.

"Why?" Tommy wanted to know.

"Perhaps because some part of our mind was seeing something horrible and repressing it," said New Jersey.

"That would explain the headaches," I said.

"We were seeing, then—?" Tommy hesitated to say it.

"The same thing Buckaroo was cognizant of seeing when he returned from the phone call," New Jersey said. "Monsters from Planet 10."

It still sounded strangely in our ears; and yet as I sat there trying to arrange my opinions in my mind, I realized there was something to this theory of New Jersey's. The sun was still shining and birds were twittering in the sky, and through the window all appeared normal and bright with happiness. Only those of us in that room, and Buckaroo Banzai, knew that anything was amiss. Just how badly amiss we could not know, but the valorous Adder John Parker was, even as we spoke, on his way to illumine us.

22

EVENTS WERE MOVING faster now, as Pinky Carruthers could attest at the main gate. Within a span of ten minutes, Professor Hikita rode up on the borrowed motorcycle and announced he was going straightaway to his laboratory and was not to be disturbed, and John Parker, the Adder, arrived on a bicycle.

Although Pinky Carruthers could see him only as a human, John Parker was nonetheless incomprehensible to him, both in language and appearance. Still in his Nova Police silver suit, John Parker got off the bike and sidled up to the gate, proceeding to offer Pinky a package resembling a hat box.

"Buckaroo Banzai," was the only intelligible word he said at first, and then he pointed to a Buckaroo Banzai comic book which he also carried and which he later told me he had used to inquire directions of people he met along the way. That he arrived at all must be considered something of a miracle: one solitary being of his race, alone on a strange planet, having to hitchhike, and then to ride a bicycle the last twenty miles to see us. I have, in my private moments, wondered whether I could have done the same, had the tables been turned. It is a hypothetical question, but it serves to remind me of his stalwart spirit and unshakable resolve which must never be forgotten.

Upon listening to the strange visitor for a few moments, Pinky Carruthers was able to make out a few more of his words—for it was English John Parker was speaking, only a heavily accented version of it which required patience of the listener. "Need see . . . Buckaroo Banzai . . . message from John Emdall, Planet 10," was the essence of what he said as Pinky took the package over the top of the gate and said:

"Sorry, pal. Everybody need see Buckaroo Banzai."

And that was the end of it, or could easily have been the end of it, if Pinky Carruthers had not in hindsight sensed something extraordinary about the visitor, the more he thought on it, and returned to the gate to look for him. Alas, he was gone! Or so it appeared. But there was still the package the fellow had brought, and without opening it (according to security procedures, all incoming packages to the Institute must be X-rayed) Pinky resolved to follow up on the matter himself.

At full gallop, he carried the package to our security section himself, and after it had been put through tests, opened it. Inside he found the well-known Planet 10 hologram disc now on display at the Smithsonian, although at the time he had not a hint of its importance or even its function. It resembled somewhat a long-playing phonograph record but was thicker and slightly oblong. Growing more excited, Pinky wrapped the object up immediately and delivered it to us.

Amid our examinations of the strange object, Buckaroo Banzai arrived. Following his introductions of Casper and Scooter Lindley and after answering a barrage of our anxious questions wanting to know the details of his adventure, his attention turned to the hologram disc.

"Have you played it?" he wanted to know.

"No, it just got here a few minutes ago," Rawhide said. "A black guy brought it to Pinky at the gate."

Buckaroo's eyes grew wide as he turned to Pinky. "A black guy? Wearing a silver suit?" Pinky nodded. "Where is he?" Buckaroo demanded.

Poor Pinky was downcast. "I let him get away," he bemoaned. "I had trouble understanding him. When I realized it might be important and went back to look for him, he was gone. I have a couple of the boys out looking for him."

"Good," said Buckaroo, indicating the irregular disc he was holding. "No matter—this was why he came. Put it on."

He handed it to Big Norse, and she laid it carefully on the turntable. We were standing in his study, and I can recall our exact positions relative to one another as she let the phonograph needle down gently. "Anything from Pecos and Seminole?" Buckaroo quickly asked.

"Nothing," I said, doing my best to put the subject out of my mind. "Not a peep. Big Norse says that strange signal from space is coming closer to Earth, resulting in worldwide communications difficulties, so that's probably the problem. Apparently it's some kind of enormous energy field."

"That's where the little ship carrying our black friends must have come from," surmised Buckaroo. "From the mother ship."

A discharge of sparks from the needle striking the grooves of the revolving disc interrupted him, and a gasp escaped our lips as there suddenly flickered from the spinning "record" the life-sized three-dimensional image of a black woman in a gleaming dress made of the same silver material worn by John Parker and the other Adders. Feature by feature, she may well have been the most beautiful woman I have ever seen. At least at that overpowering moment, I could think of none other justified to hold a light before her loveliness.

"Salutations, great Buckaroo Banzai," she said with the same accent as John Parker's, speaking extraordinarily slowly in order to be understood. "I am John Emdall from Planet 10 of the Alpha Centauri A system. I appear before you to warn that a common grave danger confronts both our worlds."

I remember glancing over at Perfect Tommy in the midst of this incredible sight and observing him with his mouth open. He had been right, as it turned out, about Planet 10 not necessarily being of our system, and perhaps he was correct also about their mode of travel. Had the space voyagers entered a rotating black hole and emerged in the future?

"After a bloody reign of terror on our planet, the hated leader of our military caste, the self-proclaimed 'Lord'

Whorfin, a bloodthirsty butcher as evil as your Hitler, was overthrown by freedom-loving forces,* tried and condemned, along with several hundred of his followers, to spend eternity in the desolation of the Eighth Dimension. Death was deemed too good for their ilk," John Emdall said and went on at some length to describe how Whorfin had escaped his place of confinement by taking possession of Doctor Lizardo's body when the latter had so unfortuitously become lodged in the wall, half in and half out of the Eighth Dimension, during the abortive Princeton experiment. Somehow the doctor was now two places at once—in this dimension as a possessed old man and in the Eighth Dimension as his youthful and vibrant former self (so that in this respect, at least, Whorfin had not been lying when he told that part of Lizardo still in this dimension that his younger self waited in the other). How John Emdall even knew what had happened during the Princeton experiment as well as all these subsequent years, I have no idea. And John Parker claimed not to know her method, although he was probably not at liberty to tell even if he had known. At all events, this "woman," this creature John Emdall, had a disquieting way of knowing everything.

"Were it not for the experiments of your father and Professor Hikita and the real Dr. Lizardo, then John Whorfin would still be locked safely away on another plane of existence," John Emdall said, all at once amazing us by pointing her finger right at our chief. "And now you, Buckaroo Banzai, have unintentionally helped John Whorfin's purposes with your Oscillation Overthruster! With it he plans to make good his escape from Earth *back* through the Eighth Dimension . . . and on to Planet 10 with his fighters! I warn you, if he should attempt this, and he will, we will have no choice but to fire a particle beam weapon from our airspace at a city in the Union of the Soviet Socialist Republics, vaporizing it instantly. I need not tell you what this means."

"Nuclear war," said Tommy, his jaw going slack.

---

* The Lectroids were bred by the Adder majority expressly for fighting wars of planetary defense, but in time the Lectroids grew ambitious and seized power for themselves, overthrowing civilian rule.

"Exactly, Perfect Tommy," said John Emdall, making us suddenly aware, if we had not been already, that we were watching no mere hologram but a live communication. "The Soviets will retaliate, your President will launch a massive counter-strike, and within twenty minutes the danger to us will be removed."

"Like a tumor," said B. Banzai.

"Quite," she said.

"Only you kill the patient," B. Banzai rightly pointed out.

"You have my general regret for the trouble this will cause the human race," she said, "but one cannot deal decorously with Lectroids. They are detestable, really; we should never have bred them."

"If your mind is made up," said Buckaroo, "why bother to inform us if there is no alternative?"

"Because there is an alternative," she replied. "Only one. You must stop John Whorfin and destroy the ship he is having built at Yoyodyne—before midnight. If you fail, then my course is clear."

"Even if I destroy the Overthruster?" Buckaroo asked.

"I cannot take the chance," she said. "You and I both know that scientific progress cannot be reversed, not long kept secret. Once the genie has escaped, it is too late to cork the bottle. Good luck, Buckaroo Banzai."

"Wait a minute—" Buckaroo said, but she had already descended back into the grooves of the disc. But now, already the sun was setting, and one did not have to be very imaginative to appreciate the gentle irony. The room filled with men and women who were truly frightened, the red glow of the sunset, perhaps our planet's last, shining from the walls—it was a scene I hope the likes of which I never witness again.

"Maybe she was just trying to scare us," Casper Lindley said, obviously trying to perk us up, even though he had the same vacant stare in his eyes as the rest of us.

"Well, she succeeded," I said.

"Is it just my imagination, or is this room getting hot?" asked Rawhide.

"It's just the sun," someone said. "It's a pleasant warmth."

"Yes, it is. Enjoy it while it lasts."

Did we all look different? Older? It seemed so to me, as Buckaroo sat down dreamily behind his desk stacked high with mathematical papers and scientific treatises. "All my life I have only been certain of one thing," he said with a sigh. "Nothing endures but the world and human nature." He paused, selecting his words carefully. "If I am wrong in this, everything else is meaningless. There is no such thing as magic, but there is such a thing as understanding and applying what abilities we have to a task, to the extent of our abilities and our understanding. Now is no time for grief or wringing our hands."

"What about getting on our knees?" asked Rawhide.

"There's nothing wrong with that," Buckaroo said, "as long as we don't remain in that posture. We have work to do."

Within five minutes, Billy had summoned every available assistant and had gone to work on a computer-simulated attack on Yoyodyne, searching out every scrap of information he could find on the aerospace firm. Casper and Scooter Lindley were dispatched to gather areial photographs of the Yoyodyne facilities, and the rest of us gathered in the small anteroom off the study. Buckaroo had already drawn up a checklist of things to be done.

"Where's Professor Hikita?" he wanted to know.

"He said he was going straight to his lab," Pinky Carruthers said. "He had ink on his forehead, so maybe he was going to wash it off."

"I hope not," said Buckaroo. "Rawhide, go check on him. See how he's doing synthesizing that formula I gave him and if he needs anything. Explain to him it's even more urgent than I thought."

"Right, but you know the professor," Rawhide said. "How he can be when he's working."

"If he buffets you with his troubles or hurls statistics at you, tell him the bus leaves in an hour for Yoyodyne, and I need that drug ready. Period."

Rawhide nodded and departed on his unenviable mission. The professor could behave like an outraged god when disturbed in his laboratory.

"Big Norse," Buckaroo said, announcing her marching orders as well. "Go on to the bus and try to establish communications with the Planet 10 father ship."

"You mean that signal source that's been monitoring us?" she said. "I've tried, but—"

"I don't want to hear that word," Buckaroo said sharply. "In fact, I don't want to hear any of these words—'try' or 'wish' or 'desire'—from any of you. We're up against aliens with superior strength and overwhelming numbers and a thousand years or so average combat experience.* If we begin making alibis, which are but a subtle form of selfishness, we have no chance against them. I do not care to discuss why something is not possible. There is no room for the intellect now. We are in mortal combat. You are all superbly trained. Forget the seriousness of the situation and forget everything you know. Be like the wooden horse of P'ang the Lay Disciple: Be of no mind and unmoved. Simply act."

Big Norse's lip was quivering. "Gee, I only meant—"

"I know," said Buckaroo, looking into her blue Scandanavian orbs. "You meant you will be surprised if you succeed. Do not be surprised at success or failure. Do not even consider them." Then, with a touch of sternness, he added: "We must communicate with the father ship, because I'm certain that's where John Emdall is. If we can establish a two-way dialogue, perhaps her cold power of judgment will not remain so cold."

Big Norse started to say something like "I'll do my best" but caught herself, straightened herself, and a quick change passed over her. "I'll use a mixture of languages to rouse their curiosity, perhaps even sing a song," she said.

"Good. Go," said Buckaroo. "The rest of us must be as tigers to lap blood."

"We're ready, Buckaroo," I declared. "How many Blue Blazes should I mobilize?"

---

* How Buckaroo Banzai knew this or various other details about the Lectroids of which the reader will become aware, I am at a loss to say. One can only assume the "phone call" from the father ship somehow imparted this information.

"No more than a dozen," he said. "Pick them carefully. With the interns that should be sufficient."

There was suddenly a familiar voice over my shoulder. "What about the interns?" Mrs. Johnson said, having just come in and knowing nothing of John Emdall's revelation.

"Get your gear together," I told her. "We're going on a mission."

She let out a cry of delight. "Something beastly, I hope!" she exclaimed.

"Beastly enough," I said. "You'd better alert the other interns."

She had already turned to leave when Buckaroo, in his psychic way, called after her: "Did you want something, Mrs. Johnson?"

"Oh, yes," she suddenly remembered. "You know that girl that came on the bus with the guys—?"

"Penny?" said Perfect Tommy.

I at once looked at Buckaroo, on whose countenance the name so happily registered. "Where is she?" he asked.

"Well, that's what I wanted to say," said Mrs. Johnson. "I can't find her. I guess I was a little hard on her. She must have run away."

Buckaroo looked as if he had been stricken dead but said nothing of what was in his heart. "Never mind. We have more important work," he said and headed for the door.

"What about me, Buckaroo?" Tommy said, in that peculiar gloomy fashion of his when he feels left out. "What do you want me to do?"

"Check with Sam in the garage," Buckaroo answered. "Tell him to get the Jet Car ready. I'm taking it out."

"Right," Tommy nodded. "Where're you goin'?"

Buckaroo kept walking. "To get my guns," he replied.

Tommy and I looked at one another, as though the idea of Buckaroo getting his revolvers somehow made official the dire portent of the moment. In a kind of awed whisper, Tommy said, "Getting his guns? Holy cow."

They were the Navy Colts he used only when going in search of Hanoi Xan, massive heavy pistols which had belonged to his father. The sun was down; for some reason I had the image of many sheeted dead, an entire generation or so, something more horrible than anything that had gone before.

Secretly I trembled.

23

THE MORE YEARS I traverse in this life, the more I am struck by the force of its beauty and fascinated by the terror of its end. Like tiny flickering flames in a mammoth cavern of darkness, we hew out lives for ourselves, experience sensations and emotions recalling countless other lives and souls who have gone before us. Gradually, we realize that life amounts to little more than sights and sounds, pain and pleasure, a few steps forward, and then . . . the cumulative effect of all our words and actions ultimately leaving as much of an imprint on the world as stockinged feet on a rocky floor. And in the end, while most of us are still wrestling with this bewildering gift of life, trying to decide what to do with it, the flame burns out. And the smoke remaining? What is that? Do we remain, but in darkness?

I am reminded of the dance of the corpse which La Negrette, the beautiful zombie, was given to performing. It had all the appearance of liveliness, but no amount of movement or pretending could hide the tortured look in her upturned eyes, the ghastly coldness of the whole spectacle.

That was how I felt as I assembled the interns hurriedly before the great hearth in the living room of the Banzai Institute common house—full of despairing energy, sufficiently sensible to realize that some of them would die in such a situation as we found ourselves.

I briefed them on our mission and had to say little for them to reflect upon its consequences, should we fail. All rational men and women, highly intelligent, with scientific backgrounds, they required no elaboration from me on the patent meaning of a global nuclear exchange. All the human progress of two thousand years would, in a blinding flash, be the remote past; and indeed whether the human species could even survive in any kind of reduced circumstances was arguable. The point was not to let it happen.

As I spoke to them, entirely detached from my words—indeed I was out of myself—my thoughts turned to Pecos, those glorious eyes, her crack-brained technological schemes and inventions. How she loved a mystery! Would I see her again? That was the question now, as suddenly I felt like a green and tender youth. I had once given her a bezel ring; I wondered if she was wearing it. I longed to feel her freshness upon my face and for an instant felt I did. Blindfolded, I could have sworn she was with me.

But those were only my feelings, preparatory to our embarkation into the great unknown. Everyone in the room had his or her own melancholy thoughts, and outside the room new events were rushing toward us, thick and heavy.

Casper and Scooter Lindley had reached Yoyodyne and succeeded in taking a series of aerial photographs of its environs despite drawing some scattered fire. They had meanwhile been notified by radio to rendezvous with our bus at a location a half hour's distant.

Billy and his computer helpers had managed to ascertain through Yoyodyne financial records those construction companies in the Grover's Mills area which had done work over the years at Yoyodyne and which might be expected to have blueprints of its buildings. A number of Blue Blazes in and around Grover's Mills were contacted and sent to the various companies to ask for the blueprints, stressing that Yoyodyne officials were under no circumstances to be notified of the unusual request. Where there was hesitation or resistance on the part of any of the companies to comply, a personal phone call from Buckaroo Banzai to the company's chief executives had its intended effect. Within half an hour, all blueprints of Yoyodyne had been collected and were on their way to the rendezvous site I have alluded to above.

And what of the activities of the other side? While John Whorfin exhorted his followers to work faster on the giant Panther ship, he fretted and fumed over the unexplained disappearance of his top three subordinates. They had not radioed their whereabouts in more than two hours, ever since they had located the Adder thermopod. What could have gone wrong? he wondered. Perhaps they had taken a wrong turn and become lost, but that could not explain why they had not radioed. Perhaps their radio was affected by the strong energy field of the Adder fleet now approaching Earth, but that only made it all the more imperative that they hurry back to base. Damn it, he needed that little Jap, Hikita! Where in hell were John Bigbooté, John O'Connor, and John Gomez? Time was running out! What was the point of completing the Panther ship without the OVERTHRUS-TER? They would be shot out of the sky like a lumbering goose. Where were those imbeciles?

He could not know, nor could we, that following the debacle of letting both B. Banzai and Professor Hikita get away, no one of the three shamefaced Lectroids was of any mind to inform John Whorfin of what had happened. Rather, in one last-gasp effort to cover themselves in glory, they headed for the Banzai Institute, where their arrival coincided with sundown and, unfortunately for us, our necessarily hasty arrangements to undertake our mission to Yoyodyne. As a result of this unhappy coincidence and our own state of momentary distractedness, the Lectroids found it simple enough to gain entry to our compound in scaling first the main wall and then an electrical fence, which in their case only whetted their appetites and had reasonably the same effect as a chocolate moat might have on ants: it delayed them, but slightly. Between the time when they entered our compound and the first sounding of the alarm by Sam in the garage, a period of roughly twenty minutes elapsed. We know this because of John Parker.

Again, I must regress to bring the reader up to date.

Following his delivery of what I will continue to refer to as the hologram, John Parker had found himself at a loss to know what to do next. His assignment had been completed to the best of his ability, and in fact there was nothing else for him to do and nowhere else for him to go. On an alien planet and lacking a way to go home, the mysterious creature simply searched out a restful spot and waited—for what, even he did not know; but with the onset of sundown, his entire cutaneous "early warning" system (I lack a more graceful way of putting it) became agitated in the extreme, and he realized that Lectroids were near. Stepping out of his hiding place (although he was not hiding), he observed Bigbooté, O'Connor, and Gomez as creeping shadows near the main wall and resolved to follow them, fully aware of their evil tendencies. He, too, climbed the wall (although "jumped" is a more accurate description), and was equally unimpeded by the electrical fence. He later told us that he was prepared at all costs to stop them from succeeding in their plot (which he was able to divine as he got closer to them, the Adder's sensitive cutaneous system functioning as a telepathic as well as his main sentient organ), and was on the point of alerting us to the Lectroids' presence when he himself was detained by mounted security. Not given a chance to explain coherently what he was trying to warn us about, he was taken into custody while the Lectroids, unseen by the intern guard, continued on their merry way.

My first notice of any of this came when the door of the common house living room sprang open as I was briefing the interns, and the escorted John Parker appeared as a silver giant before my eyes. Six-feet-ten, his long black hair woven into dreadlocks, his dark eyes smoldering, he was easily the most imposing sight I had seen since John Emdall and I connected him to the hologram immediately.

"My name is John Parker!" he shouted slowly, the words perhaps taking him ten seconds to say. "Here . . . Lectroids! Here!"

Buckaroo Banzai had used the term Lectroid as had John Emdall, and I was suddenly very ready to listen to what this "man" John Parker had to say. Before he could go further, however, alarms began to rattle everywhere and a second intern on security duty burst into the room, clamoring, "Intruders! In the garage!"

Naturally the same thought crossed all minds: in the midst of the world coming to an end, as if we didn't have enough to occupy us, someone was also trying to steal the Jet Car. The fact that John Parker had just mentioned Lectroids only served to heighten the drama as I ran past him on my way out the door and tapped him to follow. "Come on," I said. "This way!"

As we raced toward the garage, John Parker easily outdistancing me with his long loping stride, I directed the interns to fan out and used my Go-Phone to spread the word. I remembered that Tommy had just been directed by Buckaroo to tell Sam to prep the Jet Car and wondered if he had seen anything suspicious.

"I just came from there!" Tommy said over the Go-Phone.

"Did you see anything?" I asked.

"No."

"Where are you now?"

"In the bunkhouse, packing my gear."

"Well, you'd better tell Buckaroo there's trouble," I said. "And tell him I'm with the guy from Planet 10 who brought the hologram."

"You're kidding!" Tommy said, as I switched my phone off in midstride.

"Perfect Tommy?" John Parker wanted to know. I nodded. "Buckaroo?"

"Buckaroo Banzai."

"Buckaroo Banzai? You?"

"No, I'm Reno," I said.

"Ah, Reno. My favorite one."

What he meant by that I had no idea, although he later explained that whatever intelligence network these Adders had maintained on our planet these many years had included news of the exploits of Buckaroo Banzai and the Hong Kong Cavaliers as part of its regular reports back to Planet 10. We are in fact "very big" on Planet 10, he later told us.

But now suddenly he changed course. "This way!" he said, and I could not determine whether he was merely repeating my words or if he was truly onto something.

"No, this way," I said, indicating the way to the garage; whereas he pointed toward the building where Professor Hikita's lab was located.

"Over here! Lectroids!"

"Blast it, I wish you could speak faster," I said, deciding to trust his instincts and go with him.

"English bad. Spanish better," he said, and from that point on we communicated much more freely, in Spanish,* as his "hunch" about the Lectroids, or whatever it was, quickly proved correct.

"Reno?" It was the voice of Rawhide over my Go-Phone, which I immediately switched on.

"Yeah?"

"I'm at the garage. Sam's dead. I'm not sure how, but it doesn't matter."

"Any sign of who did it?"

"Looks like they're after the Overthruster. I'm on my way to check on Professor Hikita."

"Yeah, so are we," I said. "We'll meet you there."

"A poisoned barb," said John Parker, opening his mouth and making the motion with his lips of someone spitting. "Lectroids blow poisoned barbs from their esophagus. Best way to kill them . . . to shoot esophagus."

I vowed to make a note of that, as I quickly patted the pistol under my jacket for reassurance and then shifted it to my hand.

"Little gun is no good," said John Parker. "To need big gun against Lectroid."

As he was eyeing my .45 automatic when he said this, suffice it to say that I was filled immediately with a sick fear and may have unconsciously dropped back another stride or two. If a .45 was useless against them, why in God's name were we running so fast toward were we believed them to be?

Sam certainly had never had a chance. Rawhide and

---

* According to John Parker, under occasional optimum conditions, certain powerful Mexican radio stations can be picked up on Planet 10. He may have smiled when he said it—I can't remember—but his Spanish was as good as mine.

several of the interns found him in a contorted position on the floor of the garage, between the Jet Car and Peggy's old Vauxhall Wyvern, an aspect of gut-wrenching pain upon his face. He had apparently heard something outside in the darkness, had stepped briefly outside to investigate, and then pressed the button on the alarm just as the terrible yellowish barb resembling a snake's tongue had shot out of his killer's mouth and imbedded in his stomach. The end had come quickly but not quickly enough, to judge by the look of him.

I am of the opinion that shortly before the attack upon Sam, the Lectroids had already split up, an intern later recalling that before any of the commotion a man of John Bigbooté's description had stuck his head into his laboratory cubicle to ask where he might find Professor Hikita. The intern had suggested a couple of places, including the professor's laboratory at the end of the hall. The man had said thank you and departed amiably. The intern, thinking the visit somehow queer, had gotten up immediately and gone to the door to peer out. He had seen the man, if indeed it was Bigbooté, walking alone down the corridor and continually glancing back as if to be sure he was not being shadowed. He finally disappeared down the stairwell and scant seconds later the alarm sounded, whereupon the intern hurried down to the lobby, caught sight of the man briefly outside, and then inexplicably lost him. (We now assume Bigbooté climbed one of the trees surrounding the building and from there jumped to the roof, appearing soon afterward at Professor Hikita's window.)

Hikita himself was typically fused to his desk. He later said he never heard the alarm, although that is impossible. It is more likely he heard it and dismissed it because he resented the interruption. With little exertion, he could be cross even with the Almighty if He deemed to appear before him uninvited. Rawhide had found him only minutes before in such a sour mood that when he popped his head into the room, Hikita had delivered a glass retort in his general direction.

"How's it coming, Professor?" Rawhide had solicitously inquired.

"I'm busy," the professor had returned.

"If you'd be so excessively kind, Professor, Buckaroo would like to know how the formula is coming—"

"It will never be finished if you stand there."

"The bus for Yoyodyne leaves in twenty minutes, Professor. We need it."

"Stand still so I can hit you," the professor had said and quickly whirled, throwing the retort. By the time it burst against the wall, Rawhide was long gone. The professor turned back to his work, which, unlike one might have expected from his demeanor, was actually going quite well. He had created the new compound indicated by the formulae that Buckaroo had transferred to his forehead; the difficulty was in knowing what it was supposed to do and, without his being able to test it, whether it worked—whether it was in fact "correct." He brooded upon this and went over to his desk to recheck his figures, not dreaming for a moment that he would learn the efficacy of the compound sooner and at greater peril than he expected.

When deeply involved in his work, it was the professor's habit to take off his spectacles and rest his eyes by looking out the window behind him. Invariably it would raise his spirits—it had for many a year. On this strange evening, he went to the added trouble of raising the glass to allow some pure air into the room which had become musty and filled with the most bizarre chemical odor he could ever recall inhaling. Whatever the new pale green synthesized compound was, its smell was indeed stout, especially in the small room. So the professor raised his window and for a second or two, without special emotion, found himself face-to-face with a bona fide space monster. It was Bigbooté standing on the window ledge. The "antidote" had enabled the professor to see him as he really was.

In shock, the professor turned from his window and reached for his glasses. Being quite myopic without his lenses, he wore a quizzical look, but that was all, as he turned back to the window and tried to scream only to find that his voice had a catch in it. It was John O'Connor's Lectroid "hand" around his throat.

"Where's the Overthruster?" Bigbooté demanded, as the professor, thinking quickly, brought down the window as hard as he could, freeing himself of the Lectroid's hold in the process and racing for the door. Bigbooté simply crashed through the closed window and, now heated, ran in pursuit.

The professor's first impulse was understandable: to save the OSCILLATION OVERTHRUSTER. But he had no way of gauging what sort of force he was up against, other than the obvious fact that a single hideous beast was chasing him. In retrospect, of course, he should not have entered the room when the OSCILLATION OVERTHRUSTER was kept (Rawhide having returned it to its regular place of safekeeping shortly after the bus pulled in), despite his fears of it falling into their hands. I do not wish to linger on the past and recognize perfectly well the effect the face at the window must have had on a man his age, but his thoughtless move nevertheless nearly ended the planet. Instead of running to save himself and leaving the Lectroids none the wiser as far as the OVERTHRUSTER was concerned, he seized it himself and in attempting to safeguard it, almost lost it. As he emerged from the room, OVERTHRUSTER in his grasp, he found himself set upon no longer by a single Lectroid but by three, coming from opposite directions. Seeing no way out but to retrace his steps, he hurriedly went back into the room, opened the window, and went out onto the second floor ledge. As the Lectroids converged on his tenuous position, Hikita debated whether to drop the OVERTHRUSTER to the ground below and perhaps risk damaging it or having it fall into other Lectroids hands. (He had no idea how many there were.) He hesitated nearly too long, trying to decide, and in the chaotic chain of events it was here that the girl named Penny Priddy reentered the picture, having disobeyed orders and left Buckaroo Banzai's bedroom.

Once again, some explanation is in order. Following not just one but several traumatic experiences, Penny had sought safety as she had throughout her entire life—by running away. She had wandered up and down the grounds of the Institute before finally winding up at the bunkhouse and eventually in Buckaroo Banzai's bedroom. Although not by nature a stealthy person, she had lingered there the remainder of the afternoon, prying into places where she had no business poking around, excavating old scrapbooks and memorabilia, and at last, quite by accident, uncovering a picture of Peggy. She, who had always fancied herself a hard-featured realist, was reduced to tears by the smiling image of the woman whom she had spent her life mistakenly believing dead—her long-lost identical twin who was now long lost indeed; or was she? Reno had mentioned something about the mysterious circumstances surrounding Peggy's death. What if Peggy were not dead? Then there was a chance the two of them could still meet one day and get to know one another as sisters, as twins, between whom there could be no secrets. All her life Penny had felt discontented, incomplete in some way, restless without knowing why. Now at least she had a theory . . . this photograph of the beautiful woman in her lap. How pretty she was in the picture! Then that must mean I'm pretty, too, thought Penny, because we're twins. How beloved she was by Buckaroo and everyone who knew her! Then maybe they can love me, too, because I'm just like her. The oblique staring expression in Peggy's eyes fascinated her. How she longed to be inside that mind and know those thoughts! All her life many people had taken her for a perfect fool, but in her heart she had always known with proud satisfaction that there was more to her than met the eye. Not even her adoptive parents—they least of all!—would hear of the matter when she used to bring it up, but it came down to this: "I have a counterpart somewhere," she used to say. "Someone who is just like me and at the same time all the things I am not. The truth will not be hushed. Somewhere there is another me!"

"Then a mistake has been made," her bulldog-faced father would joke. "That's the girl we want."

Penny would break out into a paroxysm of sobbing and run to her room, slamming the door behind her, until that day . . . when she had slammed it the last time. She had run away in spite of the cold and wandered the back roads near Cheyenne for some three hours before a bunch of cowboys gave her a lift into town. The landscape had been so cheerless, and yet that night was the happiest of her life, until now. Now at last she had found the missing alter ego she had always known she had. It was only a picture, and yet from merely listening to stories and reading articles from Buckaroo's scrapbook about Peggy, she felt like she had known her all her life. More important, she herself was beginning to feel in some way reborn and unyoked from the terrible past. As if a sad veil had been lifted from in front of her eyes, a pleased expression crossed her face and those same slate-blue eyes began to shine; and she was untroubled for the first time she could remember . . . since the fire, anyway. She, Penny Priddy, was now penitent for her vagrant years and vowed to change. She would remain at the Institute, no matter what, and do something worthwhile with her life. What was the motto of the Banzai Institute—Science for Humanity? She would adopt it as her own as well, for had it not fallen her lot to continue where Peggy had left off? She was convinced of it and would be no shirker, she promised. She only wished she had some means of proving it, some challenge, some historic mission to accomplish so she could vindicate herself before the world.

Thus, as she was thinking some of this, down upon her knees, surrounded by Buckaroo Banzai's most treasured personal momentos, who should walk through the door but the great man himself? Knowing him as I do, I have an idea what he must have said, but I will not put inventions of my own into B. Banzai's mouth. I am certain there was a look of perplexity on his face, as there usually is at such times, and I am equally certain he avoided moralizing. Beyond that I will not hazard a guess, although obviously the subject of Peggy must have been raised.

Only minutes later when Tommy arrived at the room, in response to my suggestion that Buckaroo be notified (remember, Buckaroo had lost his Go-Phone at the pod crash site), he overheard the following exchange between the two of them which he subsequently passed on to me:

Penny Priddy: Should I deny that I sneaked in, that I went through your personal belongings, that I invaded your privacy?

Buckaroo Banzai: Perjury is no worse than what you did.

"Buckaroo," blurted out Tommy. "We've got trouble!"

Buckaroo already knew that, as capable of hearing the blaring alarm as any. It was his too good heart which made him linger a while to talk to Penny, in whose eyes tears had now risen.

"Don't cry," he said to her, a blush invading his own forehead. "It seems your fate and mine run together, Penny." Then of Tommy he asked: "Who signaled the alarm?"

"Sam at the garage," Tommy answered. "Maybe someone's fiddling with the Jet Car!"

"Let's go," Buckaroo said and started out of the room when Penny, with a shriek that meant business, pointed to a window.

"There!" she said. "There was someone there!"

Whether there was or was not anyone there, we shall never know; Penny identified John O'Connor later by his clothing as the man whose face she had seen at the glass, but, as I have said, John O'Connor was seen at more or less the same time by the unidentified intern some fifty yards away. I am not saying she didn't see him—to the uttermost depth of her being she may have been convinced she was telling the truth as Buckaroo raced to the windows with his pistol drawn. At all events it was a convenient way of keeping him in the room.

There was, however, no one at the window. "But I glimpsed him," Penny said. "Buckaroo, did you mean what you said about—?"

"Where did he go?" Buckaroo asked.

"I don't know. By the time I screamed he was gone. Did you mean what you said about our fate—?"

"He may have gone up to the roof," Buckaroo said.

"I'll go check," said Tommy.

"I'll go with you," Buckaroo insisted, telling Penny, "Wait here. Stay in this room till I get back."

She nodded, but her head throbbed with an intensity that mounted the longer she waited and he did not return. Finally, when she had endured it as long as she could—a period of perhaps thirty seconds—she undertook an expedition of her own in search of B. Banzai and "all the excitement," as she later remarked. In terms of the latter, she certainly found it.

While Buckaroo and Perfect Tommy searched for the peeping John (forgive me) and John Parker and I raced in the direction of Professor Hikita's lab, Penny Priddy, it seems, was actually the first remotely friendly face the professor saw. Drawn by his cries of help, she arrived to see him standing on the second floor ledge, holding the OVER-THRUSTER in his hand.

"Young lady!" he beseeched, looking down and preparing to toss her the priceless object. "Take this and run!"

Then he threw her the OVERTHRUSTER. I am ignorant of her moves for the next minute or so, but events would indicate that she did not run far, for in the final analysis, when the rake of the croupier had passed, we were left with two dead and no OVERTHRUSTER. This result came about in the following manner:

As John Parker and I raced up the stairs on one side of the building, Rawhide charged up those opposite and encountered one of the Lectroids coming down. A struggle doubtlessly ensued, but let us say that Rawhide's fate was upon him before he knew it. The powerful creature, most likely John Bigbooté, sank one of its poisonous barbs into our comrade's back, causing Rawhide to crumple up and fall down the steps to the floor of the lobby, where we found him moments later. In the meantime, however, John Parker and I had reached the second floor corridor and, hearing noises, ran into the room through which Professor Hikita had climbed out onto the ledge. Greeting us was John O'Connor, who spun around suddenly at the window as we entered and who, upon seeing John Parker, gave such a bloodcurdling shriek that it haunts my nightmares still. His mouth opened, and from it issued a tiny missile not unlike a fishing lure. The projectile seemed to scream as it shot past my head and imbedded itself in the wall with what to my ears at least was a small cry of pain. As John O'Connor quickly opened his mouth and "fired" another, John Parker pushed me quickly to one side and made an astonishing leap across the room, grabbing John O'Connor by the throat and throwing him down. One of the most violent titanic struggles I have ever witnessed then ensued, as the two "men" battled with a ferocity found on our planet only in the wilds. Indeed, the only event comparable to it in my memory was an occasion once in Africa when I had the rare opportunity to see a crocodile and a lion duel to the death, the lion's rapacious claws slitting the crocodile's soft underbelly in roughly the same instant that the reptile's powerful jaws clamped shut and practically bit the great cat in half. It was a sight I imagine few non-Africans have ever observed, and while it was terrible to behold, it was also awestriking and beautiful in the way that Nature's terrors often are.

The burly John O'Connor, heavy and slow in comparison to John Parker, fought recklessly in an effort to tear and crush his Adder opponent; whereas John Parker had but one hope under O'Connor's furious onslaught of blows—to maintain his pressure on that lightly armored portion of John O'Connor's throat and choke him to death. Their dialogue, to my ears reminiscent of the Magyar tongue, had no need of translation, so hateful and full of rage was it. As I stood by eagerly desiring to help my alien friend, awaiting only an opening, O'Connor somehow managed to free himself and with the uncouth, clumsy gambol of a big bear threw himself out the window. When John Parker and I rushed to look out, he had picked himself up from the ground and had also called out to John Gomez to jump, which the latter did without a second's hesitation. The two-story drop apparently had no injurious effect upon either of them, since it took them but an instant to run around the corner of the building, where they were lost from our sight.

Although over my Go-Phone I hastily alerted all interns to watch for them, I had the sinking feeling that the Lectroids had made good their getaway; but at least they hadn't succeeded in poaching anything, I thought. We had gotten off easily enough, it seemed, but that did not take into account the disastrous news about Penny Priddy which we would soon receive. Having caught the OVERTHRUSTER and stuffed it into her large plastic handbag, she had run only as far as the other side of the building where, according to her, she saw Rawhide enter. Seeking to turn the OVERTHRUSTER over to him, she had instead been forced to look on helplessly as John Bigbooté, that phantom Lectroid who seemed to be everywhere at once, met Rawhide on the stairs and left our close friend mortally wounded in his wake, and then proceed to snatch Penny Priddy when she yelled out in horror.

As John Parker and I ran down the steps to the lobby to pursue O'Connor and Gomez, we encountered Buckaroo, Perfect Tommy, and New Jersey already leaning over our dying friend, whose proud spirit at least remained unbroken.

While New Jersey gently lifted his shirt to reveal the small but deadly wound the poisoned barb had made, Rawhide fought the venom with every ounce of his strength, drawing us all closer to tell us what had happened and how he loved us.

Cupping his head in his hands, Buckaroo sought to comfort him. "It's all right. You're gonna be all right," Buckaroo whispered.

"I guess so," said Rawhide. "I've got the finest doctor in the world."

Buckaroo looked to New Jersey, who had just extracted the "stinger" from Rawhide's swollen flesh, and then turning his gaze on John Parker, raised his eyebrows in a questioning manner, as if to say, "Is there any hope?"

John Parker shook his head, took the stinger from New Jersey, and promptly stepped on it, a faintly audible death rattle escaping the organism (for it was a living thing) as John Parker squashed it repeatedly, grinding it into the floor.

"Good God," said Tommy. "What is that thing?"

"What killed Sam, I guess," uttered Rawhide, the portent of his own remark not escaping him. "What's gonna kill me."

"Don't be silly," said Buckaroo, quickly removing his own shirt to wrap it around his friend, who had begun to shiver violently, his skin turning a drawn, yellow color, as if waxen, glistening with beads of sweat.

"Tell me about death, Buckaroo," said Rawhide. "What is it?"

"I don't know, friend."

We had all begun to turn away from the sight, one by one, overcome by emotion, until at last only Buckaroo had the fortitude to continue looking upon our friend.

"Is it a cold numbness?" Rawhide asked, his eyes fixed and unseeing in their expression.

"Yes, it could be," replied Buckaroo.

"Then I'm in trouble," said Rawhide and tried to laugh, his body convulsed by the slow spread of the poison.

"Come on, Rawhide, don't give up," Buckaroo pleaded. "Don't give up hope."

Rawhide grimaced, though it had the effect of a smile. "You remember what Artistotle said about hope?"

" 'Hope is a dream by one who is awake,' " recalled Buckaroo.

"And education?"

" 'The roots of education are bitter, but the fruit is sweet.' "

"And Alexander, when he was dying, surrounded by all his companions—"

" 'I see that my funeral will be a big one,' " Buckaroo answered, prompting Rawhide to look around.

"Where'd everybody go?" he said.

"We're here," the rest of us assured him.

"Maybe I'll see Peggy," he said. "You won't be jealous, will you, Buckaroo?"

"Of course I'll be jealous."

"I wouldn't mind going there for a visit. It's like Aristippus said. Remember him, Reno?"

"A professional rhetorician. A companion of Socrates," I said. "You mean about the house of the courtesan—?"

Growing too weak to talk, he said softly, "You tell the story, Reno."

"Once when Aristippus was going into the house of a courtesan, one of the youths with him blushed, and Aristippus said, 'It's not entering that is troublemaking, but being unable to come out.' "

He smiled almost boyishly then, his eyes slowly closing. "That's death. And why is it better to be a beggar than uneducated—?"

His voice was so faint I could barely hear him, but I fought back the burning in my eyes and replied, " 'It is better to be a beggar than to be uneducated; the beggars must have money, the others need to be made human.' "

He reached out then, squeezed all our hands once, as Buckaroo shook him, unwilling to let him go. "Rawhide! No! Don't let it take you!"

"Guess I'm just lazy," he said with his dying breath. "I guess that's why I joined up in the first place—to escape the curse of toil. I can't wait to see Peggy."

He gasped, as the poison at last gripped his heart. Then, trying hastily to say something more, as if its significance he had forgotten until that moment, only the first part of his thought escaped his lips. Those cryptic words we have turned over in our minds ever since: "Buckaroo," he whispered, "the penny paradox—"*

---

* What did Rawhide mean by this? We would have no shortage of theories. Was he referring to Penny Priddy or to the penny paradox so familiar to science buffs and which can roughly be stated in something like the following terms: Since the same part of the moon always faces us, does the moon rotate on its axis as it circles the earth? The same question can be elucidated by using a pair of "pennies" or any round objects:

If a penny is rotated about a second one that is fixed in place, the question is: Does the first penny rotate once or twice around its axis when revolving around the second penny? For an observer who watches both pennies from above, the first penny rotates twice; for an observer on the fixed penny, only once. Therefore, to the eyes of an observer on the earth the moon does not rotate, although it rotates once in relation to the stars.

So what did Rawhide intend to say? Could the "penny paradox" in some way be connected to the riddle of Penny Priddy? I believe so, and the reader will learn of my theory in a future work.

And with that he was gone. Buckaroo held him tightly, and tears streamed down our cheeks. He was gone, and yet I know this: I felt his wraith among us immediately and have felt it near ever since. Such bonds as exist among those of us who live together and fight side by side cannot be torn apart by death. Anyone who doubts it does not realize the true power of the human will. As Buckaroo said later at his funeral: "He loved and slew, made music and made merry; he never possessed more than he could carry on his horse . . . and although it is said one can enter this life through one door only but can leave it through many, who is to say the door does not swing both ways?"

Who was Rawhide? I do not know. That was the only name by which I ever knew him. In all but the important ways, I was unfamiliar with everything about him. I knew from rumor or from idle comments he may have dropped in our conversations that he had once been a baseball player and continued to be fond of the sport, that he was an amateur folklorist and naturalist who had spent considerable time in La Plata. Indeed, he had traveled all over the world before meeting Buckaroo. There was a picture in his room that I recall, a photograph of him sitting on horseback in blue burnoos and veil between two similarly dressed stalwart fierce-looking Arabs—"Touaregs" he called them, true desert riders. The quiet sensitive side of him was drawn to the works of Hudson, the novelist; and although he was a top-flight scientist, a biochemist by training, he was foremost an imaginer, a man of vision, and yet unpretentious in his tastes. No matter how trying or miserable a situation might become, to Rawhide it was never worse than disagreeable. That was the extent to which I ever heard him complain. I recalled at his funeral a time when the two of us spent a week in the water of the Naruto Straits in the Inland Sea of Japan. Our rubber Zodiac with most of our provisions had been sucked into the largest tidal vortex we had ever measured and had very nearly taken us with it. Incapable of swimming against the current in the straits which at times reached a velocity of 4–5 MPS, we drifted for a week past shoreline and on out into the open sea, floating and subsisting on only the melted ice in a thermos chest, before we were spotted and our lives saved by Japanese fishermen. Once we had been given something warm to eat and had been put to bed, I asked him if he would characterize our week-long ordeal as anything other than disagreeable.

"Not so bad as a week I've known," he said, "when Mrs. ———— (his wife) and I passed a whole ten days in a friend's condominium in Los Angeles with nothing but a couple of tins of cocoa and some oatmeal to eat."

That was the sort of man he was, a stoic and a gentleman of the kind seldom seen anymore. Of his ex-wife and children, if any, I know nothing, having never met them. But, if they happen to be reading this, I offer them my condolences and my assurance that they have reason to be proud.

Our silent grieving for our fallen comrade-in-arms was quickly interrupted by two simultaneous events: the arrival of a badly shaken Professor Hikita and a call I received over my Go-Phone from Mrs. Johnson.

"Somebody's got Penny Priddy!" she exclaimed. "Three men—they're taking her out of the compound!"

"Penny?" Professor Hikita interposed. "I gave her the Overthruster!"

We were off like a shot, all of us as one possessed, but we were too late. The Lectroids, perhaps recalling Penny's impressive grasp of B. Banzai's theories from the press conference, had spirited her away on the grounds that something was better than nothing. Or perhaps they felt they could entice B. Banzai to do their bidding by holding her hostage. What they evidently did not know was that the very object they so desperately sought was at last within their reach. They had only to look through Penny Priddy's purse. That they did not find it strains human credibility, but the fact that our planet remains is proof enough.

At the time, however, we had to assume the worst. *The Lectroids and John Whorfin had the OVERTHRUSTER. John Emdall would quickly learn of it and precipitate a global nuclear war, or would perhaps destroy the earth even more quickly with whatever weapons she had at her disposal*. Thus, our position was suddenly more precarious than it had been even a few minutes before. Buckaroo ordered the bus boarded immediately for the journey to Yoyodyne, but even so, we were confronted with a fearful decision: whether to alert John Emdall that the OVER-THRUSTER had fallen into Lectroid hands or withhold the information from her. Perfect Tommy and I advocated the second choice, arguing that by telling Emdall the news she dreaded most we would in effect be waving the red flag in front of the bull, with the Earth caught in the middle. Neither of us believed that she could resist annihilating our planet for very long, armed with such information—certainly for not as long as our original deadline had entailed. Dared we entrust this unknown ruler who was not even of our species with such dismal news of our own making? In view of what would certainly seem to her to be an example of our incompetence, how could we rightly expect to be given a second chance, possibly at the expense of her planet?

I admit now that this argument was absolutely unhindered by logic and any power of clear thinking, as B. Banzai sufficiently pointed out to me. "If we cannot even pinpoint the source of her intelligence about our activities, nor have any way of knowing how that intelligence is communicated to her, we must in all likelihood assume that she knows already what has happened," he said. "At least by telling her fully ourselves, we may be able to convince her of our pure intentions and so argue for more time. Otherwise, she could only construe our silence as devious or worse, perhaps even in collusion with the Lectroids. It must have crossed her mind that there is nothing to prevent us from helping the Lectroids off our planet as quickly as possible so as to provide her with no excuse for our destruction."

"In other words, she might think we let the Lectroids have the Overthruster?" I said. "So that they could escape and we'd be off the hook?"

"Exactly." Buckaroo nodded. "Except she knows better and must have ways of keeping informed as to our every move."

"John Parker?" I asked. "Or that big radio receiver in the sky?"

"I doubt it. I doubt we'll ever know," he replied. "But

John Parker could be useful to us. Tell him I'd like to see him."

We were standing in World Watch One, our sophisticated electronics eavesdropping post aboard the bus, where Big Norse had succeeded in opening a channel of communications with what we believed was the Adder father ship. As I flicked on the intercom and told Pinky Carruthers that I'd like to see John Parker upstairs, I watched Big Norse listen to the Adder signal in her headphones and write out two words—Nova Police.

"Tell them we have a message for John Emdall," Buckaroo said.

"In their code?" Big Norse asked.

Buckaroo assented. "In their code, their language, whatever it is. Tell them it's urgent.

While she sent the message, Buckaroo simultaneously placed a call to the President. It was the first the outside world would learn of our extraordinarily perilous situation and the expedition we were embarked upon.

24

So much has been written about our raid upon Yoyodyne that I confess to having nearly succumbed to the temptation of leaving it out of this journal altogether; and yet I recognize—how can I not?—its continuing hold upon the popular imagination. One would think we would be satiated with the details by now. Certainly, its main events need no repeating, as they have been stylized and improved upon by better writers than I. Every schoolboy and girl now knows of the adventures of Scooter Lindley who at the point of a gun reclaimed the OVERTHRUSTER for the Banzai Institute. Equally incorporated into the public mythology by now is the aerial triumph of John Parker and Buckaroo Banzai over Whorfin's Panther ship in the skies of Grover's Mills, the fate of Earth literally hanging on the winner. How does a writer embellish upon such a *Wasserscheide* of human history? Whose pen can add one meaningful word to the documented result? The planet and the race were saved—this is the legacy of our deeds; the rest is only so much gossip.

However quarrelsome I might be with the idea of recovering this ground, the expected advent of this published journal has brought me numerous letters and inquiries from the public, many of them dealing specifically with the question

184

of our combat against the Lectroids . . . "How did you fight them?", "Were they as stout as advertised?", "Are any left among us?", and the like. In order, then, to allay some doubts and raise others in terms of certain falsities about the raid that have been disseminated, I now address myself to the truth of what happened, using transcripts and my own hitherto unpublished notes to keep to a minimum the naturall tendency of any writer to enhance the facts.

8:33 P.M.—B. Banzai's call to the president's hospital room at Walter Reed is patched through after great difficulty with atmospherics. With the President, the Secretary of Defense, whose almost frantic desire to get his hands on the OSCILLATION OVERTHRUSTER is well known.

Buckaroo Banzai:	Hello, Mr. President. How's my favorite patient? Any tenderness?
The President:	Buckaroo! What's it like out there . . . (unitelligible) . . . in the real world?
Buckaroo Banzai:	Not too terrific, sir. I apologize for the interruption—
Secretary of Defense:	Buckaroo—
Buckaroo Banzai:	Mr. Secretary—
The President:	What's going on?
Buckaroo Banzai:	Something very unusual. We have reason to believe that there are, moving freely among us, alien space creatures known as Lectroids, disguised as humans and the owners and operators of Yoyodyne Propulsion Systems.
The President:	Yoyodyne Propulsion?
Secretary of Defense:	The people working on our top secret Truncheon sub hunter-killer? Under control of alien nationals?
Buckaroo Banzai:	Not exactly, Mr. Secretary. Alien

Lectroids from Planet 10, a planet in a distant two-star system. There isn't much time to explain, but *camouflaged* as human beings, what they're really doing, forget your Truncheon sub hunter-killer, is building an enormous rocketship to escape back through the Eighth Dimension, and—

The President: Buckaroo, Buckaroo . . . slow down . . . (unintelligible). We go back a long way together.

(John Parker has arrived in World Watch One, and B. Banzai immediately urges him to speak.)

John Parker: Excuse me, but time is short. To prevent John Whorfin's escape, my comrades at this very moment are taking up a geostationary position over New Jersey. The situation is explosive.

The President: Who the hell are you?

John Parker: I am John Parker. Who are you?

The President: I'm the President of the United States. What are you talking about, man?

Buckaroo Banzai: This "man" as you called him, is not a human being, Mr. President. He is an Adder, a representative of the Nova Police.

Secretary of Defense: Nova Police? What's that, a rock band?

8:37 P.M.—New Jersey joins Professor Hikita at the microscope to look at a sample of Lectroid tissue taken from John Parker's "fingernail." Without the antidote synthesized by the professor, the sample appears to be human flesh. One whiff of the antidote, however, and the sample is seen as it really is . . . a dark wine-colored scaly material. Though the exact mechanism of the camouflage ability is unclear, the principle is not. True to B. Banzai's revolutionary theory of consciousness as a force transmitted by subatomic particles, the Lectroid tissue disguises itself by speeding the emission of consciousness particles, akin to speeding up a movie to the point where it is no longer visible except as an indistinct object. The human imagination does the rest, connecting the dots, as it were.

New Jersey: You mean the brain of the observer sees an indistinct human form—? A piece of clay?

Professor Hikita: Yes, on the subconscious level. An interesting experiment would be to try hypnosis on the observer.

New Jersey: I doubt it's that simple. Otherwise, why not just hypnotize all of us instead of using the antidote?

Professor Hikita: Not everyone is equally susceptible to hypnosis, and what the antidote does is amazingly simple—and effective. It increases the speed of neurons within the brain, allowing us to see the creatures in sync.

New Jersey: You mean like speeding up the turntable from 33 $1/3$ to 45?

Professor Hikita: Yes. As the neurons of the reticular activating system carry the visual information faster, the images come into focus. You see, their camouflage works because we are all under the deception that we possess sensory continuity. But that is simply not the case, given that the firing of neurons within the brain is of a finite order—like

187

frames of celluoid moving through a projector, giving the impression of uninterrupted viewing. The trick is, we cannot see the "gaps" in our vision any more than we can see the gaps between frames on the celluloid. The brain simply knits itself over these time gaps to give itself the illusion of continuity.

New Jersey: Like it knits faces and human characteristics on the Lectroids—

Professor Hikita: Yes—

New Jersey: But, that means—

Professor Hikita: Yes—?

New Jersey: If our minds invent their faces, kind of like potato heads, none of them ever looks the same to more than one person.

Professor Hikita: Right. All the people in a room would see the creature differently. In fact, if you met him yourself on separate occasions and did not know in advance who it was, you would likely see him as a totally different individual.

New Jersey: But if I knew in advance . . .

Professor Hikita: Then your mind would remember him. He would look the same, depending on how good your memory is.

New Jersey: But he would never age.

Professor Hikita: I think you're onto something, New Jersey.

New Jersey: That would explain how John Bigbooté could have run Yoyodyne since the late 1930s—nearly fifty years—and still look like a man in his forties. Isn't that right, Reno?

Reno:	I would say early forties. They all looked to be in their early forties.
Professor Hikita:	Funny. To me they appeared to be in their seventies, like me.
New Jersey:	How strange!

8:40 P.M.—The conversation with the President continues. The Secretary of Defense leaves the room to call John Bigbooté of Yoyodyne.

John Parker:	Mr. President, I have delivered a message from my own leader John Emdall, who has made it clear that unless John Whorfin is destroyed, she intends to fire an over-the-horizon particle beam weapon from your airspace at the Soviet Union, incinerating one of its cities and provoking them to attack.
The President:	My God, that's an outrage! You can't be serious. Who is this person—? John—?
Buckaroo Banzai:	John Emdall, Mr. President. I believe she is quite serious. Her ship is at this moment—
Big Norse:	Four hundred—
Buckaroo Banzai:	Four hundred miles and closing. You may have heard of the atmospheric disturbances we're experiencing.
The President:	Yes, we've been having . . . (unintelligible) . . . trouble with the Hot Line.
Buckaroo Banzai:	I'll see what I can do, Mr. President. I have a call into her now. But it may be too late for the Hot Line.
The President:	Too late for the Hot Line? Oh, my . . . (unintelligible) . . . I dont know what to say, Buckaroo. I'm flab-

bergasted. I mean, you and I go
back a long way. You're my personal physician, but . . . (unintelligible) . . . aliens from some Planet
10, nuclear extortion, a girl named
John—

8:42 P.M.—The Secretary of Defense returns to the
room.

Secretary of Defense:	Buckaroo, I couldn't reach John Bigbooté at Yoyodyne. Some other guy answered.
Buckaroo Banzai:	John Whorfin?
Secretary of Defense:	How did you know? I admit some-thing's funny over there. You say you're on your way there right now?
Buckaroo Banzai:	Right, Mr. Secretary.
Secretary of Defense:	Maybe I should meet you. We could go in together. You might need my clout to get in.
Buckaroo Banzai:	It's not exactly a social call, Mr. Secretary.
Secretary of Defense:	Well, be that as it may . . . (unintel-ligible) . . .
The President:	Yes, I think that's a good idea. The United States Government has a lot riding on that place.
Buckaroo Banzai:	Unless they are stopped, Mr. Pres-ident, there won't be a United States.
Secretary of Defense:	Fine, then. Have your aide give my aide the coordinates, and I'll be there by chopper within the hour.
Buckaroo Banzai:	We may not have an hour, Mr. President.
The President:	Well . . . (unintelligible) . . .
Secretary of Defense:	By the way, Buckaroo, where is the Jet Car?

Buckaroo Banzai:	It's with us. It's safe.
The President:	Yes, I think that's the best plan. You two meet and go in together. Maybe there's a logical explanation for all this. At any rate, they owe us an explanation why that bomber is so damn far behind schedule. The GSA is supposed to be looking into it—
Buckaroo Banzai:	Well, you're the Commander-in-Chief, Mr. President.
The President:	That's right. (to an aide) Get me SAC HQ and NORAD. See what there is to this atmospherics stuff . . . (unintelligible) . . . okay, Buckaroo?

8:44 P.M.—Communication is established with the Nova Police father ship. John Emdall is unavailable, but John Parker speaks with John Penworthy, Commander of the Fleet. Parker apprises him of the situation, at which point Buckaroo Banzai breaks off communication with the President and informs John Penworthy that the Lectroids have managed to obtain the OVERTHRUSTER but that it should take them some time to program it and that, in the interim, we are going into Yoyodyne after them. John Penworthy is noncommittal; says he must consult John Emdall. We wait.

8:46 P.M.—A phone call from someone identifying himself as Dr. Lizardo via the Institute. Buckaroo Banzai accepts the call and the charges.

"Dr. Lizardo":	Well, well . . . (unintelligible) . . . Dr. Banzai?
Buckaroo Banzai:	Speaking.
"Dr. Lizardo":	Dr. Lizardo here. Perhaps you don't remember me?

Buckaroo Banzai:	Of course I do. Professor Hikita speaks of you often.
"Dr. Lizardo":	Fond memories, I'm sure. We know the same people, don't we?
Buckaroo Banzai:	Some of them.
"Dr. Lizardo":	One of them has just arrived here in fact. Dr. Penny Priddy, your associate.
Buckaroo Banzai:	Doctor—?
"Dr. Lizardo":	Yes?
Buckaroo Banzai:	No, I meant—never mind. How is she?
"Dr. Lizardo":	Fine . . . for the moment. She claims to know nothing about the Overthruster circuitry which I need in order to get away for awhile.
Buckaroo Banzai:	She's telling the truth. She knows nothing.
"Dr. Lizardo":	Perhaps if you asked her to tell me.
Penny Priddy:	I'm not worth it, Buckaroo! Forget me! Don't try to come after me!
Buckaroo Banzai:	What makes you think I'm coming after you?

(Penny Priddy screams horribly.)

"Dr. Lizardo":	That's an excellent idea, Dr. Banzai. Shall we say "A Penny for your thoughts"? You can come in her place. alone, with the Overthruster?

(Buckaroo allows a sigh of relief. At least the Lectroids have not found the OVERTHRUSTER in Penny's purse.)

Buckaroo Banzai:	Where are you, Lizardo?
"Dr. Lizardo":	Have you ever heard of a company called Yoyodyne Propulsion Systems?
Buckaroo Banzai:	It sounds familiar.

"Dr. Lizardo":	That's where I am. (laughs, then to someone in the room) Bigboote, take her to the pit, find out what she knows.
John Bigbooté:	It's Bigbooté.
Penny Priddy:	You're Hanoi Xan! You killed my sister!
"Dr. Lizardo":	I don't know what you're talking about. Take her, Bigboote.
John Bigbooté:	It's Bigbooté.
"Dr. Lizardo":	Shut up! I'll have you put in the torture cradle with her! Come, Banzai—remember . . . alone; you and the Overthruster.

9:00 P.M.—Buckaroo informs us he will drive the Jet Car on ahead of us to Yoyodyne. At least in that way he can learn exactly where things stand. There is still no further word from John Emdall or the father ship, causing us all to be quite jittery. In Buckaroo's absence, I am to assume command of our attack. Details for our rendezvous with the Secretary of Defense are finalized. He is to meet us at the same point as Casper and Scooter Lindley and the Blue Blazes carrying the Yoyodyne blueprints. In effect, we're on our own to succeed or fail. I have never felt such fear in my life. The fear is not of losing my life but of failure and its consequences. The pressure is all but debilitating.

9:06 P.M.—The Jet Car is disengaged from the rear of the bus. Buckaroo exchanges words and hugs with us all, makes a final speech.

Buckaroo Banzai	The antidote filters the professor has whipped up will let you see the creatures as I have since yesterday. The first time you see them they can be pretty intimidating—

193

they're not as handsome as John Parker.

John Parker: Thank you, Buckaroo Banzai.

Buckaroo Banzai: But there's no time to be frightened. If we fail tonight, there's no tomorrow. Remember, shoot for their throats and don't offer them any exposed targets. My job will be to get the Overthruster before they can cause any problems for John Emdall. Reno and Perfect Tommy know what to do. You're all aware of what happened to Rawhide, so listen to them. If for any reason this is good-bye . . .

He doesn't finish. We men and women who would follow him anywhere watch as his speech becomes halting with emotion and he gets in the Jet Car and drives away. John Parker, sensing our grim mood, begins to stamp and shout with an inhuman ferocity; now yelling, now whistling furiously with a piece of audacity that at first surprises and then thrills us, filling us with the deadly abandon we will need to combat the creatures.

9:15 P.M.—We reach the rendezvous point. Casper and Scooter Lindley come aboard with aerial photographs of Yoyodyne. They are joined by a half dozen Blue Blazes who have brought the Yoyodyne blueprints and insist on joining in the attack. They have brought their own gear—a motley assortment of knives, pistols, and shotguns. I consult briefly with Tommy and, giving them antidote filters, welcome the group to our midst. Along with Casper in the chopper, they will serve as a diversionary threat while we launch the major attack. There is still no sign of the Secretary of Defense, so we wait.

194

9:33 P.M.—Buckaroo radios that he is entering Yoyodyne through the main gate, under escort of
the creatures. Then there is silence. We continue to wait for the Secretary, our patience
wearing thin. Tommy and the others are
anxious to press on with the attacks, I am
just as anxious as they, but I cannot disobey
Buckaroo's orders, which are to wait for the
Secretary of Defense until ten o'clock.

9:50 P.M.*–(Penny Priddy's note)—"I looked at my
watch as the one they called Bigbooté prepared to put me in the 'torture cradle,' a
strange open chest studded inside with long
spikes, the entire contraption resting upon
two curved ribs, like a rocking chair. Beneath the contraption was a small hollow in
the floor where a fire could be lit. In fact,
embers were kept constantly glowing. All
that needed to be done was to add more
coals. I was stripped and told to get into the
'cradle.' When I struggled, they placed me
forcibly. I felt the awful spikes as they
bound me tightly, the one called Bigbooté
smiling. 'Careful,' he said. 'The more you
fight it, the more you rock the cradle, and
the points will do their work. You see that
groove down the center?' There was a
groove cut into the bottom of the chest. 'It is
for blood.' I shivered and yet could not
move a muscle without the spikes piercing
my flesh. Then they closed the lid, more
spikes coming down on top of me, their
sharp points pressing into my skin in utter
darkness. I felt claustrophobic and horri-
fied. 'Tell us about the Overthruster,' one of
them said. 'What is the crucial missing cir-

---

* I have sought eyewitness testimony from as many sources as possible in
the compilation of this record.

cuit to overcome Goldshtik's problem?'
When I said I hadn't the faintest idea, I
knew they would soon heat up the fire and
begin to rock me. This was my introduction
to the torture cradle of the Lectroids."

9:55 P.M.—Communication reestablished with the Nova
Police father ship. It is within a hundred
miles of Earth. John Parker tells them that
Buckaroo Banzai has entered Yoyodyne
alone and must at least be given a chance to
succeed. Impressed by B. Banzai's courage
and his long-standing commitment to high
principles, John Emdall through John
Penworthy informs us that she plans no rash
acts unless John Whorfin should attempt to
escape. But there is a new danger: the Soviets. The worldwide atmospheric interference
caused by the tremendous energy field surrounding the Nova Police ship or ships (Big
Norse believes there to be three based on
their intership communications—a father
ship and a pair of fighter escorts) has played
havoc with Soviet radar and defense capabil-
ities (just as it has with our own); but the
Soviets naturally are accusing us of being
responsible. Matters are not helped by the
hostile relations presently reigning between
our two countries. How can we expect them
to believe the truth, absurd as it must sound,
about beings from outer space? I wonder if
the President has even attempted to broach
the subject to them. Perhaps they would
think him a raving madman capable of anything—even a first nuclear strike—in which
case *they* might decide to strike first! The
mind boggles in the face of such endless
permutations, and it cannot be our job to
dwell upon them. The world, without its
even knowing it, is looking to us for action;

and action we shall give them, in a matter of a few minutes more.

9:59 P.M.—As we prepare to leave without the Secretary of Defense, Big Norse calls me to the radio. Using sensitive listening phones in tandem with dozens of miniaturized microphones resembling Pepsi-Cola bottle caps dropped over Yoyodyne by Casper and Scooter Lindley, she has managed to pick up the following speech, apparently by John Whorfin to his minions:*

John Whorfin:	You see, it's Buckaroo Banzai! He is here to help us! You must work faster to finish the Panther ship, so we can enter the Eighth Dimension using the Overthruster Buckaroo Banzai is going to give us! Then we will free the rest of our comrades and return to our home! Home!
	(cheers)
	Where are we going? Tell me!
Lectroids:	To Planet 10!
John Whorfin:	When?
Lectroids:	Real soon!

10:00 P.M.—A special advance recon patrol led by Pinky Carruthers boards Casper Lindley's helicopter. Scooter will remain behind. As we prepare to roll toward Yoyodyne, a second helicopter appears overhead, bringing the Secretary of Defense. Immediately upon arrival, he attempts to bring his entourage

---

* Buckaroo confirmed later that he had been present at this speech, having been forced to stand beside Whorfin-as-Lizardo as he delivered this pep talk to his workers in the large secret hangar housing the Panther Ship. A detailed report of Buckaroo's actions once inside Yoyodyne has been widely circulated by the popular media; hence I see no need to cover the same ground.

aboard but finds his way barred at gunpoint by Perfect Tommy.

Perfect Tommy:	Only you, Mr. Secretary. Those are the orders.
Secretary of Defense:	Who the hell are you?
Perfect Tommy:	Perfect Tommy.
Reno:	And I'm Reno.
Secretary of Defense:	Reno who?
Reno:	Reno Nevada.
Secretary of Defense:	Well, let me tell you something, Mr. Perfect Tommy and Mr. Reno Nevada. I'm the secretary of Defense, the eyes and ears of the President of the United States of America! *In loco presidentis!* Which means I'm in charge here!
Perfect Tommy:	No, you're not.
Reno:	Let's go.
Secretary of Defense:	Where's Buckaroo?
Reno:	He's at Yoyodyne.
Secretary of Defense:	Then I'll go to Yoyodyne myself. I'll see what the hell is going on. I sure as hell can't get the time of day from you bozos.

(The Secretary starts to return to his helicopter when Perfect Tommy jumps him from behind and pulls him back to the bus, to the speechless shock of his retinue and bodyguards. Waving his Israeli Uzi in their direction, he forces the Secretary of Defense on board, and I order the doors closed behind them. We are off. There certainly is no turning back now, if ever there was.)

10:15 P.M.*–Buckaroo has been strapped into the "chair of delight,"** another of the Lectroids' tor-

---

* Obviously a postdated entry, as will be all references to B. Banzai during this time apart from us at Yoyodyne.

** So-called because to the Lectroids massive electrical shocks were a source of great pleasure. Among themselves, they used the chair for recreational purposes, much as we might use a sauna.

ture devices. A modified electric chair with a rheostat, hooked up to a lie detector, the function of the queer contrivance is to send electric jolts through B. Banzai whenever the polygraph deems his answer to a given question to be false. In front of him, standing at a blackboard filled with mathematical equations, is Whorfin-as-Lizardo. Every time he alters an equation, he asks Buckaroo Banzai whether the new version is correct. If B. Banzai does not reply or states other than the truth according to the machine, he receives another agonizing shock to his system. There is one exchange of dialogue in particular which B. Banzai has recalled and which I find particularly telling. I offer it here as indicative of his "grace under pressure":

John Whorfin: Where is the crucial missing circuit?

Buckaroo Banzai: The crucial missing circuit is in your head, Whorfin.

John Whorfin: "Whorfin–?" How did you know my secret identity?

Buckaroo Banzai: John Emdall spilled the beans.

According to Buckaroo, the look on John Whorfin-as-Lizardo's face* was one to be treasured. He was thoroughly shaken.

10:16 P.M.—(Penny Priddy's note)—"The fire was building beneath me. I could smell it inside the contraption, as well as feel its hot tongues lapping at the underside of my cradle which they had begun to rock, resulting in excruciating pain as the points of the spikes cut into me. They kept asking me about the OVER-

---

* Remember, reader, John Whorfin's Lectroid body was still in the Eighth Dimension. Unlike the other Lectroids, he did not appear to Buckaroo as anything but the human form of Dr. Lizardo, appearing as a human also to his fellow creatures.

THRUSTER, questions I did not understand; and yet as they continued to ask me and the pain grew nearly unbearable, I thought how easy it would be to tell them about the OVERTHRUSTER in my purse . . . no more questions, no more torture in that terrible cradle . . . perhaps death, but no more torture. I have been asked by many interviewers since, if it did not occur to me just to give the Lectroids the OVERTHRUSTER. I always answer the same: of course it occurred to me. I am only human; I am not a superwoman. But without knowing their motives, I knew they were nonetheless evil, and I wanted also to prove something, I suspect . . . not just to the other members of the Banzai organization but to myself above all . . . so that when the pain increased in intensity and I felt like giving in to them, I remembered what Mrs. Johnson had said about *Wu-shu* (sic), that Oriental discipline of putting mind over matter, mind over pain. She had said that with sufficient control of the mind, a person can walk barefoot through burning coals, can lie on daggers, can even whirl around on the point of a spear and not be harmed. So I devoted my time in the hellish blackness of the torture cradle to thinking in terms of *Wu-shu,* putting the pain as far as possible out of my mind, concentrating all my mental powers on specific parts of my body where the pain was most severe. I tried to imagine myself as impregnable steel, asbestos-coated, impervious to heat and metal. I cannot say I became a *Wu-shu* master in a couple of hours, but I can say this: had it not been for my efforts at *Wu-shu* I am certain I would not be around today."

10:17 P.M.—I see my first space creature in its natural

form—John Parker. Brutally offensive to these eyes, but at least the antidote works as advertised. The Secretary of Defense is becoming more hysterical, refuses even to try the antidote to see whether we are telling the truth . . . can talk only of his Truncheon sub hunter-killer, as Tommy and I finalize our battle plan. Using Scooter Lindley's invaluable aerial photographs and the company blueprints, as well as John Parker's uncanny insight for these things, the plan is as follows: three teams invade Yoyodyne . . . Tommy's team, my team, and a third group of the volunteer Blue Blazes led by Mrs. Johnson. Tommy's group and my group will converge on an unmarked building on the northeast edge of the camp, believed to be the principal living quarters and bivouac of the creatures. Entering stealthily, the plan is to kill as many as possible while they are still half-stunned. That is the work of the moment. It is dirty, unappealing business, but it must be done. Once we have decimated their numbers, we move on to the principal objective, which must be Whorfin and the Panther ship. Mrs. Johnson's team and Casper Lindley in the chopper will create myriad diversions to distract the creatures, while we burst upon those inside Hangar 23 (John Parker's choice as the hangar housing the Panther ship) with the speed and force of a tornado. "What is to be our watchword?" says Tommy. " 'Dark and Silent,' " I aver, "if anyone asks." "What's my job?" asks Scooter Lindley. "Can I go with Mrs. Johnson?" "Afraid not, Scooter," I say. "We need you to stay on the bus and man the radio." "The radio?" he protests. "Who's gonna call on the radio at a time like this? You guys are all out fighting." "The President might call—or John Whorfin," I reply. "It's very important that somebody answer if they do." Reluctantly, Scooter agrees. Someone shouts that we are approaching Yoyodyne. Some of the newer interns are visibly trembling. But it is the waiting that is the worst. It is time we faced the menace at last, or the waiting alone will do us in.

10:20 P.M.—Pinky Carruthers's recon team parachutes undetected into Yoyodyne under cover of darkness and immediately fans out, investigating and indentifying buildings according to our special system of pictographs.*

10:22 P.M.—The bus arrives at the main gate of Yoyodyne. The Secretary demands to be let off so he can call John Bigbooté from the guard post. Thinking that it might work to our advantage, I order the bus door opened but direct Tommy to follow him.

10:24 P.M.—While Tommy and the Secretary of Defense divert the guards (in the Secretary's case unwittingly), I give the signal to leave the bus. The rest of Tommy's team, led by John Parker, is first off, and then the Blue Blazes under the command of Mrs. Johnson. Finally, it is our turn, and as we silently scramble under cover of darkness, I hear the faint noise of Casper Lindley's chopper overhead. He has been scouting the area, and we com-

---

* Using a special paint that is visible only through a night scope, Pinky's patrol marks the sides of buildings within Yoyodyne in the following manner:

means a safe building,	means a guard dog present	means enemy within

municate by Go-Phone once my team huddles together safely fifty yards inside the perimeter. "A lot of foot traffic in and out of Hangar 23," he reports. "A load of materials pulled up there about ten minutes ago." "Right," I acknowledge. "After we take care of the bivouac, that's our next stop." "You want some excitement?" he asks. "Not yet," I reply. "I'll let you know. Wait'll they know we're here." "Roger." Getting our bearings, we move forward in darkness, communicating with John Parker of Tommy's team and Mrs. Johnson. So far, all is well. No alarms. "Dark and Silent."

10:28 P.M.—As the Secretary of Defense demands to speak to John Bigbooté, one of the guards reaches for the phone, leaving Tommy no choice but to act. Taking his favorite Wetterling gun from under his coat, he blasts both creatures cleanly through the throats and rips the phones from the wall, leaving the dumbfounded Secretary of Defense to stare in sudden terror at the dying creatures on the floor, their human camouflage fading away before his very eyes. "Tommy!" he screams. "Wait for me!" But Tommy is gone like a shadow, joining up with John Parker and a dozen black-faced interns. "Let's go in," Tommy says over his Go-Phone.

10:33 P.M.—We enter the building believed to be the creatures' bivouac only to find it deserted, at least on the surface, leading me for an instant to ask the obvious question, "Could they have left already?" "Don't worry," said John Parker over Tommy's Go-Phone. "Lectroids live underground."

10:40 P.M.—After a brief descent through a secret tunnel

uncovered by John Parker, we (or any human beings) visit the harrowing world of the Lectroids for the first time . . . an underground enclave with pervasive dampness and filth, unvented odors which can make a man sick merely by inhaling them . . . everywhere dark spaces carved out of the earth, as we make our way in single file down the stone steps that seem to lead on and on without end. Having to crouch to avoid striking our heads on the low ceilings, unable to see even the man ahead of us, testing every foot of the way, we advance toward a sound the likes of which I've never heard before. "Lectroids!" John Parker whispers over the Go-Phone. "We have caught them sleeping!" So that is what that singularly loathsome sound is. They are snoring like the living dead! We continue our journey deeper into the fetid ground, hands on weapons which have probably mildewed by now. How will we fight in this kind of place? No room to maneuver. Unclimbable walls. Is this where the last battle of our race will be decided, among jostling bodies, men advancing inch by inch, feeling their way? Is this where we have finally brought our precious burden of our world's fate, only to entomb it along with ourselves? I look at my watch. How long has it been since we entered this bottomless pit with the stench of death, real or imagined, everywhere? It is only five minutes. Like a man in a dream, I have lost all sense of time.

10:46 P.M.—Our first encounter with a Lectroid underground. I do not even see it happen, but the word quickly spreads. John Parker has saved Perfect Tommy's life. A Lectroid has dropped from a hole in the ceiling onto Tommy's back, but John Parker has slain the beast with his strangely curved blade, swinging the terrible crescent against the Lectroid's throat. But how many more lurk about? Overhead . . . underneath? Has he alerted the main body? Are they waiting for us?

10:50 P.M.—An amazing sight meets our dilated eyes, a sight so unexpected that our group is literally stopped in its tracks . . . dozens of glittering Lectroids, glowing in the dark, all seemingly asleep and cold with numbness. Unless it is my imagination at play, the room, a low-arched gallery, the "atrium" of their underground villa, is positively frigid. Some of the creatures sleep dangling from the ceiling in hammocklike webs while others are to be found literally underfoot! Still others lie on basket-lounges as if basking in the sun! They are everywhere like hibernating bears, their "snoring" raising a fearsome din, and yet . . . for some reason I am reminded of a dimly lit taproom I once stepped into by mistake in Marseilles. I recall as if it were yesterday the sensation of the rising hairs on the back of my neck as I realized too late what I had gotten myself into . . . Chinese coolies, Lascars, and ferocious Algerian women turning to scrutinize me as if I were from another world, their expressions hardening ominously as they scanned my face . . . I had escaped from that unpleasantness, but not until after a stabbing affray, and now my heart beats as fast again, the hairs standing to attention on the back of my neck once more. Oppressed by a strange foreboding, I feel eyes looking at us, the eyes of cats in the rayless night. John Parker attempts to inspire us to attack, "before they sense us." Already something like that is occurring.

The Lectroids have begun to chatter, still in their sleep, but the air begins to throb. "Kill them!" says John Parker. Of course we agree, but how does one shoot a sleeping target, even a Lectroid? Then without waiting for us, John Parker leaps into a mass of Lectroids; a whirling form with animal swiftness, he slits the throats of the sleeping creatures. But now the room is in an uproar, the creatures buzzing excitedly, opening their eyes. I thrill at John Parker's daring. He canters coolly into the middle of their enclave, killing as he goes, throwing half-awake Lectroids left and right like rats. Suddenly they are all over him, attacking in a frenzied convulsion! And not just there, but behind us! Shifty eyes and claws suddenly springing for our throats! We open fire! They keep coming until our shots find their marks. I blow the eyes out of one, and he keeps stumbling forward, only sniffing me out, his "hand" jerking upward and deflecting my weapon. We fall to the floor of the dark cavern with a rending crash, fighting in the gloom, his poisoned barbs against my knife. He opens his mouth, fires the screaming tiny missiles in short staccato bursts. I dodge, plunge my knife into him repeatedly, pieces of his scaly armor adhering to my blade as I finally shove it through the "gap" in his carapace and feel the life gurgle out of him in a long undulation. Suddenly I look up and there are two more bellowing frantically and charging directly for me. Having dropped my gun in the darkness, I order them to halt, and, astonishingly, they do! I at once make a run for it, and they, furious at being left behind, grumble and pad after me! If they weren't so deadly, these monsters would be comical; but alas, the agonizing moans of several of our fighters startle me back to reality. This is war. A dying Lectroid bites my leg, whilst an intern sobs and shakes with terror, in the grip of two of the creatures who are literally tearing him apart. The sound of his own bones breaking mercifully causes him to faint. I can do nothing but watch him die, as I have my own battle to fight.

The reader will pardon my abrupt manner and will perhaps understand why I profess to be frankly puzzled by the continuing hunger of the reading public to know ever more details about our battle with the Lectroids. I have been nearly strangled, I have been stabbed, I have seen a man decapitated, I have seen a crazed man pull his own brains out. I have seen Hanoi Xan at the Majestic Hotel in New York City wearing a Mongolian shaman's net made entirely of middle joints of the index fingers of the swordbearing arms of fallen warriors and would have killed him without qualm could I have gotten off a clean shot. But I have never felt the slightest desire to hear tales of men in battle. It is my conviction that readers who find entertainment in such bloody events deserve to sample the experience firsthand; I daresay their taste in literature would change.

I could spend hours discussing our struggle with the Lectroids; but at the risk of causing an outbreak of acute mania, I will not. It was a nightmare I do not choose to relive, and so will condense my notes further.

11:14 P.M.—The battle has raged nearly twenty minutes. We have cut off the Lectroids' retreat and have begun to get the knack of killing them. They know this and begin to take cover instead of coming right at us, making our job more time-consuming. What we still do not know is whether an alarm has been sounded. Finally, we make a last rush at them, over-coming the little improvised fort they have built for themselves and wiping them out to a "man." We have various dead and wounded. Among our dead, Mustang Sally, Deputy Dan, and the brilliant geneticist Evermore.

11:20 P.M.—Miraculously, above ground all is calm; they still have not been alerted to our presence. We proceed to Hangar 23. I notify Casper and Mrs. Johnson to hold off creating any extraneous excitement.

11:22 P.M.—(the Secretary of Defense's testimony before joint Senate-House committee hearing looking into the entire Yoyodyne affair)—"After my friend Perfect Tommy killed the two rodents at the guard house, I realized there was something to what I'd heard already from Buckaroo Banzai, and so, wanting to get at the bottom of it, I walked to the corporate building, where I found the office of John Bigbooté. When I asked him about the Truncheon bomber, he used abusive language and tried to kill me. His words were, I believe, 'It's not my planet, monkey boy.' "

Congressman Ronald Dellums (Dem. Calif.):

He didn't say anything about copping a deal?

Secretary of Defense: You mean to turn Whorfin in?

Congressman Dellums: Right.

Secretary of Defense: No, he just said it wasn't his planet. I don't think he was aware at the time that the Hong Kong Cavaliers had the place under siege.

Congressman Dellums: He was just in a bad mood.

Secretary of Defense: Right, because of Whorfin. I think they all must have realized the party was over.

Congressman Dellums: You were aware that he called the FBI attempting to cop a deal?

Secretary of Defense: I learned that later. Anyway, as I was saying, he attempted to strangle me to death and then left me for dead. I played dead and as soon as I could, got up and followed him.

11:25 P.M.—Joined by Pinky's recon patrol, the remnants of my team and Tommy's team gather at the massive doors of Hangar 23. We cannot budge them. All other doors into the hangar are also of heavy steel. We debate whether to go back to the underground labyrinth and attempt to find a tunnel leading to Hangar 23 but reject the possibility as too time-consuming and instead call Casper and Mrs. Johnson to create some excitement. It is time to blow our cover and draw the remaining Lectroids out to fight.

11:26 P.M.—(Mrs. Johnson's note)—"After getting the word from Reno, I led my troops to a building near the hangar, inside of which we surprised several Lectroids in a lunch room. They were snacking, I guess, is the only word for it. Nearby a couple of naked ones had lit a fire in the middle of the room and were performing a kind of ritual* over the fire while the others cheered them on. We tossed in a couple of grenades and kept moving. I didn't look back, but a second later all hell broke loose. There was an explosion, and then someone must have

---

* I have mentioned that Lectroids do not bathe as a rule except twice in their lives; they do have a ritual of self-fumigation, however, which also constitutes recreation for them. A fire using their excrement is started on the floor and several of them strip and shake their clothes over the flames. Small parasites which infest their bodies fall out of their clothes and into the fire where they explode with different noises, depending upon the parasite's size. The cumulative effect of all these little explosions is, to the Lectroid ear, the sweetest kind of music, akin to a symphony.

pushed the alarm because it started blowing like crazy."

11:29 P.M.—Sporadic alarms* begin sounding throughout the camp. Small groups of Lectroids begin emerging from various buildings only to be strafed by Casper Lindley. Tommy and I start to get anxious, wondering whether they have heard the alarm inside the hangar. We haven't long to wait, as several Lectroids poke their heads out a side door. We're on them immediately, John Parker expediting a couple of them while Tommy and I lead our teams inside, by now joined by Mrs. Johnson and her group.

11:40 P.M.—(Secretary of Defense's note)—"I had followed Bigbooté underground to where they had the girl locked in the rocking chest over the fire, although at the time I didn't know what was in the chest. I thought it was something they were cooking . . . Bigbooté and two of his cronies. He called one of them O'Connor. 'What has she said?' Bigbooté asked. 'Nothing,' they said. 'She won't talk.' In the meantime the telephone rang, and Bigbooté answered. He said something into the phone like 'I'll be right there' and then hung up, looking extremely agitated, like his mother just died. 'That was John Whorfin, John O'Connor,' he said. 'We're under attack by Buckaroo Banzai's boys, and he wants us to kill the girl and go up there.' 'To go home?' O'Connor said. 'With what?' said Bigbooté. 'The Overthruster John Whorfin is building with Buckaroo

---

* It has been a matter of great speculation why the alarms at Yoyodyne were not sounded sooner and why, once sounded, many failed to function. A subsequent investigation by the FBI revealed that much of the alarm-system wiring in the camp had been chewed through, presumably by the Lectroids themselves.

Banzai's help,' said O'Connor. 'Forget it,' sighed Bigbooté. 'He wants us to go up there to die with him.' 'What's wrong with that?' said O'Connor. 'If you want to die, that's your business,' said Bigbooté. 'Yoyodyne is my business, and I'm not going to stand by and watch it destroyed.' 'What can we do?' asked O'Connor. 'I've been thinking of eating Whorfin's brain, John O'Connor,' said Bigbooté, and O'Connor's eyes nearly popped out. 'Eating John Whorfin's brain? Are you crazy?' said O'Connor. 'He's our leader.' 'He's the only one they want,' said Bigbooté. 'Who?' 'The Nova Police. They left us alone all these years. They left us alone to get rich. It wasn't until John Whorfin came back that they came down. If I ate Whorfin's brain, they'd leave us alone.' 'What about Buckaroo Banzai?' asked John O'Connor. 'I can deal with Banzai,' said Bigbooté. 'I'm a born negotiator.' 'But he saw us kill the hunters and the highway patrolman,' said O'Connor. 'Are you forgetting?' Bigbooté suddenly lifted O'Connor off the floor and shook him. 'You with me or not, John O'Connor?' he screamed. O'Connor nodded. 'How about you?' Bigbooté asked the other one. 'I'm with you, John Bigbooté,' the other said. 'Then let's take the Oath of the Flying Fish,' Bigbooté said. They all raised their hands, made some kind of sign, and then started upstairs. 'What about the girl?' John O'Connor said. 'Turn up the heat,' Bigbooté said. O'Connor dropped more coals on the fire, and they left. That's when I came forward at considerable personal risk to myself and saved the girl.''

11:45 P.M.—High above the hangar floor in that room called by the Lectroids the Shock Tower,

Buckaroo Banzai is nearly unconscious and Whorfin-as-Lizardo is growing desperate, as the tide of battle turns against him. As we press the attack forward and B. Banzai refuses to help him build the OVERTHRUS-TER he craves, Whorfin-as-Lizardo reacts predictably—increasing once again the voltage of B. Banzai's shock treatments. "Devil take you, Banzai!" he screams. "Blast your eyes!" "It's no use, Whorfin," mutters B. Banzai, trying to keep from drifting into that deep twilight that makes his speech slow and heavy. "You're running out of time." "*You're* running out of time, Banzai!" But Whorfin knows he must make a decision and with quivering dread does so as John Bigbooté, John O'Connor, and John Gomez report to him. "Ready the Panther ship," he says. "We're taking off." "Where are we going?" asks Bigbooté. "When we're airborne, I'll ask your advice," says Whorfin. "Now go!" On that understanding they part, Bigbooté and O'Connor roughly pushing aside their own fighters to board the ship. "Now I'll deal with you, Banzai!" says Whorfin, his hand moving again to the rheostat when suddenly Perfect Tommy and I burst into the room and Whorfin leaps over the railing to the hangar floor several stories below. Again, Death will have none of him, as he picks up his broken bones and with the assistance of several Lectroids is taken to the Panther ship. Though weakened after his ordeal, B. Banzai shoots out the door after his prey the moment we free him from the constraints of the electric chair. He races down the steps to the hangar floor, leaping perhaps the last twenty feet, and, joined by the swift John Parker, gains the Panther ship as its last tether is dropped away. The scene is pitiful: retreating Lectroids with the knowledge that their leader is aboard the ship, the doors to which have been closed and locked to them by his cowardly concern only for himself. The raving Lectroids even for a moment succeed in moving my heart; but only for a moment, as they bang on the doors of the ship panting and snarling, blaspheming with every insult their language furnishes.

11:52 P.M.—B. Banzai and John Parker climb to the rear of the giant craft, kicking away stranded Lectroids, and succeed in shooting their way into an escape vehicle attached to the larger ship. Once inside the tiny auxiliary craft, reminiscent of the Adder thermopod which brought John Parker to Earth, they seek to gain entry to the Panther ship, only to experience the sensation of a sudden lurching movement. "We're taking off!" John Parker exclaims.

11:53 P.M.—The evil face of John Whorfin-as-Lizardo can be seen through the Panther ship window, his closest aides, Bigbooté and O'Connor beside him, and behind them with a brooding face, the unknown quantity of John Gomez. The beams of their crude OVERTHRUSTER flash out from the ship and attempt to focus on the giant hangar doors. At all events, they are not waiting for the effectiveness of the OVERTHRUSTER, as the ship lurches forward on rails once more. Only futile conjectures can be made as to the conversation inside the ship. One can imagine, even see, John Bigbooté twisting his hands with furious energy . . . Whorfin-as-Lizardo with utter disregard for their hopeless situation, order-

213

ing the ship forward while wildly trying to control the aiming beams of his primitive OVERTHRUSTER.

11:53 P.M.—(Penny Priddy's note)—"The Secretary opened the torture cradle and stood leering at me for several seconds. I then asked weakly if he would put out the fire burning beneath me and in the same breath must have mentioned something about the OVERTHRUSTER in my purse, because he immediately forgot me and began searching my purse. Once he found it, that was the last I saw of him. He ran away with the OVERTHRUSTER, leaving me in the silence and the gloom of that hard rocky place, still lying in the torture cradle. It was not until several minutes later when Mrs. Johnson came along that I could at last imagine myself to have survived."

11:54 P.M.—The Panther ship charges forward, crashing into the other dimension but only partially so, its OVERTHRUSTER clearly defective, and yet effective enough to work a miracle. As we battle the last of the Lectroids willing to resist (for now with the retreat of their masters, the fight has truly gone out of them), New Jersey, who has been fighting like one whose strength cannot be measured, yells out to me: "Reno! Look behind you!" Thinking it a warning meant to alert me, I whirl in time to behold a handsome young Italian wearing a laboratory smock and a look of the most intense consternation; despite the fact that his hair is black and he is roughly fifty years younger than he was when I last saw him, I would know him anywhere. He is the young Lizardo and has just stepped out of the wall where the Panther ship has become half-lodged in the Eighth Dimension. I shout at him to take cover, for there is still fighting and then I glance upward at the cockpit of the Panther ship, where Whorfin-as-Lizardo has been transformed into the most hideous of Lectroids, his mere appearance ample enough cause to have made his name a word of fear to all. At last, perhaps sensing that his fate is upon him, he shrieks loudly enough even to be heard where I stood, as, like so many of his race, he seeks forgetfulness of self in violent action, once more attempting to penetrate the wall of the hangar and escape into the Eighth Dimension. But something is clearly wrong. The Panther ship spurts forward again, this time the Eighth Dimension closing its door completely to him; and the ship plows through the hangar doors, simply knocking them down and lumbering on its way.

11:56 P.M.—Four minutes until midnight, our deadline, and Whorfin is airborne. He lacks an effective OVERTHRUSTER, but does John Emdall know that?

Buckaroo Banzai and John Parker, only now recovering from the shock of crashing through the hangar doors and an almost-as-brutal takeoff, are frantically back at work, trying to open the door and enter the main ship, but it is hopeless. Unknown to them, however, the cutthroats in the cockpit are about to give them an unwitting helping hand.

Because there have been so many versions and so little real evidence concerning what happened in the Panther ship cockpit during those crucial minutes of flight, it occurs to me that the reader might like to share with me a document recently sent to the Banzai Institute by Federal Express. It bears no traceable return address and must simply be attributed to that still-unearthed Adder espionage network on this planet, but after careful study of its chemical composition, I believe the parchment to be authentically Adder. It purports to be a record of cockpit communications among John Whorfin and his aides during those fateful minutes aloft monitored by the Adder father ship. It is not my purpose to quote extensively from it—it will be published in due time in its entirety. The key section, however, bears upon what happened next in our narrative, and so I will reprint it:

John Bigbooté: Where are we going?
John Whorfin: To Planet 10!
John Bigbooté: Without the Overthruster? They'll shoot us from the sky!
John Whorfin: One more word out of you, Bigboote—
John Bigbooté: It's Bigbooté.
John Gomez: Careful, Whorfin, my liege, he means to eat your brains!
John Whorfin: What?
John Bigbooté: No! Help me, John O'Connor!
John Whorfin: Stop him! Release the pod! No one leaves!

(Apparently, John Bigbooté runs from the cockpit in hopes of reaching the emergency pod and making good his escape. The pod is released as this point.)

11:57 P.M.—Buckaroo Banzai and John Parker find themselves jettisoned from the main ship and falling rapidly to Earth. Flipping switches, turning strange knobs whose functions are unclear, they grapple with the instruments in an unwieldy effort to reverse their plunge. "Can't you fly this thing, John Parker?" Buckaroo asks frantically. "It's different from ours," John Parker replies. "Anyway, I failed flight school. I'm just a cop." "In that case, try the radio," says Buckaroo Banzai.

"Messenger John Emdall, tell her Whorfin has no Overthruster. He is no threat." "I'll try," John Parker vows. While John Parker attempts to work the radio, B. Banzai continues to try his hand at the controls, in effect faced with the task of having to learn an entirely new flight system and its practical operation within the twenty seconds remaining before the pod hits the ground. (That he succeeded in doing the seemingly impossible is now universally known. It is pointless to toy with the reader and play tug-of-war with his emotions. B. Banzai simply did it; to ask how is to ask too much. One may confirm his success by simply looking out the window.) At all events, the pod's course suddenly righted, Buckaroo flies in hasty pursuit of Whorfin's ship, testing the new controls as he goes. "Any guns on these things, John Parker?" "Boy, I hope so, Buckaroo Banzai." And so it goes, the two of them, John Parker trying to reach John Emdall over the balky radio and Buckaroo Banzai at last locating the air cannon, which with each blast somersaults their round flying pod.

11:58 P.M.—John Whorfin's Panther ship spots and zeros in on by Buckaroo Banzai. John Parker is still unable to reach John Emdall but senses a grave development if Buckaroo Banzai fails. "John Emdall will destroy the world," he says. "No question about it." "Thanks. That's all I need to hear," states Buckaroo Banzai, still closing fast on the Panther ship from seven o'clock. And then he fires.

John Whorfin:	John O'Connor, you're the weakest individual I've ever known. You're unworthy of your father's blood.
John Gomez:	Something's on our tail!

John Whorfin: What was that?
John Gomez: We've been hit! We're going down!
John O'Connor: We're going down! What do we do?
John Whorfin: Die like Lectroids.
    (B. Banzai darts past them.)
John O'Connor: It's Buckaroo Banzai!
John Whorfin: I'll see you in hell, Banzai! Explode ourselves!

With a tremendous flash, the Panther ship explodes, nearly knocking the pod out of the sky as well. As Whorfin's legacy, flaming debris of the Panther ship, showers over them, Buckaroo Banzai demonstrates the controls of the pod to John Parker and informs him he is on his own. "Flying this thing is bad enough, John Parker. I don't think I can land it. Think you can find your way back to your father ship?" "We have our ways, Buckaroo Banzai." "Yes, you do," says B. Banzai. "Give my best to John Emdall. Hopefully, we can be friends now. Please tell her that." "Yes, I will," says John Parker, to which Buckaroo adds: "Come back for a visit sometime." "I would like that, Buckaroo Banzai. Where are you going?" "I'm jumping out the hatch," says B. Banzai and does just that, leaping from the pod wearing a parachute marked PROPERTY OF JOHN BIGBOOTÉ which someone had stashed conveniently beneath the chair.

25

WITHIN A MATTER of moments it seemed, the world was back to normal. Professor Hikita and the young Dr. Lizardo enjoyed a somewhat queer, although endearing reunion, Lizardo like a man on a strange planet, unable to comprehend where he was or what had happened.* The surviving Lectroids were herded together like the surly beasts they were and would soon be on their way back to the Eighth Dimension, courtesy of the Jet Car and the OVERTHRUSTER retrieved from the Secretary of Defense by the fearless Scooter Lindley. His statement follows.

Scooter Lindley: I was sitting on the bus like Reno told me, with the doors locked. I was going to follow orders no matter what, but then the President called, asked me what was happening. I said, 'I don't know. I have no idea. Reno told me to wait on the bus.' So the President said, 'Well, I'm the President of the United

_____
* Tragically, as a result of this harrowing experience, the 'young' Doctor Lizardo also went mad and ironically ended up back in the same mental hospital where Whorfin-as-Lizardo had been committed. He is still there today.

States of America, and I'm telling you to get in there and see what's happening and report back directly to me. Otherwise we could have global thermonuclear war, and it'll be your fault, Scooter. You're my eyes and ears.' 'I thought the Secretary of Defense was your eyes and ears.' I said. 'The Secretary of Defense doesn't know his a— from a hole in the ground,' the President said, so I got my gun and left the bus through a window and went on a recon patrol. There was a lot of shooting suddenly, and I ran into Perfect Tommy, but we got separated in all the smoke from the grenades, and the next thing I knew, when the smoke cleared, I saw the Secretary of Defense with the Overthruster in his hand, about to steal the Jet Car. I pointed my AR at him and said, 'Another step and I'll drink your blood.' He froze in a hurry. I held him till the guys showed up.

Perfect Tommy, perhaps our greatest fighter, had fought his greatest battle, killing a score of our enemy. I joked to him that these Lectroids were hardly as swift as the Junglemasters he kept in his room as 'pets' and on whom he practiced his reaction time.*

As for Penny Priddy, she had been found by Mrs. Johnson and taken to Buckaroo's cubicle on the bus, where Mrs. Johnson refused to leave her side even when New Jersey came into the room to treat her wounds . . . the same New Jersey who had once flinched from surgery now naked and grimy from the waist up, eyes red, carrying the marks of

---

* A cat's paw striking is quicker than sight, and yet I have seen Perfect Tommy step barefoot on the head of a poised Jungle-master. Read more of his quick reactions in the chapter "Perfect Tommy and the Argentine Miss" in the adventure *Bastardy Proved A Spur*.

numerous wounds and the gratitude and respect of his comrades. He said to me in passing, "You know, Reno, I have saved a person or two on the operating table, but it does not compare to risking my life to save a life. The two feelings are not even comparable. Today, out in the field, I learned the meaning of something Buckaroo once said to me and which at the time did not register: 'Every year we pass the anniversary of our death.' Now I know what he meant but can't explain it to anyone."

"It's best to say nothing," I replied. "We all know."

Big Norse interrupted us, calling down from World Watch One. "Reno, it's Pecos!"

As I raced upstairs to grab the call, I thought about what New Jersey had said and thought about our dead comrades and resolved to live a better and fuller life in whatever time was left to me. After Pecos had told me breathlessly about escaping Xan's death dwarves at sea with the assistance of a school of porpoises, and asked what had we been up to, I replied, "Nothing much. I miss you."

"I miss you, too," she said. "Are you going on the polar mapping expedition?"

"I don't know. I may take it easy for a while," I replied.

"You always were a lazy bones," she said. "We'll talk about it when I get back to the Institute."

"We'll talk about everything," I said, smiling at Big Norse who I could observe spying shamelessly on me from out of the corner of her eye. "Have a safe flight."

The admonition made me smile. The world was definitely back to normal, or was it? Buckaroo quickly brushed past me on his way in to see Penny, Mrs. Johnson later telling me that the two of them had kissed and Penny would be convalescing at the Institute for some time, as a series of tests would be needed.

"Tests?" I said. "What kind?"

She raised her eyebrows. "I don't know, but when I put her to bed, I found tiny scars behind her ears."

"Scars?" I said. "Surgical scars?"

She nodded. "The most skilled I've ever seen," she said.

"Well, she was burned in that fire when she was little," I

said. "She's been through quite a lot. Let's not leap to conclusions."

"I'm not," she said. "She's starting to grow on me, but you never know. How about some Karakoumiss?"*

I shrugged and joined the others to partake of the foul liquid symbolizing that in life we must take the bitter with the sweet. It had been a long day . . . I thought of Rawhide and his words "but not so long as one I've known" . . . and it was true. All things were relative. We had saved the world, but had also saved that spawn of hell Hanoi Xan, from whom much more would undoubtedly be heard.

---

* The fermented mare's milk I have mentioned.

Author's Note

Mr. Shapiro Lichtman
Artist's Manager
Beverly Hills, CA

Mr. Reno Nevada
Banzai Institute

Dear Reno:

Please be informed that our client Orson Welles denies categorically any connection with the outer space creatures mentioned in your book. At no time was he contacted by said aliens, although he does not deny the possibility that he was hypnotized and made to do things he was not aware of. Also, Orson would very much like to see any proof that you may have to the contrary.

Warmest,

Shapiro Lichtman

Shapiro Lichtman